ROBIN'S
MAID

JESSAMINE RUE

First Edition: November 2022

Rue, Jessamine
Robin's Maid / by Jessamine Rue—First edition.

AUTHOR NOTE
&
TRIGGER WARNINGS

This is a fictionalized fantasy version of a country
similar to England, not England itself. The laws of
succession and inheritance are not meant to be
perfectly accurate,
nor is the behavior of lawkeepers and church officials
intended to be absolutely correct,
nor is the timeline in history firmly established.
Many liberties have been taken.

Not only does Marian have sex with her main lovers
and multiple other male partners, but the male
partners also have sex with each other and other
characters. They share an open relationship.

Warnings

Suicidal thoughts, murder, violence, bondage, blood,
knife-play, torture, threat of rape, self-harm, spanking,
rape, consensual non-consent

1

MARIAN

Sherwood Forest looms ahead, a maze of dark trunks clad in shivering leaves. A brisk wind, more suited to winter than early autumn, catches my cloak, twisting and whirling its frayed edges before racing away into the trees, making them bend and sway.

Perhaps I should have done this the way Lord Flaymish suggested. He wanted to hire some mercenaries to chase me into the forest. They would attack me, I would scream for help, and Robin Hood would appear—maybe.

It might have worked. The Hood has been known to save women from rape before.

But it would have been a temporary meeting. The Hood would have beaten my assailants soundly, escorted me somewhere safe (if indeed such a place exists in this region), and that would be the end of it. Robin Hood would disappear again.

This way is better. This way I can worm my way in deeper, secure a spot in the outlaw's band, and learn all the secrets that Prince John craves.

Under Prince John's orders, the local sheriff has tried to ambush the Hood before. But when traps are set for him, he always wiggles out of them.

Some of those who have tried to catch him claim he can actually disappear—turn himself invisible. Others claim he can make the trees move, changing the paths of the forest, hiding his tracks and those of his men. Which is why, no matter how many times Prince John and the sheriff send men out to comb the forest, they never find any sign of the Hood or his camp.

Some claim he's a spirit. A ghost, haunting the greenwood. Though the amount of good hard gold he and his band have stolen would indicate otherwise.

I'll soon find out the truth.

Gripping my staff, I move forward into the trees, trying to keep my steps firm yet jaunty, like a youth of sixteen or so. Under my cloak and my coarse woolen tunic, my breasts have been bound flat with strips of cloth. The leather vest over my tunic helps to conceal any telltale lumps. Beneath my trousers I'm wearing a sort of codpiece, giving the vague illusion of male genitals.

My hair has been chopped short, forming dark curls around my ears. It was too fine and silky to belong to a peasant, so I roughed it up with a little dirt and grease and wedged a shapeless cap onto my head. I wrapped a scarf around my neck and my mouth as well.

Deeper into Sherwood Forest I walk, following a faint path. I used to play within the borders of this forest as a child. My familiarity with the terrain is one of the reasons Prince John allowed me this chance to dictate my own future.

Married at sixteen to a wealthy lord, I warmed his bed for only a week before he went off to war. Four years later, I'm a widow, the pawn of my late husband's uncle, Lord Flaymish, who is in turn a pawn of Prince John. Flaymish took me to court and showed me off, where I drew the attention of Lord Gisbourne, another close friend of the prince.

The mere thought of Gisbourne enrages me. Using my staff as an anchor, I leap over a rotting log, and as I leap, I curse his name.

Gisbourne is well into his fifth decade—a paunchy, bejowled, balding man with flushed bags under his eyes and a perpetually liquor-stained beard. Perhaps I could manage despite all that, if he was kind. But he isn't. I've heard what he does to female servants.

I'm part of the property left behind by my late husband, and Gisbourne wants it all—the land, the gold, and my body.

But I've been the beautiful possession, the graceful ghost of a woman left to haunt the halls of her husband's estate while he goes where he pleases and lives his own life. My married years were lonely and dark, and I refuse to be married again unless I have a say in the matter.

When Lord Flaymish told me of the match, I had the courage to speak up for myself. In fact I spoke so loudly, and with such vehement smashing of pottery and throwing of table knives, that he took me seriously for once and brought me to Prince John.

As I stood before Prince John, the only question in my head was "What does he want most?" For weeks prior, the court had been full of chatter about the outlaw Robin Hood and his constant assaults on the noble coffers of the land. And so I concocted a plan.

Lucky for me, instead of simply ordering my obedience, Prince John was pleased enough by my beauty to allow me the chance to speak. Somehow I navigated the dagger's edge between impressing the prince and infuriating him. I emphasized my youthful connection to Sherwood Forest, and I presented him with my bargain.

"Let me go to the forest and get close to the Hood. I will learn his secrets, his hiding places, and the identities of all his men. And then I will give them up to the Crown, in exchange for full possession of my late husband's goods, servants, and property, and the promise that I may wed the man of my choice. If I succeed, you get Robin Hood. If I fail, you lose nothing, and I lose everything."

To my own astonishment and Lord Flaymish's great shock, the prince agreed.

I quicken my pace through the trees, approaching the bank of another stream, a wider one, with a narrow, rickety wooden bridge across it. The bridge has a ramshackle railing woven of branches along one side.

I have a vague memory of this spot—of hanging strings of acorn caps from the twiggy railing when I was a girl—before I had to dress properly and play the lady. Before my ailing father made the match between me and my late husband. Before I became nothing but a pawn in men's hands, a chesspiece to be moved here and there as they please.

If I fail to make a report within three months' time, I forfeit everything. My husband's property will go to Gisbourne anyway. Lord Gisbourne will possess not only the fields and treasures, the house and the livestock, but also the servants who became my friends during my husband's absence. He'll do terrible things to them, I know it. I can't let that happen.

This deal, foolish though it might be, has bought me a little time. Now if only I can find Robin Hood quickly, and befriend him somehow…

Frowning, I plant one foot on the bridge, doubtfully eyeing its structure. Maybe I'd be better off trying to ford the stream. I can't risk dealing with a fall and an injury if this rotten thing gives way.

"A good morning to you, lad," says a merry voice directly ahead of me.

I lift my gaze from the bridge, scanning the newcomer's form. First, a pair of well-worn boots, made of pliable black leather, planted on the opposite end of the bridge from where I stand. The boots are tall, reaching to mid-thigh on long, lean legs.

A glimpse of a tight pair of green hose, and then the hem of a patchwork tunic, black and green, belted at the waist. A trim, well-muscled male torso under the snug-fitting tunic—his chest crossed by a strap that holds a quiver of arrows to his back.

His hand, clad in a black fingerless glove, grips a longbow, propping the bow's end on the bridge. His other hand, similarly gloved, is braced on his hip. He has a strong white throat, showing between the folds of a cowl, which is pushed back. And then—

His face.

He's pale, sharp-featured. Beautiful, like no man I've ever seen. Laughing red lips, a mocking grin, narrowed eyes that sparkle green beneath slashed black brows. His hair is glossy black, like a crow's wing. It feathers against his cheekbones and jawline.

This can't be Robin Hood. I was expecting someone rugged and beefy, with greasy hair and a thick beard, heavily tanned from a life outdoors. This man is too tall, too slender, too pale. And he's much too handsome.

He is wearing green, though, and he carries the Hood's signature weapon—a longbow.

"I'd like to cross," he says, still with that cocky smile.

I've heard stories of encounters with the Hood—how he values a good fighter, whether they're on his side or not. It's the reason I brought the staff.

What does a woman do for four years, while her husband's off to war and she's expected to stay in his castle and wait for him? She takes fighting lessons from the old stablehand, of course. Master Blunt is no knight, but he was a brawler in his day—fought with the quarterstaff and with his fists, and made decent money before he was trampled by a runaway carthorse, got his leg broken, and had to find other work.

If I step aside, this man will continue on his way and think no more of me. But if I fight—

"I grow impatient," says the man with the bow. "Give way to your betters, boy."

"Betters?" I say, as low and gruff as I can. My voice is partly muffled by the scarf. "I see no betters here."

He laughs, a merry peal that rings through the woods. "I'll let that insult pass if you back off, my little man."

"Little man? I am seventeen, fully grown. Why, I could be married if I chose," I growl into my scarf.

"That would be a pity. Marriage ruins all the best young men, I swear."

"How so?"

"They bind themselves to a woman before experiencing the full delights of both genders, or of multiple partners."

My cheeks flush hot beneath the scarf. "The Church would call such things sin."

"The Church calls many things sin. To me, there are only a handful of true sins—and one of those is disrespect to your elders. Step back."

"Age makes you better than me? I think not. *You* step back."

"My patience is waning. Yield, and move."

"And why should I move for a preening cock dressed in his mother's quilts?"

The man's black brows pin together, and I wonder if I went too far. My goals won't be served if he kills me for my insolence.

He stalks forward, white teeth set in a savage smile. "A preening cock, am I?"

I stand firm, shifting the staff to a two-handed grip.

His gaze drops to it. "That's a sturdy weapon. You'd fight me, boy? I could shoot you through the heart and think nothing of it."

"A longbow against a quarterstaff? You'd be a coward and a villain to use that advantage."

"A coward?" He arches an eyebrow. "Wait here, you little wretch."

He spins on his heel, sets his bow against a tree, and strides into the undergrowth, whipping a knife from some hidden sheath. In moments he has a sturdy sapling cut and trimmed.

"My staff." He holds it up. "And I'll wager mine is longer than yours. Thicker, too." He winks at me, and a thrill ripples through my stomach. My pulse is pounding in my throat, in my skull. I've practiced with this staff for years, but I've never battled someone like him. What if he beats me easily? What if he sees through my disguise?

"Now," he says, "by my preening cock and my mother's quilts, I'll fight you, and the winner crosses the bridge first."

2

ROBIN

The young man faces me across the bridge, brandishing his staff. He's an odd-looking fellow, with a squashed cap, a scarf covering his neck and jaw, a mop of dark curls, and a set of coarse, ill-fitting garments.

Still, something about his stance is pleasing, and his eyes—fuck me, they're beautiful. Huge, deep brown, and thickly fringed with black lashes.

Seventeen is nearly too young for my taste, but as he said, in this land he's considered of full-grown legal age. Capable of taking a wife—or a lover.

Perhaps I could be persuaded to teach him a few things, if he proves himself worthy of my time.

"Come on, lad," I tell him. "Prove your mettle."

He hesitates, surveying my stance, the way I hold my weapon lightly in both hands.

I lick my lips and smile at him. "Will you come for me or not?"

Above the scarf, his cheekbones redden. Clearly he understood my double meaning. Not a complete innocent after all, then.

He charges, a clumsy onslaught fueled by a low cry of frustration. I sigh, carelessly holding up my staff to block him.

But at the last half-second he ducks. Jabs. Strikes just beneath my guard, at the side of my knee. Bone creaks under the force of the quick blow.

I yelp like a whipped pup—a sound I've not made in a long time—and I lunge into a hail of angry strikes. But the lad meets me blow for blow, quick and sure, with the expertise of a man who has been training in the art of the quarterstaff for a good number of years.

The first clumsy charge was meant to fool me, to make me believe he was no more than a farm-clod who plays at stick-fighting with his friends. Clearly he's much more than that.

My injured knee pains me. It will heal soon, but not fast enough, which means I'm slightly off balance for this fight; and on a narrow bridge like this one, that's unfortunate. The bridge groans and shakes beneath our quick steps and the weight of our blows. It won't last long, I'll wager.

"You've been well-trained," I tell the young man. "Who was your teacher?"

"Perhaps I am yours," he snaps. "Since I'm schooling you so thoroughly."

"How about a lesson for a lesson? You're showing me your best skill—I'll show you mine afterward."

"And what's your best skill?"

"It involves an altogether different kind of staff."

His eyes flash up to mine, startled—a moment's inattention—and I thunk him soundly in the chest with the butt of my staff.

A breathless cry of pain jolts out of him. He bends over slightly, so I whip my staff around and sting his left ass cheek. "Such a fine little ass. It would be a pity to bruise one cheek and not the other." Whirling, I strike the right cheek as well. "There now. A matched set of rosy blossoms you'll have. Perhaps you'll show me my handiwork later."

"After I've rung your skull with this good staff, you won't be able to see anything," he retorts, charging into the fray again.

Once more it's blow for blow, until his eyes widen suddenly and he looks down, between my legs. "My god, man, have you pissed yourself?"

Frowning, I glance down. It's instinctive—yet even as I do it, my mind lights up with a warning. *A trick, a trick!*

The youth's staff clanks against the top of my skull. It's a ferocious blow, one that would knock me out cold if I weren't what I am.

Even so, despite my resilience, I'm dazed, and he follows up with a smashing blow to my ribs—whereupon I topple sideways off the bridge into the stream.

The stream runs through a gully, and there are rocks studding the water below. Rocks that I crash onto, full force. Two ribs crunch upon impact. Shit. Those will take hours to heal.

I landed with my face in the water, too. Lucky for me I can hold my breath far longer than the average human.

I could leap up at once and end the insolent youth with an arrow to the heart. But I slump down, feigning unconsciousness, curious what he'll do next. Will he steal my bow and begone? If he does, he won't get far. Or perhaps he'll simply walk on, leaving the stranger he bested to drown in a shallow stream.

As a fighter, I like him. And as a fine piece of ass, I like him even more. But I have both excellent fighters and fine asses in my company. What I could use more of is men with compassion. Men too soft-hearted to leave an injured man to die.

What the young man does next will determine whether or not he gets an invitation to the Gloaming.

So I wait.

3

MARIAN

Shit.

Shit shit *shit*.

I may have killed Robin Hood. And while proof of his death might buy me some measure of goodwill with Prince John, it's not what we agreed upon. I was to deliver *all* of the Hood's band to the Crown.

Without Robin Hood alive, I have no way to find the others, to learn their hiding places, or to discover how they stay invisible from the Sheriff and his men.

And what if this is not Robin Hood at all? What if I've killed an innocent man?

I hurry across the bridge, pull off my boots, and scramble down the steep, rocky bank. Bracing myself with my staff, I wade into the stream.

The man is lying face-down in the water. I seize his black hair and haul his face up, and then I shove his shoulder until I manage to turn him over. He's half on, half off a boulder in the stream.

Heart rattling with anxiety, I bend over him and feel along his throat for a pulse. I can't tell if there is one. Perhaps I'm putting my fingers in the wrong spot. Is that *my* pulse I'm feeling, or his?

Forget the pulse.

I wet my wrist and hold it in front of his perfect red lips. They're slightly parted, showing a hint of his white teeth.

I can't feel any air on my wrist. Wait—is that a puff of breath? Or is it the breeze?

God's bones, I'm no good at this.

He doesn't seem to have a heartbeat or a pulse, so he must be dead.

"Holy Mother forgive me," I whisper. And then, for good measure, I call on the old gods too. My mother taught me their names in secret, before she died. "Eriu forgive me, Brigit bless me. May the Dagda grant me his mercy, may Arawn guide this poor soul into his rest—" My voice catches. "He was a foul-minded, licentious, prideful knob, but he did not deserve death."

Did the man's mouth quiver?

I lean close again, but there's no movement, no breath. Must have been a trick of the light.

Now, what to do with him. Should I leave him here? He's so tall there is no way I can get him out of this gully.

Undecided, I stand in the stream, staring at the beautiful stranger, my toes ice-cold in the flowing water. Pebbles are digging into my feet, and the bottom edge of my thin cloak is soaked, dragging heavily along the surface.

The trees soar above me like the statues of judgmental saints in the church near my late husband's castle. I went to church often, just to have something different to do, something beautiful to look at. These trees are as beautiful as the sanctuary, but they are wild and untamed, whispering curses to the breeze—a curse upon me, the lying murderess.

Among the treetops and throughout the forest undergrowth, the occasional bird twitters. Not all of them have flown to warmer country yet. There's an especially loud, annoying bird that keeps calling, over and over. Which seems inappropriate considering there's a dead man here.

Perhaps it's several birds—the same call seems to be coming from different places. And it's getting closer.

A memory flickers in my mind—one of the servants telling a story of Robin Hood and his band. "They're part of the forest by now," she said. "They're one with the trees and the animals. It's said they can speak the language of the creatures, and they call to each other in the voices of birds."

Shit. If those calls are from Robin Hood's men, and I have killed their leader—yes, they might take me to their hiding place, but it won't be to invite me into the band. They'll be dragging me there to kill me.

I should have married Lord Guisbourne.

No—I couldn't bear that. Better to die free out here than die slowly every day, while he pawed at me, rutted into me, abused my servants, and wasted my money.

This is better. Whatever is coming, I'll face it like a man. No—like a woman. Women are a damn sight braver and more clever than men, and stronger too, where it counts.

"Apologies for murdering you, stranger," I whisper. "It was all in good sport."

The twittering calls are much closer now. Nearly on top of me.

I wrap my scarf tighter, ram my hat harder onto my head, and grip my staff.

The bird-calls I heard among the trees resolve into crunching footsteps and male voices.

"Here's Robin's bow!" calls someone.

I wince, glancing at the man's body. So this *is* Robin Hood. I killed him.

He looks very uncomfortable lying there, draped over the boulder, with his quiver of arrows pinned between him and the rock. The staff he used has already floated downstream.

A tall figure leans over the edge of the gully. His skin is brown, his eyes liquid and dark. Black scruff shades his jaw, and silky black curls cluster over his head. Every feature, from his smooth brow to his aquiline nose, has a regal cast—a touch of elegance.

He has an arrow pointed at my heart before I can take a breath.

"Don't move," he says, his voice thick with emotion. "Gentlemen, to me."

Several more figures line the gully—men dressed mostly in shades of green. One of them, however, wears a flamboyant scarlet tunic, doublet, and hose. He's fine-featured, blue-eyed, with a short golden beard. His hair pours over his shoulder in a golden flood as he peers down at the stream.

He's breathtaking as sunshine.

"My god!" he cries. "Robin!" And he plunges down the bank, careless of his fine clothes smearing through the mud and snagging on rocks. "Robin—" He pushes past me as if I'm a dragonfly hovering over the surface of the water. "Robin, my darling—gods, no—"

"You," snaps the dark-eyed man to me. "Out of the stream, boy, and speak. What happened?"

Driving my staff into the bank, I manage to climb out of the gully. Sullenly I mutter behind my scarf, "He and I wanted to cross the bridge at the same time. We fought for the privilege, a battle of staves. He lost. But I did not intend to kill him. I must have struck his head harder than I thought."

I risk a glance backward and down, where the scarlet-clad man is bending over Robin's body. I can't see either of their faces.

The dark-eyed man tucks his arrow back into his quiver, and for a moment I think he might believe the death was an accident. But then he draws a massive dagger, with a crooked blade as wide as my palm. He strides forward, places a hand on my chest just above my breasts, and walks me backward until my spine strikes a tree trunk. Then he sets the tip of the shining blade against my temple.

"Don't move," he warns. "Will? What say you of Robin?"

I can't see the stream anymore. I'd rather not anyway. I never want to see the body of the man I murdered, ever again. This is a nightmare straight from the pit of Hell.

"Come and see for yourself, David," Will calls from the gully. "All of you, come here."

"A moment," says the dark-eyed man—David. He cocks his head, eyeing me as if he's trying to figure something out. He sheathes his dagger and unhooks a coil of thin rope from his belt. "Drop the staff and give me your hands, boy."

I hesitate, wondering if I should try to fight him. But I'm outnumbered, and if I start fighting back, one of the other men might shoot an arrow through me on the spot. Better to wait and see if I can talk my way out of this. If all else fails, I'll tell them I'm a woman and see if that makes any difference.

I drop the staff and hold out my hands. "I'll be needing the staff back later."

"Shut up." David binds my wrists and tethers the rope to a high branch. Then he goes down into the gully with the rest of the men.

When they climb out again, their faces are sober, and the scarlet-clad man, Will, is brushing away tears.

David marches back to me, his jaw clenched, and unties the rope tethering me to the tree. He holds the end, jerking it as if I'm a horse to be led. "Come on, filth. Time to face judgment." He nods to the men. "A few of you bring Robin's body out of there, and carry him back to camp. Gently."

"So he is really dead then? I killed Robin Hood?" I clamp my lips shut—I forgot to disguise my voice. Maybe they will excuse the shrillness as the nerves of a beardless boy.

"The Hood is dead as a doornail," mutters one of the band. "Fucking bad luck, that."

A band of black cloth drops over my eyes, and someone knots it at the back of my head. The blindfold is too tight, but I don't dare complain.

I'm jerked along by the man David, forced to stumble blind through the woods. No one asked if I wanted to put my boots back on. The twigs, thorns, and roots scrape and slash my feet as I walk. The wet hem of my cloak slaps my ankles, just below the cuffs of my soaked trousers.

"It was an accident," I venture. "I never meant to kill him, only to beat him."

"And beat him you did." A smooth, mellow, golden sort of voice—sweet and mournful. I think it's Will, the man dressed in scarlet. "That is the only reason you're still alive. We must kill you, of course, but since the death occurred through honest combat, we'll kill you in an honest way."

"There's an honest way to kill someone?"

"Of course. Slitting the throat. The old sword-in-the-gut. A quick decapitation. All done face-to-face of course—no behind-the-back shenanigans. Unless you like taking it from behind."

I have no words at first, because I think Will just made a sexual comment. In rather poor taste after what just happened to his leader, but I suppose thieving ruffians in the woods wouldn't know taste if it bit them in the ass. "Behind or in front, it doesn't matter to me."

"Perhaps we'll have you open wide and we'll take turns shooting into your mouth," says Will.

My stomach double-flips. "Shooting—arrows?" I ask shakily.

"Of course arrows. What else?"

What else indeed? The thought of what else a troop of lusty men might shoot into my mouth sends a wanton quiver along my sex.

I have not been touched intimately by a man in years. I've played with myself, of course, but sometimes that's dull. Sometimes I want a handsome man to touch, to look at. Something to stimulate me to greater pleasure.

I will probably never have pleasure again.
Because I'm going to die.

An 'honest death,' apparently. Small comfort.

4

It's all I can do not to burst out laughing as Will Scarlet teases the lad. When my men came down into the gully, I whispered to them to go along with the trick I've devised. They will pretend I'm dead, bring the little staff-wielding wretch to his execution, and then I will leap out and reveal myself.

A delightful joke—one my opponent deserves for giving me two broken ribs and a sore skull.

The other men have spread out and they will return to the Gloaming by different paths. It's just David, Will and I with the prisoner. David marches ahead, yanking the rope mercilessly, forcing the boy to walk barefoot over the rough forest floor. I did not realize the lad was barefoot until we got under way, and I can't speak aloud to stop our progress, or he will know I'm alive. He will have to endure the pain until we reach camp. I'll ask the Friar to apply a healing poultice to the boy's feet later.

The young man certainly has a nicely shaped ass—almost feminine in its roundness, like Will's. Speaking of which—I step forward and squeeze one of Will's ass cheeks. He rounds on me immediately, eyes bright, and he collides with me, chest to chest, searing my mouth with a silent kiss.

David trudges on, leading the prisoner, while I lose my senses in the liquid heat of Will's mouth.

He pulls away, breathless, and whispers by my ear, "I thought you were really dead, for a moment."

"I know. You ruined your lovely clothes coming to check on me. So touching."

"You owe me a new outfit." He trails his tongue across my mouth, letting the tip quiver between my lips. My cock hardens at once, and I rock my hips into his.

With an eager murmur, he rubs his own firm bulge against mine. His tunic rides up, leaving only his thin hose to cover the ridge of his erection.

I caress his face, savoring the graze of his golden beard. His fingers dive into my hair, and we kiss again, slower this time, a molten delight. I'm taller than him, and I like how he has to tilt his face slightly up to kiss me.

"Will, my love," I murmur against his cheek.

"Yes…" He's breathless for me, slave to my desire. He would let me take him right now.

"I'm attracted to the lad."

"The one who beat you?" Will pulls back. "He's young."

"He's past seventeen."

"Ah. Still, though." He chuckles hoarsely. "David and I, the occasional tavern wench, and all the Merry Men aren't enough for you?"

"You know what I am."

"You're insatiable. And you're fortunate I'm not the jealous kind." He smiles. "As long as you don't entirely replace me, you can have your fun."

"Our fun," I correct him. "And you're as big a fool as that Sheriff of Nottingham if you think I'd ever replace you."

I glance ahead, noting that David and the prisoner have long since disappeared. With a sharp grin at Will, I drop to my knees, ignoring the twinge of pain through my ribs.

"Robin," he hisses. "Robin… oh… gods-fucking shit…"

His cock tastes delicately sweet, as always. Will Scarlet, so fastidious about cleanliness, even out here in the greenwood. He uses soaps with flower petals and brown sugar in them, and if any man but me or David dares laugh at him for it, they get their heads cracked for the mockery.

"Your mouth is magic, I swear," gasps Will.

I bob my head faster, occasionally taking a good deep dive so his length goes partway down my throat. His hips are tilting forward—his hands clutch my head as he comes, jetting over my tongue. I swallow, and swallow, my cheeks hollowing out as I suck him dry.

When I pull off, his cock is slick from my mouth, glistening in the shade-dappled light of the greenwood. Not so much green now, with fall coming on, but we call it so anyway. I've seen few things more beautiful than Will Scarlet with his cock out, dressed in red, panting through his fading orgasm with a rapturous look on his face, while scarlet leaves from the trees overhead drift down around him.

I want to keep this image of him secure in my heart forever.

Tenderly I tuck him back into his hose and adjust his tunic and doublet.

"Come on," I tell him. "We need to catch up. I don't want to miss the fun with the prisoner. What good fortune that we had no thieving to do today!"

"Ah, but there must needs be thieving tomorrow," Will reminds me as we set off through the forest again. "You remember? The gold from the abbey?"

"Ah yes. Gold filched from the pockets of good hard-working families by the Holy Church. A travesty we must rectify before the 'tithe' goes to swell the coffers of Prince John."

"Indeed. But you know Friar Tuck won't like it."

"He's an idealist," I muse. "Still not entirely one of us yet, though he pays us many visits and gives me excellent information. I must think of a way to secure his loyalty for good."

"Perhaps a seduction." Will nudges my elbow.

"I've tried that." I wince. "I believe his leanings are toward women. And it would take a special sort of woman to persuade him to break his vows, if he ever does. No, I think we must find a different way of binding him to us. I'll think on it, later. After we have a little fun with our guest."

I clap Will on the shoulder, and then I twitch my fingers at a tree standing in our way. It shifts obediently backward, its roots rolling beneath the turf and the forest litter.

A clear, straight path to the Gloaming, and then we will show our new friend how we entertain visitors here in Sherwood Forest.

5

MARIAN

I hurt everywhere.

My buttocks hurt where Robin smacked me, and my right breast aches where the end of his staff struck me. The rope chafes my wrists. My feet are so lacerated I can barely stand the pain; tears are soaking my blindfold as I stumble along. And at the end of all this agony—death.

My toe catches on a root and I fall headlong, crashing into the bristly plants. I don't bother trying to get up. If they expect me to walk to my doom on my damaged feet, too bad. I'm not taking another step.

"Get up," growls the man leading me, the man called David.

I don't reply.

His large hand closes on my shoulder, dragging me to my feet, but when my torn soles press the mulchy ground, I cry out sharply at the pain and collapse again.

David's fingers close around my ankle. "You have the tender feet of a noble, boy. Not used to trudging through the woods, are we? Who are you, anyway?"

His gruff question is laced with suspicion.

I'm prepared for this. I designed a story to go along with the character I plan to play.

"I am from a noble family sir—or I was. We've been disgraced for our loyalty to King Richard. My father was hanged for his insolence to Prince John, and my mother died of a broken heart shortly after. I've been disinherited, my lands and money seized by the Crown. I heard a man could make his own way in these parts. I suppose I was looking for my fortune." I sniff, lifting my bound wrists to wipe my nose on my sleeve.

"You found a fortune indeed. An ill one, though. Had you told Robin Hood your tale instead of fighting him, things might have been different."

A very real sob hitches in my throat. I truly have the worst luck.

The next minute I'm being lifted, my body swinging through air as I'm draped over David's shoulder. My legs are pinned to his chest, wrapped by his muscled arm, while the rest of me hangs at his back.

I have never been treated like this in my life. His shoulder presses into my gut, and after a couple dozen steps I start to feel sick. Will this shithole of a day never end?

After what feels like an interminable walk through the forest, I begin to hear the murmur of men's voices, the crackle of fires, and the clang of pots. The warm fragrance of woodsmoke fills my nostrils, and the aroma of roasting venison makes my stomach churn harder against David's shoulder.

Someone breezes past me, and I hear the golden tones of Will, the man in red. "Weep and mourn, men of Sherwood, for your daring leader has fallen. Robin Hood was killed in combat upon a bridge in the greenwood. Behold his murderer! Let us gather for the judgment."

Sightless and nauseated, I don't resist as I'm shifted off David's shoulder and forced to kneel on the ground. I try not to rock back on my torn heels, but my thighs are shaking from holding myself upright on my knees. My hands are still bound in front of me.

"He's just a boy!" says someone, and "Tell us of the fight! Was Robin truly bested?" cries another. "Bested by a stripling," someone snorts nearby.

I frown beneath my blindfold. I'm not hearing the outcry, rage, and weeping that should follow the announcement of Robin Hood's death.

"What should we do to the young man who beat our sweet Robin?" Will calls out. "Shall his throat be slit, his heart pierced, or his head cut off?"

A cacophony of different opinions rises around me, and I cringe at the roar. I have never heard so many male voices raised at once. Such a large gathering of outlaws—warriors who, by all reports, owe their allegiance to King Richard.

I don't care for kings or princes. I don't worry myself with the plight of peasants or farmers. All I care about is my own future, and the future of the servants back at my castle. That's all I can afford to concern myself with. I don't care if Robin Hood's cause was a just one—whether he was a morally-upright hero or a low-down sneakthief. He was my chance at independence, and he's gone. So that's me fucked.

"Throat-slitting it is, then," crows Will. "For the honor of dear, sweet Robin."

Someone tears off my cap. Sinks their fingers into my curls and jerks my head up. My scarf is dragged down, and a cold, sharp edge presses against my neck. I can feel it biting at the surface of my skin.

I hardly dare to breathe.

This is it. The end of me. I'm about to be split open and poured out.

Then a voice, mocking and merry, so close I can feel his breath on my cheek. "By my preening cock, you look frightened."

My breath stops altogether.

My blindfold is pulled off.

Crouched before me, his red lips stretched in a laughing smile, is the beautiful black-haired man I met on the bridge.

Robin Hood.

"A fine joke, eh?" Robin Hood drags the tip of the dagger up my throat to my chin. "And worth it, to see this pretty face. Look at you, lad." He whistles, low. "You're devastating."

"Fuck you." My voice is hoarse. I'm trembling, fighting the roiling nausea in my stomach.

"You may, if you say 'please,'" he purrs.

The innuendo sends a fountain of hot fury into my brain.

"This was all a joke?" I can't hold myself back; I'm practically yelling in his face. "You pretended you were dead—and then what? They *all* played along with it? To fool a stranger into thinking he was doomed to death? You're sick, all of you. You're as mad and cruel and wicked as they say."

"Is that what they say about me?" Robin rises, looking down at me with a slightly less pleasant smile. "You must have been passing time with the rich nobles and blood-fattened courtiers whose only labor involves licking Prince John's dick."

"The lad said he was of a noble family," interjects David. "They fell afoul of Prince John and he has nothing left. He was seeking his fortune when you came upon him at the bridge."

Robin Hood's dark eyes pierce mine. "To whom do you owe allegiance, lad? Say 'Prince John' and we will blindfold you again and escort you safely to the border of the greenwood. Say 'King Richard,' and you may stay for dinner and for sport afterward."

It's a test, of course. I can see it in the eager tension of the men behind him—one of whom is holding my staff.

"I want that back," I say, pointing to it.

"In good time," says Robin coolly. "Answer the question."

When I look into his eyes again, I sense a strange pull in my chest, a zing of warning through my very bones. Something tells me this man is going to see right through any lies I offer him.

So I give him the truth.

"I owe allegiance to none but myself," I reply. "But I have no love for Prince John."

Silence shivers in the clearing for a moment— and then Robin Hood nods and leans forward, sawing through my ropes with his blade. "Good enough. You'll be our guest this night. Give the boy his staff, and Will, my love, take him to the Friar's tent to have those feet seen to. Then we dine, good fellows!"

The men cheer as Robin turns away from me. But he whirls back immediately. "A pox upon me, I forgot! What's your name, boy?"

I have prepared for this too. "John."

"John? John what?"

"I told you, I've been disinherited. I have no other name, no title."

"Yes, yes," he says impatiently. "But we all have two names here. I am Robin Hood—" he touches his cowl— "This is David of Doncaster. That's Will Scarlet, and so on. Since you lack a second part to your name, I will give you one. You're young, and small—so you'll be called 'Little John.' Welcome to the Gloaming, Little John!"

The other men laugh uproariously, but I merely shrug. I grab my staff from the man who holds it and I hobble after Will Scarlet.

The camp is the strangest one I've ever seen. It's made up of a few dozen dwellings, at least, but it's hard to tell the exact number because some of the hovels seem to be formed of living trees and vines. Some are shaped entirely from hedges, with arched openings instead of doors and domed rooms within. Several times, out of the corner of my eye, I think I see the twigs and vines moving, adjusting their positions in the tightly woven walls.

Must be a trick of the light.

Of course that's what I told myself earlier when I saw Robin's mouth twitch as he lay on the rock, when I called him "a licentious, prideful knob." Now I know that his lips really did twitch—he heard everything I said, including my prayer to the old gods. Which does not bode well for me. In this land, worshiping the old gods is punishable by death.

I can only hope an outlaw like him can excuse my deviant religious habits.

Besides the dwellings formed from the forest, there are regular tents, too, made of animal hides. Will Scarlet leads me into the largest of these. Candles burn in a cluster of weeping wax on a broad plank laid across two large barrels. There's a mound of furs and fabrics nearby, too, too shadowed for me to see it clearly. A rumbling, hissing sound emerges from it.

Will kicks the shadowy heap. "Friar Tuck! I have a patient for you."

The pile of furs and cloth shifts with a snort. From its center rises the mountainous bare shoulders and muscled-packed torso of the biggest man I have ever seen. Instead of a friar's tonsure, his entire head is clean-shaven, including his jaw. Dark brows bend as he pinches the bridge of his nose.

He's different from the others, the way a magnificent mountain is different from a sparkling gem or a frothy waterfall. David of Doncaster has a regal handsomeness to his features; Will Scarlet is golden and gorgeous; and Robin himself has a sharp beauty, like a blade. But Friar Tuck is roughly, ruggedly handsome—granite features, a chin dented in the center, a bold nose, and hazel eyes draped in soft brown lashes—the only soft thing in his face. Even his mouth looks coarse and rough.

I want that coarse, rough mouth on my mouth. The involuntary thought shocks me.

His chest is shaved, too—thick collarbones, bulging pectorals, and abs that ripple distractingly as he reaches over, grabs a brown woolen robe, and pulls it over his head.

"I was sleeping, Will," he grumbles. When he stands up, he has to bend so his head doesn't brush the top of the tent. Before his robe falls into place, I glimpse a dangling cock so massive, I can hardly believe what I just saw.

"Sleeping off another few tankards of good ale, eh?" Will Scarlet laughs. "Well, clear your mind, my holy friend. We have a lad here who could use your ministrations. His feet are a bit worse for wear. Show the Friar, boy."

Leaning on my staff, I lift one foot and angle it so the Friar can see the damage.

"Did you trek through Sherwood barefoot?" The Friar's eyebrows lift.

"They didn't let me put on my boots." I cast a scathing look at Will Scarlet.

"Now then, Will." The Friar frowns at him. "Was that the good Christian thing to do?"

"I was preoccupied, Tuck." Will lifts his hands in mock self-defense. "And when have I ever been a good Christian?"

"You've got me there." Friar Tuck laughs, a deep, hearty sound. Two clefts wink into existence in his cheeks—dimples so deep I could lose myself in them. "What's this lad's story?"

"Took some knocks from Robin Hood on the Wicker Bridge. Gave better than he got, though, by all accounts. Robin named him 'Little John.' We'll have the christening later." Will Scarlet winks at me.

Tuck nods. "Go on, you reprobate. Leave the boy to me."

6

The boy Will Scarlet brought in is the most attractive lad I've ever seen. Features delicate as a snowflake. Cheeks as rosy as a peony in full bloom. Lips like plump ripe berries I want to savor—

I turn away, wrapping my rope belt around my waist and tying it. My thoughts have not been pure lately. I have always struggled to keep my mind constrained to God's Word and to His will, but recently it has been more of a battle, and I know why. It's my association with this band of outlaws. Every time I leave their company, I tell myself I will never return, that I won't pass Robin any more information or consume any more of the good liquor that's so plentiful in the Gloaming.

But each time I make that vow to myself, I break it.

I watch their sinful antics, but I don't participate. And I confess later—I say prayer upon prayer, lash my back in penance. I've come close to blinding myself, so wretched was my guilt at watching the open fornication they indulge in every night after dinner.

After tonight I'll go away again for a while. Maybe this time I can settle into my duties without feeling the grating, itching restlessness that drives me back to Sherwood again and again.

For now, I have something to distract me.

"Sit on the plank there, lad," I say, rummaging through my satchel. "Mind the candles. Little John, is it?"

"Yes." The boy obeys, settling himself on the makeshift table. He's short, and the barrels are large, so his feet don't brush the ground.

I have poultices and tonics aplenty, in bottles and small pots tucked within the satchel. That's another reason I come to the greenwood. There are certain poultice ingredients I can only find here. And there's one element that renders each poultice and tonic miraculously effective when applied to any injury or disease—an element only Robin can provide.

None of the people I serve know what makes my remedies so effective, nor can I ever tell them about the secret ingredient. They would be appalled.

After locating the cream I want, I drop to one knee before the lad and catch his ankle. He has a strangely dainty foot, thatched with bloody cuts. As I smear a bit of the cream onto his heel, he makes a small, distressed sound. A very feminine sound.

My head snaps up, my eyes locking with his. He looks away, a guilty flush coloring his cheeks.

My gaze drops to his chest—flat, no bosom to be seen—and then between his legs, where there's a slight bulge. I eye his neck—slim, no sign of an Adam's apple. It isn't obvious in all males, so that's not definitive proof.

"Have you been injured anywhere else?" I ask.

He shrugs.

"I don't imagine you walked away from an encounter with Robin Hood without some bruised bones. You can tell me about your injuries, or I can call Robin in here to inform me exactly where he struck you."

"I'm fine, truly." The lad is squirming now, redder than ever, and I'm becoming more certain by the second that he's not a lad at all.

"Right then. I'll strip you and look for bruises myself. We don't stand on ceremony here in the greenwood."

Little John's eyes blaze with sudden fire. "I'll strike you if you lay a hand on me—other than fixing my feet, of course." His slender fingers tighten on his staff—but then he winces.

I snort a laugh, astonished that this twig would threaten me. "Think you could beat me, eh?" I smear more ointment on his foot. "Growing a bit cocky after winning your bout with the Hood? You must have used some trickery—Robin doesn't lose often."

The boy won't meet my eyes. "It was a fair fight."

"Indeed. And now that the sparrow has beaten the robin, he thinks he can take on the hawk." I press cream into a deeper cut, and Little John cries out, muffling the sound with his palm.

"Where else are you hurt?" I ask again, firmly.

The answer comes low and unwilling. "Robin struck me twice on the ass and once in the chest. Just bruises. I'm fine."

"Lift your tunic."

"No."

I wipe my hands on my robe and stand up. I'm a threatening bulk compared to his slim form. He moves as if to strike me with the staff, but I catch his wrist, apply quick leverage, and force him to drop the weapon.

I bend, bringing my face close to his… no, *hers*. I'm sure of it now. "Lift your tunic."

"You already know what you're going to find," she whispers. "I can see it in your eyes."

"Do it." I release her wrist.

Lips pressed together, eyes hard and bright, she rolls up the tunic, revealing cloth wrapping. Several padded strips are thickly wound around her waist and her lower ribcage to bulk up that area, and more are tightly wrapped around her upper chest to flatten what must be some rather fine breasts.

"Satisfied?" she snaps.

I nod at her crotch. "So you have something in there to make the right shape?"

"Yes."

"And why the ruse?"

The girl sighs. "As I told the others, I am the offspring of a noble house, disinherited and disgraced. I want revenge on Prince John for the role he has played in my family's downfall. I've heard of Robin Hood, how he fights against the Prince, and I thought if I could become one of his band—"

"But Robin steals from the rich. If you were still wealthy and titled you'd be a fair target for him."

"I know. But I see the world differently now that I'm poor myself."

I snort. "Fair enough. But Robin doesn't allow women in his band. Women do sometimes come to camp, but when they do, they know exactly why they're here. To serve the lust of Robin and his people."

She tilts her head. "You're not one of the band?"

"I am a friar. I serve a few small hamlets near Nottingham, helping out where I can, sharing my remedies with the sick and wounded."

"But you got drunk in this place. And you were sleeping here—ow!" She squeals as I seize her other foot and swab it with cream. "That ointment stings."

"Only for a moment. You'll sting much worse when Robin figures out the truth."

She flushes deeper. "I thought he was kind and respectful to women."

"He is, to women who need his help. Not to those who tell him lies and play him for a fool." I chuckle. "I look forward to seeing his face when he realizes he's been tricked."

"You're not going to tell him?"

I shrug. "I find it amusing you've fooled them all this long. I'd like to see how much longer it takes for them to figure out the truth. But you should know— this 'christening' Will Scarlet mentioned, and the activities after dinner—they are of a salacious and sinful nature. Nothing any God-fearing woman should endure, or watch."

"Do *you* watch?" Those beautiful brown eyes sparkle at me with suspicion and sly humor. Her plump mouth curves up at the corner, and a bolt of arousal shoots through my cock, stiffening it.

Mother Mary, forgive me...

"What—what do you mean?" I say hoarsely.

"Do you watch these salacious, sinful activities, Friar Tuck?" she murmurs. Her little toes twitch in my hand. "Do you partake?"

"No," I say quickly. "I do not partake. But I—I watch sometimes."

"And you like it, what they do?"

"Yes." I'm not sure how she elicited that confession from me. I swallow hard, avoiding her eyes, conscious of blood and heat rising to my face as well as filling my cock.

The girl doesn't laugh, or censure me. She leans forward, inspecting the first foot I treated. "It feels better already. They both do. Thank you."

I nod and straighten as much as I can in the low tent. I feel suddenly ponderous and clumsy next to her. "I will go and find you some shoes or slippers."

"And you'll keep my secret?" She stares up at me, those enormous eyes holding me captive. "Because I truly want to be one of the band. I'm an excellent fighter, as I've proven. Please say you'll keep this quiet."

I bend down, planting my hands on the table on either side of her thighs. Her lips part on a soft gasp, and she leans back as I move into her space.

"Swear you mean no harm to Robin Hood," I demand. "Swear it on your parents' souls."

"How do you know my parents are dead?" she falters.

"I assume they are. You're a woman unprotected." My heart is beating heavily, thunderously, and my blood roars to close the distance between us, to touch her, to cut away her disguise and view her pliant flesh myself. I've never seen a woman naked except for crude sketches. Parts of naked women, yes—but never a whole one at once. Usually I can subdue my desire, but this slim, sly creature in trousers tempts me beyond reason, and almost beyond resistance.

Maybe part of her charm is the way she's staring at my face. She wears a half-wondering, half-alarmed expression, but there's an edge to it—one I recognize. Desire.

"I like your mouth," she breathes. "God's bones, I spoke that aloud."

"You did." My own voice is barely more than a breath. "I like yours, as well."

My nose touches the tip of hers, a light brush of skin that sends a tingling flare of heat along my cock.

"Friar Tuck—" she whispers.

"Just Tuck."

"Tuck—shouldn't you get me those slippers you mentioned?"

"I should." Gulping, I force myself to back away, to turn my back on her, to leave the tent.

Only when I'm rooting through the supply tent for spare footwear do I realize—

She never swore on her parents' souls.

7

MARIAN

When Tuck returns with a pair of leather
slippers, he starts to ask me something, but then two
of Robin's band noisily enter the tent, holding out
thorn-studded palms and arguing about who shoved
whom into the bricklebush first. *Like a pair of children,*
I think, amused, and I slip out of the tent before Tuck
can stop me.

He probably wanted to elicit a vow from me—
that I don't intend harm to Robin Hood.

But I do intend harm, of course, and I'm
religious enough to dislike the idea of swearing a lie
on my parents' souls.

It's not that I hate what the Hood does—taking wealth from the rich and doling it out to the poor. It's a laudable cause. But it's not mine. My sole duty is to hold onto my late husband's castle and keep my servants safe.

My late husband—I always call him that in my head. I don't like saying his name, even in my thoughts. I'm not sure why.

Or maybe I know why, and I simply don't want to face it.

Upon leaving the friar's tent, I'd hoped to look around, maybe gain a clue as to where exactly we are in the forest. But the center of camp is a bustle of plank tables being moved around, stumps and fallen logs being set up as stools and benches, and wooden platters being stacked up near pots of food and trays of bread.

"The guest of honor!" someone shouts, and immediately I'm encircled by rough, grinning, green-clad men who hustle me to the head of a table. There's a sort of throne there, made of vines and branches so tightly pressed together it's as if they were woven. And they, too, seem to be fully alive. How were they made to grow like this? It's impossible.

I'm pushed into the throne and brought a tankard of something that stings my nostrils when I experimentally sniff it. I can tell instantly that it's stronger than the mead or wine I'm used to. When I take a sip, I'm ready for the burn, and I manage not to choke and gasp, which seems to impress the Merry Men. But my eyes water, and I have to fight to keep down that one swallow.

At least one source of discomfort is gone. My feet are nearly pain-free now, which is astounding. Whatever was in the friar's ointment, I wish I had an internal version to help me with my monthly cramps.

Robin Hood dashes up and hitches himself onto a tree stump to my right, one foot propped against the edge of the table. He barely looks at me—too busy laughing with his men and describing the battle on the bridge in great detail. When the meal begins, he passes me a bowl of stew, a hunk of bread, an apple, and a sugary cake without ever stopping the stream of glib words flowing from his mouth.

I watch his sharp, beautiful face in profile, drinking in every expression. I'm enamored with him—impossible to deny it. The flash of his white teeth through his blood-red lips, the feathery black of his hair, the unnaturally bright green of his eyes—it all entrances me, as if he's a glittering lantern and I'm the fragile moth, beating nearer and nearer on soft, vulnerable wings, until his flame lashes out and devours me.

I hate myself for the obsession with his beauty, but I can't stop it. I'm used to grimy, weather-worn, sweaty men. And this lithe, long-limbed outlaw, who smells of fresh rain and leaves whenever he moves—I can't help desiring him.

But in spite of my fixation, I manage to eat a little. It has been a long day.

At last everyone has eaten their fill, and the men are getting deeper into their cups. The attention has shifted to Will Scarlet, who's regaling everyone with a bawdy tale of him seducing first an innkeeper's daughter, and then his son.

And while they are all distracted, Robin Hood finally turns to me.

The force of his eyes strikes me like an arrow. I'm pierced, pinned, quivering under that bright green gaze.

"You spoke to the old gods when we were in the gully," he says, so low I can barely hear him.

I swallow, then clear my throat, taking care to keep my own voice low and rough. "My mother believed in the Old Ones. Worshiped them in secret, so my father wouldn't know. She taught me about them. Forgive me, I was shaken. I'm a true daughter of the Church."

"Are you? How disappointing." He sips from his cup, his eyes glinting over the rim.

"You're not shocked? I could be burned or hung for speaking the gods' names."

"Not here." Robin leans toward me, and his face seems to sharpen, to grow even wilder and more beautiful. "Here we revere all gods. Some more than others."

Something brushes my wrist, and when I look down, the twiggy throne I'm seated on is extruding green leaves and white flowers. They're growing as I watch, unfurling and multiplying as the entire seat bursts into leafy bloom.

My eyes lift to Robin's and he grins. A grin of ownership, of exultation, of authority.

He did that. I don't know how, or what it means, but he made the throne grow leaves and flowers.

"What are you?" I breathe.

Robin doesn't explain the flowering throne, or answer my question. Instead he bounds up and leaps onto the top of the stump he's been sitting on.

"My brothers, lovers, fellow warriors," he calls out. "I've told you the tale, how Little John and I met on the bridge, and how I was bested by wit and by skill."

Everyone assents with a cheer.

"I now offer our guest a choice—to leave this place tomorrow, no worse for wear—or to remain with us here in the greenwood." He looks down at me. "Little John, I can offer you good ale, hearty meals, a safe place to lay your head, and the love and loyalty of the best men in the land. I can promise we'll make the prince and his ilk suffer. You'll have good honest work to do, and battles to fight if that stirs your blood. And your cock will never lack a willing hole to fill. We've men aplenty here for that task, and women who visit us as well."

The last bit shocks me, but I try not to show it.

"What say you?" Robin says, a little softer. "Will you leave, or join us?"

This is what I want. To be welcomed into the band so I can learn the secrets of the greenwood.

"I will join," I say firmly.

Robin rams a fist into the air, and the entire company cheers and hammers on the tables.

When the noise dies down a bit, Robin cries, "Now we must welcome Little John properly, and confirm his new name among us. How shall he be christened?"

The men bellow so loudly I can't discern word from word.

But when Robin lifts his hands, they quiet, and he says, "Three choices, lad. First option—you strip and we dunk you in the Bottomless Pool a short walk from here. Second choice, we douse you in Much the Miller's best fiery ale. It stings like a net of thorns and you'll smell like a brewery for days. Third choice, three of us anoint your face."

He smirks, and his hand drops to his crotch, a bold hint about what kind of anointing I can expect.

I can't choose the first option. Stripping is out of the question if I want to keep my place here, as a male, as one of the band.

The second option sounds painful, and I've had enough pain today.

Surprisingly, the third choice is the least objectionable. A flare of delicious heat spreads through my lower belly at the thought of three men coming on my face. My arousal scares me more than the act they will perform. What kind of person must I be, to feel this way about sexual encounters with strangers, in front of a crowd of men? I'm a whore, a harlot, just like *he* used to say...

Maybe I *want* to be a harlot, at least once.

Strange how the greenwood makes everything seem like an eternal secret, one that will never come to light. Odd how free that makes me feel.

Robin is looking down at me with a resigned expression, as if he's sure which one I'll select.

I hold his gaze. "Third option."

His green eyes widen with surprise as the men bellow their approval at my choice.

"Each man shall mark a piece of bark with his sign or initial and put it in that empty pot," Robin says. "I'll choose two."

"And who will be the third anointer?" someone shouts.

"Me." His lips twist, a wicked, insolent smile. He's still gazing at me.

My stomach soars, a thrill that leaves me breathless. Wetness is seeping between my legs already, and a slow ache pulses at my core.

A few short hours ago I thought I had killed him, and that I would die for it.

Now I'm more aroused than I've been in years.

I can barely permit myself to think the words, to admit the truth—

That I want Robin Hood's cum on my face.

8

WILL

Robin picks my piece of bark and David's from the pot.

It's no accident—I'm sure of that. I know more of his magic than anyone in camp, and I know he chose the two of us on purpose. He doesn't want anyone else coming on the boy's face—just him and the two men he cares for the most. Something about this young stranger is special—he has a hold on Robin already, and that concerns me.

I'm not a jealous man. I've watched Robin fuck countless pussies and assholes here in the greenwood, or in the shadowed back halls of taverns. But perhaps

I wasn't jealous then because I knew the acts meant nothing to him. He doesn't fuck anyone else the way he takes me and David.

Watching him come on the beautiful boy's face might hurt, though.

The greenwood is dark now, swirling with inky shadows. Our campfires and lanterns keep the night at bay, encircling us in a pool of golden light. And in that light, Robin undresses before us all.

He has already laid aside his bow and quiver for the night, but now he removes the rest—vest, tunic, hose, boots. Every one of us has seen him naked many times, yet we never tire of the sight. Most men seem to grow more vulnerable the more clothes they remove, but Robin gains power. His nude form is sleekly muscled—milk-white, silky skin over stone. Earlier he must have switched his gloves for jewelry—his fingers glitter with thick gold rings, a match for the tiny gold piercing near the tip of his perfect cock.

He leaps onto the table, standing over Little John, who sits paralyzed and wide-eyed in the flowery throne. He has likely never seen a dick as long and lovely as Robin's.

Alan of Dale is playing his lute, and a couple others join in with drums and pipes, filling the air with a thrumming, devilish dance tune. Drinks slosh as men jig and jostle, arms over each other's shoulders, some kissing or cupping each other's cocks through trousers. But they won't strip until Robin is done with our guest.

Robin stands wide-legged on the table, his cock pointing straight out, toward our petrified guest. He cuts a look at me, crooks a finger. "Come here, Will."

My chest warms, and my own cock stiffens with pleasure. Robin knows I need to be involved in this. He understands me like no one else.

I disrobe to the waist and approach the throne where Little John sits, his face as scarlet as my clothes.

"What shall I do, Robin?" I ask.

"Kiss him," Robin says, breathless, curling his fingers around his shaft, beginning to stroke.

I step in, leaning over the young man on the throne. He is beautiful, almost girlish, and bright-eyed with desire.

"May I?" I whisper.

He nods, his eyes enormous, lips parted.

First I kiss his cheek. It's velvet-soft and hot.

"Have you ever seen such a magnificent man as Robin?" I breathe into his ear.

John shakes his head. But his eyes skip from Robin's face to mine, and admiration heats in his gaze as he looks at me. I know I'm handsome, but it's always gratifying to have it recognized.

Laying my hand against John's cheek, I turn his face further toward me so Robin can see us both in profile. Slowly I move in, my lips hovering over his. A soft graze of skin. My tongue flicks along the opening, teasing the edge of his teeth.

Then I close the space between us. My eyes drift shut as I sink into the luscious heat of his mouth. These sweet, plump lips—the way his mouth and tongue respond eagerly to mine—a flood of sparkling desire rushes along my limbs, and my cock hardens.

Humming in my throat, I kiss him deeper, sliding my tongue over his. My hand drifts from his cheek, travels down his belly—he's not stopping me, I doubt he even notices. He's too busy sucking my lips, savoring my tongue.

I cup him between the legs.

And immediately I know something is wrong.

Where an erect cock should be, there is an odd lump between Little John's legs. A lump that doesn't feel right.

I plunge my hand into his trousers, and I find—a curved leather codpiece, secured by strips of cloth.

Little John makes a startled, panicked sound into my mouth.

Pulling back from the kiss, I stare into our guest's frantic dark eyes.

"Yes," says Robin from the table, still pumping a fist along his cock. "Touch him, Will."

He can't see what my fingers have discovered—that beneath the codpiece there is a soft little pussy. A wet, quivering, desperate little pussy.

A woman, here. A woman, pretending to be a man, accepting a place among us.

The girl in the throne stares at me, desperate, pleading. She doesn't want me to tell.

Suspicion coils darkly in my heart. But she looks so innocent, so frightened, so flushed.

So fucking beautiful.

I happened to find souls I love inside the bodies of two handsome men, but I like women's bodies just as much. So delicate in places, so soft and kissable, yet with an inner strength most men underestimate—passion like a storm waiting to be unleashed by the right touch.

And this one—the boldness of her, to wear such a disguise and walk right into the greenwood. She challenged Robin Hood himself—and she beat him. That alone is enough to make me admire her.

Suspicion and questions can wait. First I am going to make this little trickster come on my fingers.

My hand is concealed by the girl's trousers and tunic. Robin is watching our faces, and the men are watching him, so I doubt anyone will notice any oddity in the style of my movements.

I kiss her again, gently, reassuringly. She gives a little relieved sob, and I can't help myself—I grip the back of her skull with my free hand and crush my lips to hers, my tongue thrashing deep inside her mouth.

Meanwhile my hand moves in her trousers, under the cloth strips holding the codpiece in place, over her tender pussy. I can feel her clit, a little peak at the top of the triangle of sensitive flesh. I massage it gently, then faster, and she whimpers over my tongue.

I go deeper, until my fingertips glide over her soaked entrance. The heel of my hand is rocking against her clit.

I slip two fingers inside her, dipping in and out.

Her whole body goes rigid, shaking with her intense desire to come.

One more kiss on her mouth, and I slide my wet fingers out of her pussy, swirling them over her clit before rubbing firmly, rhythmically. Then I whisper in her ear, "Come for me, you wicked little beauty. But quietly. Softly as you can."

I can feel the spasms of her pussy against my fingers as she comes—in perfect, obedient silence. Her muscles tighten, and her thighs compress my hand hard before she relaxes, breathing through the aftershock of her climax.

"Good girl," I breathe against her ear.

Gathering more of her wetness, I withdraw my hand and smear the liquid over the front of her trousers.

"He came for me," I tell Robin.

"He did? Fuck," Robin says in a strangled voice. "I'm coming too, Will. I'm—"

The girl leans forward suddenly, tilting her face up, meeting his gaze. Something latches into place between them, a violent, almost tangible connection. Passion, vibrating in the taut air.

She opens her mouth.

The men around us groan in appreciation and surprise.

"You don't have to—" Robin pants, but he can't hold back, not when such a sweet invitation is offered, not when her little pink tongue slides out, ready to be anointed.

Robin moans, his beautiful body hardening all over, his balls jumping and tightening as he shoots ropes of hot cum into the girl's mouth, onto her face and hair. Because of who he is, he produces more cum than the average man, and his orgasm goes on for several seconds.

Some of the men in the group come in their pants every time he does this, and this occasion is no exception. Moans and grunts erupt through the clearing, echoing Robin's gasps. I don't blame them— I'm about to explode myself.

The girl is dripping from his release, but she doesn't look disgusted—she's gasping, too, almost laughing. I hand her a cloth to wipe her lashes. And then I hitch one foot onto the armrest of the living throne, and I pull my cock out of my hose.

A few pumps of my hand and I come hard, aiming upward so my release paints the girl's face afresh. Drops and lines of my cum slide down her cheek, into the creamy glaze of Robin's release.

It's a good orgasm, but I feel vaguely unsatisfied afterward. I want to strip that girl down to her bare skin. I want to take her apart slowly and find out who she is and what she wants, while she comes on my cock.

I don't think I'll be satisfied until I can have her, whole. Until I find out if she's a threat to Robin, to me, to all of us.

9

DAVID

I am a whore for pain. Inflicting it, and receiving it.

Some in our band know my affinity for such acts. But only Robin and Will truly understand the depth of my dance with agony, how far I'll go to ensure the keenest pleasure for myself or the one I'm fucking.

I can't usually come unless someone is hurting me, or I'm hurting them.

Pain is most deliciously intense in private, when its art is practiced between two people, or maybe three. Which is why, when the other Merry Men are whooping and guffawing and rutting cheerfully into each other's asses or mouths, I usually drag someone aside, into the blackness under the trees, and I hurt them until they come so hard they see stars.

I don't like to fuck openly and share my proclivities with everyone in the band. And Robin knows that. So why the fuck did he pick my name out of the pot?

Why the fuck did I even put my name in?

But I did. I wrote my initials on a piece of birch bark, and I put that papery scrap into the pot with the others.

Maybe it's because of the way our guest felt under my palm when I pushed her against the tree by the bridge—resistant yet pliant. A strong spirit that yearns to be dominated.

Yes, I suspected she was a woman then. I suspected more strongly when I caught her ankle and felt the delicacy of the bones. I saw her sliced-up feet and I grew instantly rock-hard. She'd been in such pain the whole time we were walking, yet she barely made a sound.

When I draped her over my shoulder, I knew beyond all doubt she was a woman. Her body was warm, soft, and solid—strong, yes, but toned in a different way than a man's.

I am intimately familiar with bones and muscle groups, with fat and flesh. I know every pleasure point, from the tender spot beneath the ear to the thin skin of the inner wrist—from the sensitive taint behind a man's balls to the pleasure spot deep in a woman's channel. There wasn't much chance of her fooling me.

But no one else seems to realize her gender except Will. He put his hand into her trousers and discovered the truth—but instead of shouting the revelation to everyone, he made her come. And the others were too distracted by Robin's beauty to observe the way Will moved his hand under the fabric—not the up-and-down rubbing or stroking he would have used on a cock, but a variety of other movements—especially the circular motion one might use on a nicely swollen clit.

I'm surprised Robin didn't notice. But Robin was too busy chasing his own climax. And the males of his kind tend to be pretty, fine-featured, and beardless anyway, so the girl's face wouldn't have been a telltale sign for him. In his view, humans tend to dress in specific, prescribed ways, as dictated by their society, and he accepted what was presented to him. She dressed in trousers, so he saw a man.

Robin fucking Hood. So intelligent that sometimes he cannot see what is right in front of his face.

The girl is in front of *my* face now. Her delicate features are wet with Robin's cum and Will's, and she keeps licking her lips as though she likes the way they taste.

I've tasted both of them. They're fucking delicious.

The other men have quieted, though low moans still roll through the clearing as a few couples take pleasure with each other. The rest are watching me and "Little John," curious to see me take myself in hand before them all.

"Get down here, boy." I point to the ground. "Kneel."

She obeys, her legs wobbling a little as she sinks onto the grassy turf. She's off-balance from the orgasm Will gave her. Probably craving another.

When she looks up at me, my breath catches. I'm overcome with the need to give her every exquisite pulse of agony and ecstasy I've learned to elicit.

Back in my homeland, I studied the science of healing. I wanted to help people.

But war wrecked all my good intentions. Prison shredded my goodwill toward humanity. When I met Robin Hood, I was broken. Hadn't felt a trace of desire in a long time. But his glittering smile and savage beauty promised a torturous delight I'd only dreamed of achieving. At my request, he fucked me over and over, with endless stamina, while I clawed and swore at him—until finally I lay in a pool of my cum and his, my blood and his, and I was finally healed. Transformed. At peace.

He broke me apart, and then he and Will put me back together. With them, I found that sex can heal, deeply and permanently. Love can repair the wounds of hate.

In this girl's eyes I see lust, but beyond that I see pain. The terror of ruination, the sour ache of despair, the raw wretchedness of deep humiliation. She has endured something dreadful, and the fear of more agony vibrates at her core.

She needs me to hurt her. To strip away that fear, the terror that she'll lose control. She needs me to *take* the control away from her, and dismantle her, and show her how to walk through the fire into true freedom.

But that will have to wait until another time, when she and I can be alone. When I have plenty of time to perform the exorcism of her fear.

For now, all I have to do is come. In front of them all. Without the aid of my usual tricks.

I'm not sure I can manage it alone.

10

MARIAN

David takes out his cock.

It's big—thicker than either Robin's or Will's—though admittedly I didn't get a good look at Will's. Will of the magic fingers…

But I can't think about him right now. I'll think about him again later, when I'm alone. And I'll think about Robin coming and coming on my face… so much of him spurting into my mouth, bursting uncontrollably across my skin, my hair. I loved it, because I'm terribly wicked.

I'm glad no one outside the greenwood knows how very wicked I am.

David hasn't undressed, and he doesn't seem as rigidly erect as the other two were. He's stroking himself grimly, as if determined to accomplish a distasteful task.

Robin Hood is draped in a fine purple robe, probably stolen from some noble, and he has taken a seat in the throne I just vacated. His eyes flick from David to me by turns.

Will Scarlet is dressed again, standing near Friar Tuck at the edge of the firelight. They're murmuring to each other, watching me. They both know my secret. At this rate, everyone in Sherwood Forest will know by morning.

David grunts low, a sound of frustration, not passion.

Some of the Merry Men are beginning to notice how long it's taking him to climax. They're eyeing him, speaking aside to one other, smirking. And for some reason, I don't like it. I don't want him to be humiliated.

David was rough with me. Tied me up, called me "filth." But he also carried me into camp so I wouldn't have to walk any farther on my injured feet.

"Thank you," I murmur, so quietly only David can hear—and perhaps Robin, whose place on the throne puts him nearest to us. "Thank you for carrying me."

"Your feet were hurt," David growls.

"They were. So many cuts."

"The pain you must have been in." He strokes a little faster. "Tell me about it."

"The soles of my feet were practically sliced apart."

"Yes." He practically groans the word.

My eyebrows lift as I realize that hearing about my pain arouses him. If it means helping him, getting both of us through this more quickly, I can play that game.

"You saw the blood," I say softly. "The scratches all over my ankles from the thorns. The lacerations on my heels. The pain was like licks of fire. Like teeth biting into my feet."

"Teeth, biting your feet," he rasps, and his cock jumps a little.

"Would you like to sink your teeth into my feet, David?" I whisper. And then, on impulse, "Or maybe you'd like to bite my ass."

His jaw locks. Breath drags through his flared nostrils. The tip of his cock is leaking clear, glistening fluid.

"Robin smacked me there, you know. Struck me with his staff, once on each ass cheek. I think I have bruises." My heartbeat is wild, wanton. I have never spoken like this in my life. Not aloud, anyway. Perhaps I've had inclinations, thoughts—nothing I would ever vocalize. But here—I can't stop myself.

"Imagine the bruises," I murmur. "The marks of Robin's staff on my smooth bottom. The flesh is sore there—"

He cries out, rough and ragged, and a spurt of cum strikes my cheek. I jerk back a little, but with a moan he grips my curls and holds my head steady while he comes all over my lips, pulse after pulse, warm wetness glazing my mouth, until he releases a long sigh of relief. Then he wipes the head of his cock on my chin.

I'm helplessly wet, my face coated with cum. Tentatively I lick my lips. He tastes saltier than the others, richer.

David tucks himself away and steps back.

"The anointing is complete!" Robin calls out, rising from the throne. "Little John is now one of us! I will take him to wash up, and the rest of you—to bed! We have thieving to do tomorrow."

Without another word, Robin Hood catches my arm, pulls me to my feet, and hustles me away, toward the dark forest. He seems caught in some fierce current of purpose, and my stomach drops. What if he has found me out somehow? I spoke too gently to David just now, I think. Shit.

The night is chilly, but not as chilly as I'd feared it would be, since the breeze has all but died away. Still, there's a nip in the air that speaks of much colder nights to come. As Robin and I hurry through the trees, the occasional dark leaf detaches from overhead and flutters down to the crunchy carpet under our feet.

"Where are we going?" I venture.

"There's a pool nearby, where you can wash your face. I doubt you want to sleep like that." Robin's tone is crisp, but there's a strain in it.

"You're angry," I say, low. "Are you going to hurt me?"

"Now you're talking like a frail little farm boy," Robin seethes. "You're not fighting back like you did on the bridge."

"Maybe I've grown wiser."

"Maybe you've lost your mettle. You've turned docile."

I stop suddenly, jerking my arm from his grip. "You want me to fight back?" I shove his chest, hard. He shifts half a step.

Then he lunges, and I lift both arms defensively. He grabs my forearms and pushes me backward, crowding me against a huge tree, his chest pressed to mine.

"That's better," he hisses between clenched white teeth. In his stolen robes of embroidered purple, he looks like a mad prince, reckless and beautiful. "But for now, you should be still, or I may hurt you."

There's a wild gleam in his eyes that confirms the warning. This is not the jovial man I fought on the sun-dappled bridge. Here in the forest, in the flakes of silvered moonlight, he is entirely different. Someone feral—someone truly dangerous.

I go still as the tree trunk.

My borrowed shoes offer protection from the undergrowth, but there's nothing to protect me from Robin Hood and whatever he plans to do to me.

"How did you do that?" he asks, low and urgent. "How did you know what David wanted—what he needed? Have you met him before?"

Again, I get the sense that he'll know if I'm lying. "No. I haven't met him before."

"Truth." His eyes narrow. "Then how did you know he likes pain?"

"I'm not sure. I guess I felt it."

"Felt it?" He frowns, shakes his head in disbelief.

"Yes, I felt it, or sensed it from his stance, his expression. How do *you* know when I'm lying?"

"It's a talent, not some nebulous feeling," he retorts. "When you told me your age on the bridge, I could tell you were lying, that you were older than seventeen."

"Yet you didn't challenge me."

"I thought you didn't want to admit it because you're still beardless. What are you—eighteen? Nineteen? Have you been through the change? Do you have hair in all the places human men get it when they leave boyhood? Have your balls dropped yet, or are you sexually stunted somehow?"

"What?" I gasp through an incredulous laugh. "Why are you asking that? And what do you mean '*human* men?' *You're* a human man—aren't you?"

But the moment I say it, I understand that he isn't.

He truly isn't human. Not at all.

He has no extra body hair that I could see, even when he was naked—not even a trace of scruff along his jaw. He controls living things, makes them move and blossom at his will. His climax is longer and more copious than any human male—though granted, I've had a very small sampling from which to judge. He can discern lies from truth. Which means I need to be extremely careful. There is much more going on here than a simple outlaw and his rugged band.

"Human, am I?" Robin whispers, his lean body pressing me harder against the tree. Through the silky robe I can feel the prod of his erection against my lower belly.

"What are you?" I breathe.

He's bending his head, his mouth hovering near mine. The pull between our lips is delicate, yet visceral. Irresistible.

His hands land on my waist. "You're not ready for what I am, Little John."

"Ridiculous name," I murmur.

"Indeed." His nose skims my cheek. "I can smell all of us on your skin. Gods, you're filthy, covered in our cum."

"I would do it again." I breathe the wicked words, and he chuckles faintly.

His mouth grazes mine.

"Robin?" A voice, sharp with concern. "Where are you?"

He sighs and steps back from me. "Here, Will."

Will Scarlet steps out of the trees. "The miller and the tinker are fighting again, and if they're allowed to continue, they'll suck all the others into a brawl. We can't have that, not after you told everyone to turn in. You're the only one they'll heed. Go—I can escort Little John to the pool."

"Very well." Robin doesn't seem pleased, but he pushes himself away from me and stalks off into the trees.

Will Scarlet hauls in a deep breath. His long hair is like a river of white gold in the moonlight. "Now, darling," he says. "You and I are going to have a chat."

Will leads me through a thin belt of trees, down a hill, to the pebbly shore of a pool.

"Is this the Bottomless Pool that Robin mentioned?" I ask.

"No, that one is deeper in the forest." Will kneels by the waterside, scoops a palmful of liquid, and rinses his own face. I follow his example, kneeling and bathing the cum from my cheeks, lips, and hair.

When I'm done, I turn to face Will, who's still on his knees, looking at me.

"Why?" he asks simply.

I know what he's asking. Why did I dress as a boy and come into these woods?

"I know what you told Tuck," he adds. "We spoke, he and I, while you were with David. Is this really the only path you could see to your revenge? Dressing like a man and joining this lawless band?"

"Who else but Robin Hood is strong enough to threaten Prince John and his lackeys?" I ask. "None but the true king, and he's away. Imprisoned, some say, and others claim he's dead. I was desperate."

Will nods, stroking his close-trimmed golden beard. He has lovely eyes, blue and honest and strangely innocent for someone who came on my face a short while ago.

"Many are desperate now," he muses. "Trapped in the hands of a merciless ruler, dragging through a day's work only to see most of their wages go to the Church or the Crown—which some would argue are the same thing. The people are sad, angry, and wretched. We've seen a recent swelling of the ranks here in the greenwood."

"And all of them participate in the—nightly activities?"

"Not all, and not every night. Some who are loyal to Robin stay in their own homes, on their farms or in their villages, and they come only when he calls. Others revel in the freedom the greenwood brings. The absence of judgment."

I nod, heat seeping into my cheeks. "I understand that."

"You enjoyed yourself, didn't you?" Will's long fingers clasp my knee, a soothing squeeze. "The noble lady, giving herself over to debauchery."

"I shouldn't have enjoyed it so much," I whisper. My face is probably as scarlet as his clothes.

"I used to tell myself the same thing." He shifts his position, planting his rear on the pebbled beach and draping his arm over one bent knee. "Several years ago, I had just begun recognizing my liking for men as well as women. I thought myself terribly wicked. I'd go to confession and sit in the booth trembling, afraid to tell the priest my sin lest I be shunned and punished, or even killed. The guilt and shame gnawed at my soul like acid, for a long time. Until I realized that the God who gave me these loving impulses toward all His people would not shame me for acting on them. I suppose I created my own religion, in a way. A different version of God from the one I was taught."

"But—can you do that?" I crook an eyebrow at him. "Create your own version of God? Isn't that also wrong?"

"The lines of right and wrong are more blurred than you think, darling." He reaches out, running his fingers through my short curls. "Your hair must have been beautiful when it was long. Did it pain you to cut it?"

"Not really."

"Hm." He gazes at me, his blue eyes soft beneath heavy lashes. "I'm sure you're weary and grimy after this long day. And your breasts must hurt, if you have them bound as tightly as I think you do. If you'd like to wash, I can promise no one else will disturb you at this hour. Robin will have them all under control by now, and he'll be occupied for a while, making sure they get to their rest. It's safe for you to bathe. I have scented soap in my hut—I can fetch it, if you like."

The water is cold, but a wash does sound like heaven. "If you'd be so kind."

"Back in a moment." He leaps up and disappears into the trees.

I peer around, searching out every shadow in the gloomy forest. I see no one anywhere. Just a few rocks, the trees, the sloping beach, and the shimmering water.

In the chilly starlight I shuck off my cloak, trousers, vest, and tunic, as well as the clumsy codpiece and the borrowed shoes. When I inspect my feet, I'm shocked to find that they are nearly healed. Just the faintest of scratches remain.

That is not natural. Not normal. Mark it down on the list of strange things I've seen and heard since I arrived in the greenwood.

Slowly I unbind my breasts. As the blood flow returns, my flesh screams with pain. Tears burst in my eyes, and I whimper quietly as I make for the water.

When I wade in, the liquid bites more sharply than I expected. It didn't feel so icy when I was washing my face.

Gasping, heart racing, I force myself in deeper. I need to be neck-deep by the time Will comes back with the soap, so he can't see my body. Of course, he did already coax me to orgasm, so perhaps my modesty is foolish.

A few moments later Will strides out of the trees, carrying a couple of blankets, which he lays over a rock. He tosses me the bar of soap, which I catch, thankfully.

And then he begins disrobing.

"What are you doing?" I gasp through chattering teeth.

"Bathing."

"You said I could bathe safely here."

"I said no one *else* would disturb you. And neither will I, darling. I simply want to be clean."

I noticed earlier that Will's skin is a shade more tanned than Robin's, though that's hard to discern in the pale glow of the moon and stars. He has a swirling tattoo up his left side, from his jutting hipbone all the way to his breast. It's a mingling of leaves, vines, and symbols I don't know the meaning of. The back of his right calf is also tattooed—a skull, a moth, and some flowers and herbs.

His hair is straight, and long enough to brush his buttocks when he stands upright.

When he enters the water, he hisses. "Gods' bones, that's fucking cold. Ah, my balls have tucked themselves into my gut, I do believe."

I can't help giggling, and he flashes me a smile. His smiles are gentler than Robin's, but they're still tinged with lust. And the lust weighs his long lashes as he moves toward me through the water.

His expression ignites a mirrored desire in me, fuel for a new kind of boldness.

Maybe I don't mind if he sees me, after all.

When he's waist-deep, he asks, "May I borrow the soap?"

"In a moment." Taking a deep breath, I walk closer to him, toward the shallows, until my breasts emerge from the surface. I keep walking until the waterline hovers at my ribcage, and then I slide the soap over my arms, my neck, my chest. Lathering one hand, I dip it beneath the water and wash between my legs.

When I risk a glance at Will, he looks entranced—lips parted, blue eyes glowing with desire.

I lather up my hands again and pass the soap to him. Then I rub the lather over both my breasts, slowly, delighting in the freedom from those horrible bindings. My nipples harden to painful points in the chilly night air.

Much as my wicked heart would like to stay out here with Will, my body is sending very strong signals that it's much too cold. My jaw aches because I'm trying to keep my teeth from chattering.

"I think I'm freezing to death," I pant, splashing water over my soapy shoulders to rinse them.

"Get out then," Will says with a laugh.

"Where can I sleep?"

"Normally you'd be assigned a pallet in one of the huts, but I think we can make an exception. Would you care to join me in my hut? It's rather more comfortable than the others, and seeing as you're nobility, used to a certain level of accommodation, I thought it might suit you."

My stomach flips. "I—um—"

He lifts both hands, one holding the soap. "I won't touch you unless you want me to."

I want you to. I have to bite back the words. "Thank you, that's very kind."

"Take a blanket, then, and put your shoes back on. Don't forget your bindings and such." He gives the order casually but warmly. He's commanding me for my own good, like he did when he told me to come quietly.

And like then, I feel compelled to obey him.

I wade out of the pool, wrap myself up in a blanket, and put on my shoes. Then I collect my things, tucking them under the blanket, close to my bare body.

Will comes out of the pool a moment later, glistening like a beautiful god, water streaming from his hair. I can't tell if the moisture between my legs is from the pool or from my attraction to him.

When I'm with him, I feel strangely settled. As if I'm safe, and I can trust him to take care of me. It's something I haven't felt in—well… perhaps never. Certainly never with a complete stranger.

Robed in our blankets, we walk through the trees again, heading for camp.

"You do look rather like a boy, with that tousled mop of curls," Will murmurs. "An unusually pretty boy." He sighs. "Tuck doesn't want me to tell Robin about you. He wants to wait until Robin discovers it himself."

"I think Robin is close to guessing the truth," I admit. "Earlier he was asking about my age, if I'd been through the normal physical changes yet. Hair between my legs and all that."

"You're joking." Will muffles a laugh into his blanket. "Human growth and fertility has always fascinated him, but he has never gotten a firm grasp on it."

"He's not human, is he?"

Will's laugh dies immediately. "What makes you say that?"

"He made the throne flower around me. He can tell when I'm lying—which I suppose is helpful for an outlaw leader. And—just looking at him—I can tell."

Will nods slowly. "That's one reason he wears the cowl when we go beyond the greenwood. His face draws too much attention."

"But you won't tell me what he is?"

"It's his secret to tell." We're at the edge of the camp now, and Will places a finger against his lips.

The air in this part of the forest is warmer, and I don't think it's solely because of the bonfires. They're burning much lower, banked up for the night, just embers and stubby flames. Noting the unnatural warmth, my skin prickles with the awareness of something *else* at work, something I'm not prepared to name just yet, because acknowledging it is going to change everything I know and believe.

Before I let myself believe it, I need sleep.

Will leads me through the tents and huts. He points to the largest hut of them all, a huge dome made from woven branches threaded with vines. There's no entrance that I can see.

"Robin's," whispers Will. "He must have gone to bed already."

I'm a little sorry Robin didn't return to check on me, his guest, his new Merry Man. But perhaps he grew frustrated after dealing with his rowdy band, and decided I was a problem that could wait until tomorrow.

The hut next to Robin's proves to be Will's chamber. He holds aside the deerskin covering over the door and ushers me into a space lit by two candles and furnished with a couple of low chairs, a wicker table, and an abundance of large cushions and finely woven blankets.

"Stolen from noblemen's carriages," Will says softly. "As are all these." He gestures to gleaming copper pots, shining candelabra, a tray of sparkling jewelry, and an open chest packed with neatly rolled silks and other fine fabrics.

He steps over to a small washstand and places the soap we used in a wide bowl that holds several more bars of soap. Their rich floral scent pervades the whole chamber with the aroma of luxury.

"There's only one bed, I'm afraid." Will gestures toward the shadowed part of the room. "We'll have to—oh shit."

I follow his gaze—and there, lying on his stomach on a wide wooden bed, among tasseled pillows and velvety blankets, is David of Doncaster, very naked and very fast asleep.

"Why is David sleeping here?" I whisper to Will.

"He has his own hut, but he comes to me sometimes, for comfort."

"Oh." I lift my eyebrows.

"Not just *that* kind of comfort." There's a softness in Will's eyes, a tenderness that cracks my heart. I would love to have someone look at me the way he's looking at David right now. "The bed is big enough. We can all share it."

"But he'll find out," I whisper. "About me."

"He may already know. David has an instinct about people—about bodies. But if it makes you feel better, I can help you wrap up these lovely breasts again." He touches the hollow of my throat, trails a finger downward into the valley between my breasts. The blanket I'm clutching stops him from going any lower.

But I wish he would. I'm still cold. My legs are so chilled that my knees keep knocking together.

Will frowns. "You're shivering. Enough talk— you need to get in the bed and get warm. Now."

"Help me bind my chest first," I plead.

With a sigh, Will nods, knotting his own blanket around his waist. I do the same with my blanket and hand over the cloth strips, noting how his gaze sweeps over my upper body.

"You're beautiful," he murmurs. "What's your name? Your real name?"

But I shake my head, smiling. "It's Little John to you."

I lift my arms, and Will moves in. His breathing is shallow, his cheeks rosy in the candlelight. He's eyeing my breasts.

"May I touch them first?" he whispers.

My throat is so tight with suppressed desire I can't speak. I only nod.

He slides a warm hand up my ribs, over my right breast. My nipple slips between two of his fingers, pressed and rolled as he squeezes my flesh gently. Arousal licks along my pussy like a white flame.

Will Scarlet leans nearer and takes the nipple of my left breast into his mouth.

I gasp, shrill and broken, my clit tingling with wild need.

He laves the bead with his tongue, coaxing it tighter, harder. Sucks my breast into his mouth, as much as he can take.

No one has touched me like this, tended me like this. I wanted this from my husband—asked him timidly for it, and I was told my cravings were strange and sinful, that I was a wicked whore for wanting that kind of attention. To him, I was only a hole to be taken. Nothing more.

"Do other women like this?" I ask suddenly, desperately.

Will releases my breast and straightens, confusion and concern swirling in his eyes. "Did I hurt you? Did you not like it?"

"I love it." Tears are pooling in my eyes and I can't stop them. "But I thought—I was told—only harlots and madwomen like this sort of thing. I must be both."

Will looks shocked, and a little angry. "Who told you that?"

"My late husband," I whisper. "He died in the war. But during the week we shared a bed, I asked him to touch me in certain places, and he was furious. He made me confess my request to the priest the next day, and do penance afterward. And he—" But I can't tell Will what else my husband did. I can't.

"Listen to me." Will cups the back of my neck, looking earnestly into my eyes. "Not all women enjoy touch. But most do. You are neither mad nor wicked. You are as God made you—a beautiful, sensitive, luscious woman. And as for being a harlot or a whore—those words are not so shameful as some people think. Some whores are forced to please men—that's a painful truth—but others enjoy the task and derive pleasure from it. They are not ashamed. Nor should you be."

I nod, tears brimming in my eyes. Never have I felt more raw and open than now, with this man.

I didn't plan for this, didn't expect this.

My mind goes suddenly dark, a terrible image swirling in my head. Will Scarlet, his handsome face purpled and swollen, his neck constricted by a hangman's noose, his lovely blue eyes vacant in death.

Sickness roils in my gut.

I'm not sure I can betray him. Perhaps I'll leave his name off the list I give to the Sheriff.

In my mind I repeat the names of the people for whom I'm doing this, the people I need to save.

There's Martha, the young cook with twin tousle-headed boys. Only with me does she have freedom to set aside her work and spend time with her children whenever she likes. She confided in me that the boys' father isn't dead, as she tells everyone. In fact they were never married, and once he found out she was pregnant, he never spoke to her again. Without my patronage, she would be shunned, or worse.

Then there's Master Blunt, with his twisted leg. I took him on as stablehand when no one else would give him work.

Sarah and Ruth are my maids. I've suspected for a long time that they are in love with each other. Nowhere else would they have the privacy and safety I give them. Lord Guisborne would rape them both, and Martha too, I have no doubt.

Then there's George the gardener, a quiet man. His son Otto cannot walk—he sits in a chair in the garden while his father works. I pay the cost of anything Otto requires, and I allow his father all the time he needs to care for him.

They are my family. They are the people I must protect. No salacious whispers, no wild sexual pleasures in this dark, distant wood can distract me from the purpose I must fulfill.

Will is stroking my sides lightly with his palms. "Where did you go just now?" he asks softly.

"Thinking about the past," I whisper.

"Don't think," he murmurs, sliding an arm around my body, pulling my chilled skin against his warm, bare chest. His pectorals are dusted with fine golden hair. "Just feel."

His lips brush against mine before sinking deeper, and I sigh into the relief of the kiss. We're both naked to the waist, pressed together, and it feels more wonderful than anything else ever has. Perhaps I can enjoy it, just a little, and think about my responsibilities later.

Will's mouth tastes like warm sunshine, faintly spiced—like sweet honey sliding over my tongue, gliding down my throat. His lips are a tingling delight.

I could kiss him forever, all the way into hell— and from the way he's mouthing me, devouring me, swirling his tongue over mine, I think he's enjoying this just as deeply.

But a grumbling voice interrupts our kisses.

"Are you two ever coming to bed?"

11

"Shit." I break the kiss with the girl and turn around.

David is propped on his elbow, glaring at us—a gorgeous, disapproving god with silky black hair. Scars thatch his brown skin. Robin and I cut him sometimes, for pleasure, but he is always healed after our sessions. The scars are from his life before he met Robin Hood. Some are from the war, some were self-inflicted.

"Yes, Little John is a woman, and I've known since I carried her over my shoulder," says David.

"Let's move on. And by moving on, I mean the two of you will get into this bed and shut up."

"You came to me," I say, relinquishing the girl and moving toward David. "Did you need—" I lift an eyebrow.

"I need sleep," he growls. "And a warm body in bed."

It's a dichotomy of David's that, while he prefers weaving pleasure with pain, he also likes to cuddle with someone, especially on certain nights when his past becomes wretchedly vivid in his mind.

I glance at the girl again. "Will you trust me? I believe I have an idea that will bring all of us comfort."

After a moment's hesitation, she nods.

Gently I disengage the knot holding her blanket around her waist. It drops, revealing her to David and me.

She is exquisite. Lovely shoulders and sharp collarbones. Full breasts, still flushed from their bindings and my ministrations. Slim, toned arms. A tapered waist and a flat, smooth stomach inset with a kissable dot of a navel. Long, shapely legs, delicate ankles, dainty feet. And between her legs, beneath a light dusting of curls, is the pretty pussy I teased after dinner. I want to kiss it.

The sorrowful, self-loathing way she spoke of her needs earlier—it broke my heart. I want to show her how normal and wonderful she is. I want to reveal all the pleasure she's capable of.

And it starts with her trusting me now.

I drop my own blanket and scoop her into my arms. She's anxious, her body rigid as I carry her to the bed. David scoots back, making space for us. His jaw is tight, a muscle flexing near his temple.

"So resistant, the two of you," I murmur. "So tight and tense. Just relax. We're only going to snuggle together and share warmth as we fall asleep. No one will wake up with anyone else in their holes. Agreed?"

"Agreed," rumbles David.

The girl actually looks a little disappointed, and judging by the way David's eyes snap to mine, he notices. She relaxes as I lay her down next to David. I can feel the heat rolling off him, and the musky, spicy scent that turns me on every time. My cock is already painfully hard from fondling the girl's breasts and seeing them both naked.

David and the girl eye my cock as I walk over to the candles.

"That looks painful, Scarlet," says David. "Need a hand?"

"I'll calm down soon enough. Go to sleep." I blow the candles out and settle onto the bed, pulling the blankets over us before lying down on my back, with my shoulder pressed to the girl's.

I lie perfectly still, my heart beating double-time. To calm myself, I recall days of fear and penance. I remember the deaths of Merry Men at the hands of the Sheriff's men. I muse over my own fears that someday, Robin will truly fall—or that he'll leave us, and wander off to wherever the rest of his kind went.

In the cocooned warmth, I hear David shifting his position. And then the girl shifts hers, turning her back to David and her front to me.

A moment later, her silky fingers glide over my breast. My eyes drift shut at the tentative touch. She's copying what I did to her, squeezing lightly, then rolling my nipple with her fingers. The stimulation goes straight to my dick, and I let out a low, rasping sigh.

She cuddles nearer with a little satisfied wriggle. She's learning quickly, this one. Desperate for contact, for pleasure. She must have been deprived for years.

David moves again, and the girl releases a tiny mew. His answering rumble sends another thrill through my cock.

So we *are* going to play before we sleep, after all.

12

MARIAN

In my most sinfully sensual moments, alone in
the enormous bed in my husband's castle, I dreamed
of being surrounded by male bodies. Hot smooth
skin, surging muscle, a light graze of hair from chests
and legs. Strong fingers probing into my secret places,
palms cupping my bottom, thick warm cocks
prodding my flesh.

This is the closest I've ever gotten to that dream.

When Will places me in the bed, gets in himself,
and covers us all up, I lie perfectly still for a few
moments. But the glow of David's heat is more than I

can resist, and I begin to shift my chilled arm slowly toward him.

I forgot he was lying on his side, facing me.

My questing fingers touch the tip of his cock, slipping through a bead of wetness there.

I pull my hand back.

He doesn't move. Neither do I.

And then I wiggle my fingers toward him again, and I touch his erection. Beneath the thin skin, his shaft is rock hard. Gently I trace the bulging vein I can feel along its length.

David's hand finds my hip. He hitches himself closer to me, then pushes me over onto my side so my back is to him and I'm facing Will. His grasp on my hip tightens as he urges my bottom up and outward, toward him.

Judging by Will's quick breathing, he's still awake and aroused. I don't want him to be left out of this. After all, his fingers made me come on Robin's throne tonight.

Cautiously I smooth my hand over his breast, imitating the movements that gave me so much pleasure earlier. I saw one man fondling another's chest during the "christening." It must be something all genders like.

Will's nipple beads at my touch. He lets out a shaky sigh, and impulsively I move closer, my breast pushing against his shoulder. He wants this—needs it.

And here in the quiet darkness, in the depths of the greenwood, there is no one to tell us *no*.

Behind me, David moves forward. My legs are bent, tucked up slightly, my ass toward him, and when he comes closer, the flat of his lower belly contacts my bottom. His cock lies parallel to my sex now, its length lightly touching my pussy folds. He rocks gently, and his cock slides through my outer lips—not entering me, just nudging along the seam, teasing more wetness from my body. It feels so good I release a small sound, which David answers with a low, pleased growl.

Will rolls toward me, his profile nuzzling mine in the darkness. His breast against my breast, his belly seamed to mine, his cock pinned between us. I hook my leg over his hip, drawing him closer and giving David better access to my pussy.

We are blind to what we're doing. We are sightless bodies writhing and humping and burning together. I wonder if that's why so many sinful deeds are done in the dark—because we think God cannot see us here.

But if He exists, He must see.

The thought should make me pause. It should make me leap from this bed and flee into the woods, begging a lightning bolt to strike me down or some ravenous beast to devour me. It should prompt me to say prayers, to do penance, to work for righteousness so I might escape the fiery result of my fornication.

But I don't do any of that. Because in my soul thrums the unshakable certainty that this is exactly where I belong—that these two men—strangers I just met today—are pieces of me. They belong with me, inside me. Not forever—nothing so dramatic as that. Just for tonight.

Will is kissing my nose, my cheeks. He finds my mouth and voices an urgent hum as he rubs his cock between our stomachs.

David reaches between my legs, thick fingers fumbling. He finds my buzzing clit and pinches it hard.

I squeak against Will's mouth, and David's heavy cock bobs against my sex.

A harsh whisper from him. "I want to be in you."

In answer I clutch Will's shoulder, and I angle myself so the tip of David's cock is poised over my slit.

"You're so fucking wet," David whispers. And he thrusts inside.

My pussy lips are slippery, but he's so thick it still stretches me almost to the point of pain. I whimper, and Will hushes me with his mouth.

"Tell me it hurts," says David hoarsely.

"It hurts so much. Don't stop. Keep hurting me, please, please."

He squeezes my ass cheek, right where Robin bruised it, and I let out a small yelp of real pain. A deep groan rakes from his throat.

Will releases a light moan, his cock twitching between us. Then he sits up and leans over me, his chest brushing my shoulder. I can hear him kissing

David while David moves inside me, rolling heavy and slow, in and out.

"Lift her leg, my heart," Will urges, and David seizes my leg, holding it up high and straight. The blankets are half off us, and a breath of chill air wafts across my heated pussy.

The next moment, there are lips in that same spot, and the graze of a golden beard. Will's mouth and nose, nuzzling my sex.

I was forced to suck my husband's cock a few times, before the terrible night when I asked him to put his mouth on me in a similar way, and bring me to pleasure. I asked him to touch my breasts and lick my pussy. And he reviled me. Struck me. Shamed me.

I've known Will for less than a day, and already he's more devoted to my pleasure than my spouse ever was.

"How does she taste?" asks David.

"Divine." Will's breath flutters over my sensitized clit. He moves a little, his beard tantalizing my quivering sex unbearably. Somehow I can tell he's licking the underside of David's cock as it slides in and out of me. "You're delicious too, David my darling, as always."

David's cock flexes hard inside me. So he likes praise as well as pain.

Will returns to nibbling my clit as wild need spirals through my belly. I can feel myself tightening and fluttering inside.

"She's close," David murmurs. "Keep going, Scarlet." He hitches my leg higher, opening me wider, and he starts thrusting inside me with bruising force, deep, deep—the massive fullness of him is almost more than I can take.

"Come on my tongue, little trickster. Come all over David." Will suckles my clit just as David's cock thrums against a new spot far inside my body, and I spark—I shatter—I *crack*, vibrating into helpless pieces as bliss cascades through me.

13

DAVID

The girl's pussy sucks my cock, working me closer to a climax. But I can't come like this. I climaxed once today, just by imagining the girl's damaged feet, but I got lucky. I can feel that it's not going to happen again.

I need more pain. And she isn't ready for that.

I slide out of her, wet with her juices, and I ease back into my place on the bed.

Will sits up too, and the girl rolls onto her back, her arm flopping against me. I smile a little, because she's boneless now, spent with pleasure.

In the dark I hear Will whisper, "May I have a turn, darling?" A tongue of silver, that one. I may look like a prince—and I may have royal ancestry—but time has stolen the elegant phrases from my mouth. I keep my speech concise now. No sense wasting words. People rarely listen anyway.

I swing myself off the end of the bed and find my way to the candles again. There's a tinderbox beside them, so I light one of the wicks. "If you're going to fuck her," I tell Will, "I want to watch."

The light is barely enough to see both of them, their bodies bathed in dancing shadow. The girl's dark eyes are glazed with pleasure, and Will wears a delighted grin.

"Look." He runs a fingertip along her glistening sex. When he pulls it away, a shining string of her wetness joins his skin to hers.

"Fuck," I murmur.

Will kneels between the girl's legs, lining himself up. He lifts her bottom, angling her pelvis so he can enter at the right angle. "I'm going to fill you up now, darling."

The girl nods, and then, as he eases into her, she tips her head back and her eyes close blissfully.

"You can tell me what you want," Will says as he begins to move.

Her eyes open. She's surprised. Shy, but there's a delighted avarice in her eyes. She's greedy for this. "Can I?"

"Yes, treasure. Tell me what you like." Will's voice carries a note of pain.

I know him. He's upset that no one has taught her she has a voice in such moments. Too many women in our time are used as holes, and neither understood nor cherished. But when they come to Sherwood Forest, they receive more pleasure than they give. Robin makes sure of that. Every time we have an orgy, he instructs the newer members of the band on pleasing both women and men. He demonstrates the techniques, too.

"I don't know what I like," the girl whispers. "I think I like everything." Her gaze travels to me, where I stand with my cock jutting out. "I want him to come for me," she says.

A bolt of need throbs in my cock.

"Shit," moans Will. "Yes, David. We both want you to come, love."

"I can't come unless I hurt you—or you hurt me," I confess to the girl.

"I know. Like the christening. You had to think about my pain. I understand. Do it, please. Whatever you need."

"Gently now, David." Will meets my eyes as he pumps his hips, balls-deep in the girl. "She isn't used to your games."

Of course I know that. With a glare at him, I climb onto the bed beside the girl, leaning one on elbow. I play with her breasts, carefully at first, while Will thrusts rhythmic little sighs of pleasure out of her. She's going to come again for us soon. Her third climax in the greenwood.

I tweak her nipple hard. She gasps, her cheeks flushing redder.

Her reaction sends a buzz straight to my cock. I can't stop myself; I bury my face against her breast and bite into the softness. Not hard enough to release blood, but enough to hurt. Enough to leave my mark.

"Oh!" she cries, seizing my head in a frenzied grasp. "Oh god—do that again."

Will stops his thrusting, and I lift my head, shocked.

"What?" she frowns. "You said I can tell you what I want."

"Yes, but—" I'm astonished. Usually women don't like my roughness, not at first. They have to be trained to enjoy it.

This one seems too perfect. Too good to be real.

"Please don't stop," she quavers, tears pooling in her enormous eyes. "I'm sorry if I said something wrong…"

"Wrong? No, darling." Will strokes her thighs. "You are exactly the woman we need. Bite her again, David."

I nibble the sweet flesh of her other breast and bite her again, sucking and soothing the flesh I injure. Will is pounding into her now, and the slapping sound fills the room, deadened somewhat by the thick woven walls. Sleeping humans probably wouldn't notice the sound. But someone else might.

"He's going to hear us," I warn Will.

"Fuck, I know. I'm coming—shit, I'm coming—" he moans, throwing his head back. I reach over and clamp one hand to his ass, shoving him deeper inside her, feeling the tension of his orgasm through his taut muscles. He's so fucking glorious.

When he comes down from the peak, gasping, I rise up on my knees on the bed, and I shove my mouth against his, a snarl of possession ripping through my chest. He bites my tongue, and my dick jerks. I nearly come on the girl's belly.

Will pulls out of her. "Look." He grabs my face, points to the girl's pussy, which is spread wide for us. Some of his white cum oozes in a large pearly drop at the mouth of her opening.

"Fuck," I mutter. "That's goddamn beautiful." I lift my gaze to her face; she's biting her lip, squirming. I think she almost came again—she's writhing at the precipice of a climax. She wants more.

14

I'm used to the frustration of *nearly* getting what I want. I'm always in that place of *almost*, of never quite having.

But I've had two climaxes today, which is more than I've managed on my own in weeks—I've been too busy, too scared, too depressed. I've been planning this venture, this escape from a dreadful future.

I should be satisfied now. I should be able to stop at two. But it's as if someone dormant has wakened inside me, and she's ravenous, insatiable.

She craves every surge of pleasure, every spasming, glittering crest of the wave.

So when David of Doncaster leans over me and looks into my eyes, I am ready to beg for his cock.

"I'm going to push Will's cum back into your little pussy," he says. "I'm going to fuck it deep into your womb. And then I'm going to fill you up with my cum, too."

"Yes," I whine, more needy than I ever thought I could be. I'm not the girl who met Robin on the bridge—I'm someone else entirely. Or maybe I am both. Maybe I hold many Marians inside me—each one wholly *me*, and each one worthy.

David moves my body easily, as if I'm a child's rag doll. He turns me onto my stomach, drags me to the edge of the bed. My eyes roll back in my head as his thick cock pushes inside me again.

My body recognizes him, welcomes him. I am warm and glimmering inside—I was riding a mounting wave of pleasure before Will came inside me and then pulled out. I don't blame him—he has certainly done his part.

I can see Will easily from my new position, with my cheek pressed to the mattress. He's standing at the foot of the bed, his tattoos on full display, inhaling from a pipe he must have lit while David was rearranging me.

"This is the best night I've had in a long time," he murmurs.

I smile at him, and his eyes widen with delight.

"Beautiful trickster," he whispers. "Fuck her well, David. Make her come again."

"No," I gasp, my words jerking out of me with David's hard thrusts. "I won't come, not until he comes for me."

David groans. Then he smacks one of my bruised ass cheeks, hard. I cry out, and Will quickly sits down on the bed and puts two of his fingers in my mouth. "Hush, love," he whispers. "Silently, now. Be a good girl for me, like you were during the christening."

David squeezes both my buttocks in his hands, savaging the bruised flesh while he thrusts at a frenzied pace. The slapping sound of his thighs against mine, the painful grip, the slick squelch of my juices around his length—it's raw and visceral and wildly erotic, and every squeeze of his great hands is pulling me, hauling me closer to the peak. I'm moaning erratically around Will's fingers—yes yes yes yes yes—oh—oh—*yes*—and I tip over that edge, crashing, convulsing—I scream, and Will's palm slams over my mouth, and David erupts inside me, gush after throbbing gush of his hot cum shooting into my core.

I'm bruised, pulsing, nerveless. Tears are streaming from my eyes and I have never felt so fucking wonderful.

David half-collapses against my spine, pushing himself deep, wringing out the last of his pleasure.

Will removes his hand from my mouth and bends over to kiss my forehead. "Are you well, sweet one?" he asks.

But all I can manage is two broken words. "Thank you."

"Oh darling." He brushes back my curls, that sweet, pained sadness entering his eyes again. "It was our pleasure."

David pulls out silently. But he kisses my back in two different places, and each kiss zings through my skin, a warm sizzling dot of delight.

No one has ever kissed me like that before.

Will gives me a handkerchief to wipe up the cum dripping from my pussy, and then he finds me a baggy nightshirt to wear. "In case someone comes in tomorrow morning, before you're ready," he says.

We all climb into bed, and this time David pulls Will's back against his chest, while I curl up in Will's arms.

I am not truly safe here, nor am I actually loved. But I feel as if both are true.

I can't betray either Will or David. When I give my list of names to the Sheriff of Nottingham, I will leave both of them out of it.

Though if I go through with this, and tell Robin's secrets to the Crown, both of the men who came inside me tonight will become my mortal enemies.

15

WILL

When I wake, it's chilly, with the very faintest bit of light leaking around the deerskins covering the doorway. David is clumsily leaving the bed.

"I'm off to set the trap with Robin and the others," he whispers.

I press a finger to my lips and glance at the girl. Both her arms are flung up, above her head; her rosy mouth is open, and her cheeks are flushed with sleep.

I look up at David again, and see my delight mirrored in his eyes.

"She's so fucking cute," he whispers.

"Go, before you wake her," I hiss. "You big noisy brute."

He grins. Gives me a sloppy kiss that tastes terrible. I love it.

I settle back into the covers and try to drift into sleep again while David dresses quietly and leaves the tent.

We take turns going on these thieving forays with Robin. I was in the group last time, so I'm not expected to join today. And neither is "Little John," being so new to the band. She'll need instruction in the way we conduct our thievery.

According to our information, this particular mark is passing through a narrow belt of the forest, far from here, probably trying to avoid us. But no precautions can save them. Thanks to Robin's powers, Sherwood Forest can extend anywhere he pleases. Belts of trees have been known to march into place overnight, creating Sherwood where no Sherwood was the day before. And the Merry Men can travel through the woods at a shockingly quick pace, since Robin can clear paths easily and then close them up again.

Most of the Merry Men don't realize the truth of his powers. Many believe he's blessed of God, working miracles on behalf of the impoverished peasants. Others believe the forest is in league with Robin, that the very turf and trees of England herself are loyal to King Richard and therefore to the Hood as well. A few know the truth. But all have benefited in countless ways from their allegiance to Robin Hood, and their loyalty runs deep.

I still believe Robin is too trusting, that he accepts men too easily into our band. His talent for discerning truth from lies has made him cocky. Sooner or later, someone is bound to turn on him.

Sleep is eluding me, so I push myself to a sitting position. David left the tent flap slightly disarranged, and a soft pale light filters into the room, bathing the girl's sleeping face.

She looks so innocent. So relaxed.

I loved being inside her. She felt like silk and roses, and she tasted like apples and wine. Yet I cannot shake the sense that something is wrong with her story. Not a lie—Robin would have detected that. But something unsettles me.

Today I will reinforce her trust in me. And I will discover what she's hiding.

Naked, I walk outside behind the hut to piss. When I re-enter, I close the flap securely and light some candles while I brush out my hair and braid it. I have a nice selection of jewelry from which to choose, thanks to our many fruitful missions. Robin insists we give most of our loot to the poorest people of the region, while the rest is divided evenly among the Merry Men. But he cannot resist indulging me with a few choice gifts now and then.

I will never get over the wonder of it, that a man like him loves me.

"Will." The soft voice from the bed makes my heart jump. When I turn, the girl is sitting up, her short hair tousled and her lashes blinking drowsily over those beautiful eyes.

She needs to be licked gently, right now, coaxed into the softest and most delicate orgasm.

"I need to relieve myself," she says, and I almost laugh. My plan to pleasure her and then interrogate her will have to wait.

She can't go outside without her bindings, and I'm not willing to wrap her up yet, so I show her the bedpan and turn my back. I take it outside and empty it afterward, then return to her. She's naked now, refreshing herself at the washstand.

Naughty girl. She wants me to be tempted. She craves my touch.

I step behind her and let my hands flow up her body, framing her shape.

"I thought it might have been a dream," she whispers, yielding, swaying against me.

I press my lips to her shoulder, letting my erection nudge her lower back. "No. Not a dream."

She revolves in my arms, hitching herself against my body with a little mew of want.

Cupping the nape of her neck, I kiss her, walking us both to the bed, where I lay her down. She bends and lifts her legs at once, exposing her shining hole to me. I tease her clit with the head of my cock for a moment before easing inside.

She gloves me perfectly, lighting up every nerve ending along my shaft. I can barely remember what I planned to do.

"What was your father's name?" I ask, gliding through her folds.

"Hm?"

"Your father. You said he was a noble, that Prince John hanged him, yes? David mentioned something of the kind during dinner last night."

"Oh... yes." She's panting, flushing deeper as I thumb her tiny pleasure bud.

"His name, darling. Perhaps we can help you reclaim some of your wealth, if not your land."

"Oh, I don't think you can. But thank you."

I pull out of her and slide my cock over her wet pussy lips, rubbing her clit again. "Last night you told me you were married. Does your late husband have no family, no one who will care for you and see your parents' death avenged?"

"Yes—no—"

"Which is it?" I pop my cock head back into her, running my length deep in her velvety channel. "Yes or no?"

"I was married, briefly."

"How briefly?"

"A week, and then he went off to war. He died."

"Surely he left you something."

"I—I know what you're doing." She props herself on her elbows, staring accusingly at me while I sink deeper into her pussy. "You're interrogating me while you're fucking me."

I smile at her. "Sexual interrogations are far more pleasurable and productive than torture."

"So you don't trust me."

"I trust very few people. That's what happens when your family tries to drown you for being unnatural and immoral."

Her eyes widen. "That's awful."

"I know you're hiding something, little one." I come down to her, still seated deep, and I kiss her mouth. "I'm going to find out what it is. You may as well tell me now."

She shakes her head. "There's nothing but what I've told you. I want to be one of you. I want to fight injustice and help the poor."

Looking into those big innocent eyes, I almost believe her. I want to believe her.

My hips rock, a final thrust, and the tingling rush of the orgasm floods through my cock, my belly, my legs. I fill her up slowly, pulse after gentle pulse, while she lets out a wondering little sigh.

After a moment I slide out of her heat and recline beside her on the bed. Reaching over, I manipulate her clit, working her closer to her climax.

"When Robin comes home today, I will tell him your gender," I whisper. "The rest will be between you and him. But I warn you, if you're spying for anyone, I will kill you." Softly I kiss her neck. "I'll take this slender throat in my hands, and I'll choke the breath out of you, love. Do you understand?"

She nods desperately, and then her clit throbs, her pussy quivers—she's coming for me. I press my hand over her sex while she trembles through the orgasm, and I revel in every little flutter against my palm.

"Good girl," I breathe, nuzzling her cheek. "Such a good girl. Now we should bind you up again. We have work to do."

16

ROBIN

It's a small carriage this time. Barely large enough
for one person and a chest of gold, driven by a
nervous-looking man and flanked by six guards. The
driver is whipping the horses mercilessly, trying to
hasten their progress through this dangerous part of
their journey.

When they're almost below me, I leap.

I drop from the branch on which I was perched,
right onto the top of the carriage, and from there I
slide down to the driver's seat, jostling the man aside
to make room for myself.

"Lovely day in the greenwood," I say casually. "A pity you're rushing through a place of such natural beauty. You should stop and enjoy yourselves."

The man screams, dropping the reins and trying to clamber away from me, up onto the roof of the carriage.

"Good Lord." I pick up the reins and begin drawing the horses to a stop. "Why so terrified, good sir? I'm merely inviting you to a picnic lunch by the river. We've cold mutton, salt, fresh biscuits, and a fine wheel of cheese. And ale! Lots of ale."

The carriage has slowed to a crawl, and the six guards are shouting at me, pointing their crossbows or swords at my chest.

"Easy, lads." When the horses stop, I lift both hands. "I'm unarmed, see?"

"But—but you're Robin Hood," stammers one of the guards. "You have a longbow."

"I do?" I feign confusion, looking all around, patting my pockets. "Pray tell, where is it? I should probably make use of it before you kill me."

The guards stare at each other.

"He's mad," says one.

"He's mocking us," snaps another. "Let's kill him now."

"No, the Sheriff and Prince John want him alive," adds a third. "No reward otherwise. They want to be the ones who end him."

"A shame," I say. "And here I was looking forward to dying at the hands of *that* fine-looking fellow." I point to one of the guards, giving him a saucy wink. "I think we've met before, haven't we, handsome?"

The man's companions stare at him suspiciously, and he withdraws a step, shaking his head. "I've never met him. He's mad, like Cobb said."

"Pretending you don't know me?" I clutch my chest in mock pain. "Fine, then I suppose I must die. What say you, my love? Will you take your sword and pierce this heart of mine? Here's my breast, bared to your weapon. Have at me. Fair warning, I may come in my pants when you penetrate me. Could get messy."

"He *is* mad," the driver chokes out, from his dubious retreat atop the carriage.

"Robin Hood ain't mad." Another man wags his head sagely. "He's a right devil. Seduces good men and teaches 'em to take his cock up their asses. I've heard about some goings-on in the greenwood. Nothing no good Christian should abide. I say we cut off *his* cock and stick it up his ass before we give him to the Sheriff. That way he can't do no more abomerations. Abernations. I mean—"

"The word you're looking for is abominations," I say helpfully.

"Right. Bomb-nations. That's the one. Can't do no bomb-nations without a dick, can you, Hood?"

"Oh, I don't know," I drawl. "I've made a man come with just one finger up his backside. I'm happy to demonstrate."

A quiet twitter in the trees catches my ear. It's David, warning me to hurry things along. He gets impatient when I tease my prey.

"Oh, very well." I get to my feet on the driver's bench. "The signal, I suppose."

"Signal?" The guards glance at each other.

"Really, you're all complete idiots. You know I rarely work alone." I lift my hand and snap my fingers.

With a cheerful roar, my men swing down from the trees on ropes disguised with leaves. They're all masked, all armed. Some strike the guards with their boots as they descend—others tackle the soldiers bodily, bearing them down to the ground. There's a brief flurry of weapons and some cries of pain, but I pay them no mind. Instead I yank open the door of the carriage, smiling at the thought of the gold inside.

I'm expecting some sort of panicked defense from the passenger—a wild jab with a dagger or some such effort.

What I don't expect is a crossbow bolt searing through my gut.

Followed by a knife-slash across my throat.

The knife-slash is shallow, ill-aimed, because I'm already moving, dodging. The man in the carriage drops his crossbow and whips out a second knife. He's wickedly fast, but I'm faster. A flurry of slashes—pain blooming along my arms and chest— and then I have him by the throat, and I'm crushing out his life with manic force far beyond that of any normal human.

He's an assassin, planted in the carriage to kill me.

The man stabs me again and again, but I don't let go. His larynx is giving way, crumpling under the force of my fingers. He gurgles, and his eyes unfocus.

It's been a long time since anyone came this close to killing me.

I've grown careless, like Will is always saying. Careless, cocky, and foolish.

The man in the carriage is dead, but I can't let go of his throat.

He tried to kill me. *Me.*

I should have left him alive so I could torture him.

"Robin." David's voice. David—my rock, my—

"David," I whisper.

"You can let go now, Robin," he says calmly.

Releasing the corpse, I stagger back, out of the carriage. The Merry Men are standing around, not whooping and taunting their prisoners as they usually do after a successful raid. They're staring at me.

David catches me as I sway, off-balance, my body threaded with agony.

"He stabbed me," I say hoarsely. "He shot me with a bolt. There's a *hole* in me, David."

"I know. We'll get you home. What are your orders for this lot?" He gestures to the six guards and the driver, all of whom are lying with their chins in the dirt. The driver is sobbing, snot dribbling from his nose.

Normally we would take them into the greenwood for a hearty luncheon, after which we'd attempt to seduce them. Usually a few succumb to the temptation of a little secret pleasure. Afterward we let them go, thoroughly plundered in more ways than one.

This time I'm in no mood for mercy.

"Kill them all," I order.

David doesn't protest. "Gentlemen, you heard the Hood. Get to work, and make it quick. Some of you grab the gold as well. All disperse afterward and meet back at camp. There will be no straight paths through the forest today."

He's right. I can't use my powers to create a path for the men when I'm in this state. Every bit of magic I have must go toward healing myself. I'm not sure it will be enough. Blood is flowing from my neck a little too freely, and whenever I take a step, the bolt in my gut shifts, a sickening wrench.

David helps me along, his jaw tight. "I'm taking you to Tuck. He'll be setting up the picnic by the river. He has some of his medical supplies there, and he can help me get you home. Fuck, Robin. You need to be more careful."

"Maybe I do." The ground is wavering, and I have to squint to see clearly. "Maybe Will is right. I've grown cocky."

David snorts. "You've always been cocky. But yes, it's worse lately."

When David and I stagger onto the grassy, open meadow by the river, Friar Tuck leaps up. He's bigger than David, beefy and handsome and a fucking virgin. I fully intend to have him someday. I've seen the size of his dick, and I want it inside me, even if it tears me apart.

"What happened?" Tuck strides over, lending his shoulder.

"An assassin was riding in the carriage with the gold. I was taken by surprise."

"Yet you still bested him." Tuck shakes his head wonderingly. "And you're still on your feet, despite one, two, three, four—several wounds. Let's lay him down here, David. On the blanket. Undress him so I can see what I'm dealing with."

David helps me strip to the waist, and he holds me while Tuck jerks out the crossbow bolt. He jams a wad of thick cloth over the wound. "Hold this tightly in place," he orders David. "I'll need a tonic—ah, here we are."

"You're treating me with a tonic that's laced with my own cum?" I rock my head back against David's shoulder. "I can heal on my own, fool."

"This might help you heal faster." He nods to David, who moves the cloth wadding so Tuck can pour a little of the tonic into the hole in my gut. My blood bubbles a little, and I wince at the burn.

Tuck applies some salve from his bag to the cut on my neck and bandages it. Then he smears more salve on my other knife wounds.

"What would the people you treat say if they knew they were smearing my cum on their scrapes and drinking it down for their fevers?" I manage a weak smile.

"They'd string me up at once," Tuck admits. "But it's my mission to help and heal, and if a Fae bastard's cum can soothe pain and save lives, that's what I'll use. Put pressure on the bolt wound again, David."

"Maybe you have—some ailments—that I could treat for you, eh, Tuck?" I wheeze. "Sore bowels, perhaps, or a raspy throat. I'd be happy to make a direct application of healing fluid to either area."

"You've made me that offer before, Robin, and my answer remains the same: *no*. Now stop trying to talk. Focus on healing."

"Fine." I adjust my position, settling my head on David's thigh. There's a notable protrusion against the front of his pants, and I tilt my head back to look up at him.

"You like the sight of me torn and bleeding," I murmur.

He winces. "Can't help it."

"I know." I reach up, grimacing through the pain of several cuts on my arm, and I stroke him through his trousers. "Take it out, love. Come for me."

"You're hurt."

"Watching you come will make me feel better. Please."

I rarely say 'please,' to him or to anyone, and his eyebrows lift. "What about our virginal friar here?"

"Tuck can take a walk," I mutter. "Or—he can watch." I meet the friar's eyes. "I know you like to watch."

"God help me." The words break from him in a hoarse groan. "You'll be the ruin of me, Robin. You'll damn my soul straight to Hell."

"I've told you before—Hell doesn't exist, only the Afterlife. But if I'm wrong, and there is such a place, I'll meet you there, Tuck. I'll walk through the fire to you, and then maybe you'll give me a kiss."

At the last word, my lungs spasm, and my chest heaves with a painful cough.

"Easy, Robin." David holds me through the coughing fit. "Rest easy, and heal."

"I'll rest if I can watch you stroking yourself. 'Twould be a pity to waste so much lovely pain when I know how beautifully it could make you come. I know you're concerned for me, love. Distract yourself for a few moments."

"Fuck," he says in a strangled voice, and he unbuttons the flap of his pants.

"Such a nice thick cock David has, don't you think so, Tuck?" I wink at the friar, who has walked several paces away but is still watching. "The head is so fat, so well-shaped. It's a stretch to take him, honestly, but it's so good once you have him all the way up your ass. He has big balls, too. I love the feel of them in my hand. Stroke yourself, David. Look at me."

17

Robin Hood has the foulest mouth of anyone I've ever heard, I swear. I feel the itching need to confess and whip my back in penance every time I have a conversation with him. He's describing David's thick, juicy cock to me when I can see it myself. I think he knows the words turn me on.

Every time I've heard a confession related to a sexual sin, I've asked the sinner to go into explicit detail. I told them God wanted them to face the specifics of what they'd done. But it was all for my benefit. I'd grow hard listening to the account, and I'd muse over the details later.

My sexual urges have been a constant source of mental anguish and guilt for me. I've touched myself a few times since I took my orders, and every time I had to pay with my own pain and blood afterward.

But lately, even acts of penance have begun to make me hard, as if my body, like David's, is beginning to associate pain with arousal.

I should look away from the scene before me, but I don't.

The river is a broad shimmering ribbon, winding lazily between grassy banks, still green despite the waning of summer. On a cream-colored woolen blanket amid the vivid grass sits David, his raven hair gleaming and his brown skin practically glowing in the midday sun. His hand is wrapped around his cock, stroking along it—slow leisurely pumps. His dark lashes are lowered as he gazes at Robin, who lies, beautiful and damaged, on the blanket beside him. A bloodstain is smeared along Robin's sharp cheekbone, and he's pressing the cloth to his own gut wound. His perfectly sculpted torso and toned arms are thatched with cuts, some deep, others merely scratches.

His black hair has fallen away from his ears, and their fine points, usually concealed, are bared to the golden daylight. He looks like an injured Fae prince. Which is exactly what he is.

For a while after I met him, after he told me his true origins, I struggled to accept his existence. Then I reconciled it by telling myself he was some sort of demon. I browsed the Old Testament for references to demons and ancient gods, and finally I came to the conclusion that other gods *are* real, and that if they are real, why not the Fae? After all, Robin claims the Fae are descended from the old pagan gods of this land.

It's rare to see him like this. Though I believe his underlying intentions and goals are good, he is a prankster and a thief by nature. It's his delight in teasing and tricking others that made Will and I agree to keep the girl's secret from Robin. Let our mischievous leader feel the sting of trickery himself for once.

Will suspects the girl of ill intent, but to me she seems harmless enough. Her gender is not the danger, so it's no risk to Robin, letting him find out on his own.

David leans over and Robin tips his head back, accepting the other man's mouth. They kiss tenderly, languidly, in the golden haze, with the slow gurgle of the river and the rustle of leaves as music for the moment.

And this is what makes me so hard it's painful. I want the aching pulse of climax, and the blessed relief that follows—but I want it *without* the acidic guilt. And I want it *with* the love I've seen among David, Will, and Robin. They can roar and clap each other's backs, guzzle ale and make coarse jokes, wrestle and spit and curse. But they can also be tender, like this. And I want this tenderness. I keep seeking it from God, but He is so far away.

Sometimes I wonder if He is gone entirely, like Robin's people who traveled North or crossed the sea to another land.

David is pumping his cock faster now, and Robin moans, real pain mingled with his own arousal. He opens his mouth, and David grunts, lashes of white cum spraying Robin's lips and tongue. With his thumb Robin collects the excess around his mouth, then sucks it off as if he relishes the taste.

What does cum taste like? What do a woman's juices taste like? I crave both. My body is burning up under my friar's garment, my cock stiff as a quarterstaff. It's all I can do not to rake up my robes and clasp the hot, swollen shaft in my hand. I think I might die from the strain of not yielding to my desires.

David is pushing Robin's legs apart, unbuttoning his trousers. The tiny gold orb near the tip of Robin's cock glints briefly in the sunlight before most of the erect length disappears into David's mouth.

"Never stop doing that, David," Robin gasps. "The pain is less when you—ah—ah, gods—fuck, fuck—"

David's head keeps bobbing between Robin's legs, while Robin writhes in mingled agony and pleasure. The stomach muscles are involved in orgasmic release, so the gut wound must be paining him.

"Stop," he cries, breathless. "Stop, David—I'm going to come."

David pulls off, and Robin seizes his own cock, pointing it toward himself. A few frenzied jerks, and he ejaculates, streams of his cum painting his own chest and abdomen. He keeps coming and coming, half-sobbing with the force of the orgasm and the pain. David holds him while he writhes, beautiful and bloody and slicked with sweat, and still coming.

My balls tighten, and I spurt, my cock throbbing against the inside of my robe. I dare not touch myself—can't let them know I caved to physical weakness. The climax is incomplete, unsatisfying.

David smooths the fresh cum into Robin's wounds, while Robin lies spent, his gasps shrill with pain, his chest heaving. I quietly pack up the food into the two baskets, which have straps so they can be slung onto someone's back. I try to ignore the sticky discomfort inside my robes, along my thighs.

There's a worse discomfort in my soul. Longing, and craving, and a wretched guilt.

If this goes on, the desire and the remorse will eat me alive.

Robin falls asleep shortly after I finish packing the luncheon. I saved out some ale and mutton for me and David, and we eat in silence, staring at the river. Over the next two hours we check on Robin several times—he is alive, and healing. David reassures me that when he's more seriously wounded, he goes into a deep sleep to recover.

"We should get him back to camp," David tells me quietly. "I would leave him here and let him rest, but everyone will be worried. When Will hears the news, he'll be out of his mind."

I nod. "You take the baskets. I'll carry Robin."

David doesn't protest. Strong and fit though he is, I'm the bigger and bulkier of us two.

I scoop Robin's long, limp body into my arms. His head lolls, so I readjust him, tipping his head against my shoulder. The silky brush of his hair against my jaw makes me shiver.

If he was awake, he would torment me with innuendo and naughty words and salacious looks. Unconscious, he is no less agonizing because the slack softness of his mouth makes me want to kiss him.

That is something I am not allowed to do. I may never cross that line, with anyone.

"You got the gold, I assume?" I mutter aside to David as we walk.

"We did. I'm surprised you came along this time, seeing as the loot is from an abbey."

"I did not come to fight or steal," I clarify. "Just to provide a repast for your victims. Robin must have let them run off without luncheon this time, eh?"

David glances up at me, discomfort in his eyes. "Robin ordered us to kill them."

Shock steals my words. Robin may be wicked, and he may love a cruel joke, but he does not kill unless he must.

My stomach roils. "How many?"

"Six guards, one driver, and he killed the assassin in the carriage himself."

"Saints forgive us," I whisper.

"Your saints may forgive *you*," says David. "I need no such pardon."

"Because you've renounced your god, and you do not believe in ours."

"I believe in Robin Hood," David says, with a kind of fierce desperation. "Robin was my salvation. He is my friend, my leader, my lover. I will protect him at all costs. Even without his order, I would have avenged his sweet blood on all of them. He is my safe place, whatever wars may tear apart the world."

I have never heard him speak like this. Then again, he and I have never really talked alone.

"I saw you last week, when we all swam in the Bottomless Pool," he continues. "Your back. Covered with scars. You believe that pain purges your sins."

My arms tighten around Robin's body. "That is what we are taught, yes. Not all practice it, but—I try to cleanse myself, to atone, to punish my body so I may escape the fires of Hell."

"You speak of them often, these fires. But perhaps there is a worse fire. One that will consume you to nothing if you keep denying who you are."

"You don't know who I am." I speak as calmly as I can, but anger and panic are rising together in my chest.

"Have you considered what it will be like, living with these vows you have taken and this lust you conceal, for decades? With Robin's magic at our disposal we are immune to disease, we can heal wounds, and the effects of aging are slowed. Which means you are looking at a very, very long life of painful lust and self-denial. I hate to think what your back will look like by the end of it."

I cannot find the words to answer him.

I can only picture myself, weary and broken, bowed under the weight of my guilt, my back so lacerated it will bleed, and bleed, and never heal.

"Better to let the guilt go." David's voice is gentle. There's an elegance to him at times, a regal bearing, a highly educated manner of speech that occasionally slips through his usual gruff manner. He seems, in a word, royal. Fitting that he and Robin should have found each other, I suppose—and Will, too, who is also well-educated, with fine manners.

I've had some education, but I am not nearly as graceful of speech as they are. Perhaps in my mind sometimes, but not aloud. I am big, clumsy, and sometimes foolish. Since I cannot be a lech, I'm a drunkard and a glutton. I would never fit with the three of them, with their fine faces and slim, toned bodies.

There is no use hoping for it. I must cling to what I have, to the security of my place in the Church. I must not wish for what can never be.

18

MARIAN

Will Scarlet bound my breasts up snugly today
and dressed me in such baggy, coarse clothes no one
would ever suspect anything attractive lay beneath. I
know it pained him to do it, because of the
disappointed pout on his face.

We've spent the morning and part of the
afternoon touring the camp and the wide clearings
beyond it, where Robin and his men train. There's an
archery range too—a long strip of clear ground
bordered by thick hedges so no one can wander too
close and be accidentally injured. Will made me

practice with the longbow a while, but we both agreed I'm no good. The quarterstaff is my weapon.

I want to ask questions about Robin's strategies, his sources of information, and the supernatural oddities I've seen. But Will already suspects me. He said as much outright, while he was buried inside me. I'm not sure why his admission and his threats made me even more aroused.

It's midafternoon, and we're with some of the others, lounging around one of the great tables in the center of camp, when a couple of men tramp out of the forest, looking grim.

"What news?" Will jumps up, almost knocking over his tankard.

"We laid the trap, caught the carriage, and took down the guards," says one man, panting. "But there was an assassin hiding in the carriage, not some helpless priest or noble. He hurt Robin badly."

"How badly?" Will's face is white.

"Crossbow bolt through the gut. Several knife wounds. Slashed his throat, too."

"Is he alive?"

"He was when we left. He ordered us to kill everyone and bring the gold. David was going to take him to Tuck for healing."

"Blow the horn when they return." Will spins abruptly and stalks away from the table, into the woods. After a moment's hesitation, I follow him. I keep my distance, though, in case he wants to be alone.

He walks a long time, while papery yellow leaves flutter through the pale trunks of the birches and elms. A crisp breeze tugs at the end of my scarf, which is once again wrapped around my neck and my lower face. My shoes crunch with every step, so Will must know I'm following him.

"Twice in two days," he says at last, stopping in front of a towering oak. "Twice I've feared him dead. It's unbearable, this constant worry for him. And it would be even worse if he was human. Why is love so unbearably vulnerable?"

I think of my friends back at my late husband's castle. They are people I love. And yes, they are vulnerable.

"When something becomes precious to you, you fear its loss," I answer. "Even if you care for nothing, you'll still lose what you have. That's part of life. But maybe it would hurt less." I bite my lip until I taste salt and metal. "I am trying not to care."

I'm trying not to care about Will. About David. About Robin. About the gentle giant Friar Tuck, who kept my secret and healed my feet.

I don't want a second family. I already have one. Well, not exactly family… they are servants, and as close as I try to get to them, they keep a certain distance from me. They fear the consequences if they step out of their "place." And no matter how hard I've tried to close that gap, it's beyond my power.

Maybe I need more than the tenuous connection between a landlady and her hired workers, more than the cautious friendship I've developed with the people back home. I believe they truly care for me, as I care about them—but in this volatile world, it's everyone for themselves. I have risked everything to secure my servants' future, but I'm not sure any of them would do the same for me. They might be grateful for my kindness, but in truth, I'm not sure how loyal they would be if they had to make a sacrifice to save me.

I want someone who *would* sacrifice for me. Someone I can be close to physically and emotionally, in a way I never could have been with my husband, and never can be with Lord Guisbourne.

I want love—the love that I see in Will right now, as he leans his forehead against a birch tree, dressed in his fine scarlet clothes. The long braid draped over his shoulder is exactly the color of the bright leaves overhead.

He is the portrait of love's agony. And I want what he has, even if it hurts.

19

ROBIN

When my eyes open I see a dark blue sky speckled with stars, fringed by the black branches of trees. Lower down, those branches turn dusky gold, uplit by the glow of bonfires. Orange sparks dance and sail high before winking out—golden motes aspiring to be stars, never reaching their dream.

When I'm falling asleep, or when I wake, the low, ever-present ache inside me is worse. Every time I'm still and contemplative, it begins again. That quiet ache is the reason I keep myself always occupied, always prowling the greenwood and robbing the rich, always giving to the poor and making merry with my band. It's the reason I fuck so hard every night, whether in public or private—so I'll tire myself out and have no time for thinking when I finally lie down.

Sometimes it works.

I may be Fae, but I am not immortal. I can be killed. And I'm never more conscious of my own mortality than when I'm lying under the immensity of an open sky.

Slowly I turn my head aside. I'm on some kind of cot or makeshift bed, cushioned by pillows and surrounded by leafy branches. My connection to Sherwood Forest fuels my magic, and my lovers know it. They must have surrounded me with these sticks and leaves, thinking it might help me. It's sweet, and foolish, and adorable.

A short distance away, blurred by firelight and my own weariness, are the broad tables we use for dining, gambling, and fucking. Men cluster around them, talking and drinking, but there is no revel tonight, and the laughter is subdued, not uproarious. It's all out of respect for me.

I sigh, letting my eyes close again. Right now I do not feel powerful, or cheerful, or clever. I feel very, very tired.

I love my life with these men. But sometimes the ache in my soul makes me wonder how long I can go on like this. The Fae are meant to live in groups, and while I've gathered a group of my own, they are only human, after all.

"You're awake," says a soft voice near my head—at my other side, opposite the campfires and the men.

I turn toward the sound, and there is our newest member, the boy who is not a man and yet is older than seventeen, his face concealed behind that horrible scarf and the squashed hat on his head. I cannot figure him out. If he has Fae blood, I cannot sense it. Yet he does not seem to have developed like most human men, with their beards and deeper voices. Perhaps he is part Fae and does not know it. He wouldn't be the first child born secretly to a human and a Fae. He's beautiful enough to be one of us.

Why do I so desperately hope that he is?

"Where is Will?" I ask.

"He and David were here, but I made them go get some food. They've been sitting beside you for hours. Are you—are you well again?"

Twigs shift and tumble aside as I move, running my hand along my bare torso. "No wounds. I have healed."

"Because you're not human." Little John's eyebrows pull together, as if he's unhappy about that. Or perhaps restraining something he wants to say.

"I think my inhuman nature is fairly obvious by now." I sit up, cracking my neck. I don't hurt anywhere, but my joints feel stiff.

"You're a god." Little John bites out the words.

"Close." I pinch the bridge of my nose. "I am Fae. Not many of us remain. Some were killed, and most left for other lands. I know of a handful of Fae scattered up north, and one to the south, but none of them are very friendly. As you can see, I like the company of humans."

It's true, more or less. I love humans, but I crave my own kind as well. Unfortunately none of the Fae who remain in this land share my affinity for the human race. They'd rather dine on human babies or sew coats out the skins of grown men. Some of them are fading, becoming one with the trees, rocks, or lakes they frequent. One or two of them have feuds against my bloodline and would as soon kill me as join me.

"I didn't want to admit it to myself," Little John murmurs. "Magic, the Fae, the old gods. The Church teaches us they aren't real. But here you are. And I've seen your magic. You can move the forest, can't you? And heal yourself, and—"

"And I can heal others. My cum acts as a salve, curing most illnesses and quickening the repair of wounds. Tuck uses it in his tonics and ointments."

Little John's mouth gapes. "So when the friar put that cream on my feet—"

"It was laced with my essence, yes." I give him a wink.

"I have so many questions." His beautiful eyes are churning with interest, conflict, and a hint of despair that confuses me. Such a strange young man.

"We should take a walk, you and I, so I can answer your questions." But before I can say anything else, a figure in scarlet dashes up to me, nearly sloshing the stew from his bowl in his haste. Will falls to his knees beside my bed. "Robin! You're awake!"

"He woke just now." Little John rises quietly from his stool and retreats, melting into the shadows as David and Tuck approach. David squeezes my shoulder, Will kisses my forehead, and Tuck makes a show of checking me for residual wounds, though I'm fairly sure he's just ogling my body.

"I'm healed." I force a smile, waving them away as I swing my legs from the bed, scattering twigs and leaves with the movement. "Calm down, all of you."

"You should eat something." Will shoves his bowl of food toward me.

"Has *he* eaten?" I jerk my head toward the trees where Little John disappeared.

"Not yet."

"Then I'll take this to him. He and I need to have a conversation. I think he's hiding something."

"Do you?" Will's face is bland. A little too bland. He's usually the one warning me about possible interlopers.

Narrowing my eyes at him, I snatch the bowl of stew. "Yes, I have the sense he isn't exactly who he's portraying himself to be."

"If he's hiding anything, I'm sure you'll uncover it," says David. Will makes a snorting sound.

"You're all behaving very oddly. I shall punish you for it later." I swat David's backside with my free hand as I pass him.

"Yes, please," he says, low.

I wink at Tuck, who's blushing again.

"A pleasure to see you in such good spirits, Hood," he says.

"A *pleasure*, eh?" I press my hand lightly to his broad robed chest, and I let my tongue flick across my lips. He swallows hard. Perhaps he is weakening to my charms after all.

Smiling, I stride away into the forest.

20

MARIAN

"Little trickster," calls a singsong male voice through the trees, and my heart thrills.

I'm sitting on a rock beside the pool where Will and I bathed. I didn't expect to be followed—I thought Robin would be involved with his lovers awhile.

A tumult of butterflies erupt in my chest at the thought that Robin left them to come to me.

He still thinks I am male. What will he do when he finds out the truth? And I must tell him tonight. While Robin was resting, Will made me promise to reveal my secret once he woke.

I hope Robin will let me stay anyway. I've already been inducted into the band. He knows I can fight. And I can offer to fuck, as well. Maybe then he will let me remain here until I've gathered all the names and information I need.

The biggest secret I've gleaned is that Robin Hood is Fae. That is probably enough to buy some favor with Prince John. But I have to be sure I hold up my end of the bargain to the fullest, or the prince certainly won't honor his part.

"Hungry?" Robin seats himself on the rock beside me. It's not a large rock, so his hip and butt cheek are pressed against mine, and I'm far too aware of the contact.

"Thank you." I take the bowl of stew he offers and eat a few bites before handing it back. He polishes off the rest in silence.

He's still shirtless, like he was when they brought him back. Will sponged the blood off his body, though, so every bit of Robin's skin is pristine, white as moonlight. Not a hair to be seen, except the tousled, feathery black mane on his head.

Sensing my gaze, he tucks some of his hair back, revealing the pointed tip of his ear. He has two miniscule gems along the edge.

"Are you frightened of what I am?" he asks.

"No."

"If I scared you yesterday, I'm sorry for it," he says. "Night makes me volatile. Makes me ravenous to fight and fuck. The Fae hold orgies, sparring matches, and revels nightly to sate their urges, but I'm alone here, so—"

"So you revel with the Merry Men."

"We spar and fight most nights, but not on the nights before a raid," he explains. "Often I join in the wrestling matches or the quarterstaff tournaments. And if anyone is injured, well—they can use Tuck's supplies, or I can provide immediate healing." He gives me a sly smile. "Fae males can ejaculate fifty times in a night and still get hard afterward."

Gulping, I look away from him, across the gently rippling water.

"I have shocked you," Robin whispers. "Yet you opened your mouth for me when I came. You wanted to taste me."

His long fingers touch my cheek, turning my face toward him. His lips are dark velvet in the starlight.

"I have something to tell you," I breathe.

"I have guessed it."

Shock blazes along my limbs. "You—you have?"

"Yes. Your story didn't seem quite right to me. I believe you came here for the reasons you mentioned, but I think there is more. You realized you were different, didn't you? You could not conform to the expectations of human civilization—their stunted beliefs, repressive laws, and restrictive roles. You are beyond all of that. You are special."

The butterflies have settled in my belly, tremulous and whispering. I am stunned by his words, marveling by how deeply he understands me.

"Did you grow up near here, perhaps?" he asks.

"I did." I falter over the words a little, trying to think if I should tell him this, if yielding the information might give me away somehow. I cannot see the harm. "I played along the edge of Sherwood Forest as a child. Later I was prevented from doing so, and then I—moved away. I never went this deep in the greenwood, but it does feel good to be back in this area again."

"Because this is the beloved haunt of our people," he says eagerly. "It's natural it should feel like coming home to you, even if you are not a full-blooded Fae."

My pulse stutters. "What?"

"Some Fae despise those of blended race, but not me," he says hastily. "I am thrilled to have found you. It took me too long to realize why you have no beard at your age, why you're so beautiful that you feel you must hide your face—why you sought me out, why you kept pressing me to reveal my identity. You were drawn by instinct, no doubt. Fae calls to Fae. And I understand why you were shy about revealing yourself—"

"Revealing myself..." I vent a little hysterical laugh and leap up from the rock, turning to face him. "Robin, you have misread everything. I'm no Fae."

The look on his face—a startled, vulnerable pain, like someone whose greatest hope has just been stolen away—it wounds me. I can't bear it.

"Close your eyes," I tell him. "And don't look until I tell you to open them."

"Are you going to kill me, little trickster?" There's a pathetic note in his voice. "I just might let you. I don't want to go through healing myself again—it's so dreadfully boring."

"Close your eyes," I repeat.

Sighing, he obeys.

With trembling fingers I strip myself, as quickly as I can, from the squashed cap all the way down to my shoes. Then I cast away the codpiece and unwrap the bindings from my breasts.

"I think you're getting naked," Robin says. "That's what it sounds like, and I heartily approve. I've been wondering what that adorable ass of yours would look like bared to me. Oh, I must find another staff so I can redden your cheeks again, as I did on the bridge. Or are they still bruised?"

Thrills keep skating through my chest and belly, and my sex is tingling with arousal. Turning my back to Robin, I try to slow my breathing. "You can open your eyes now."

His hum of delight tells me his eyes are open and he's devouring the sight of my backside. "Gods, you're a fine specimen. You're sure you aren't Fae? I suspect you are. Perhaps someone lied to you about your true parentage—"

"Robin." I abandon the low, slightly hoarse tone I've been using all day and let my real voice emerge. "Look at my shape. Really look."

Silence.

I stand with my arms at my sides, my legs pressed together. My toes curl into the gravel, and goosebumps stipple my skin as the night breeze washes over my bare body.

There's a light scrape of fabric against rock as Robin stirs and rises. Then the crunch of his steps on the narrow bit of beach.

Out of the corner of my eye I see him bend and pick up the cloth strips, my bindings.

He's walking around—he's standing in front of me. Taking in everything. My breasts, peaked by the chill. My pussy, pressed into a small triangle by my thighs.

I meet his eyes and catch my breath at the furious intensity in them. His handsome face is wilder and more wicked than ever.

"What is your name?" The question is a low threat, a savage compulsion. "And do not lie to me. I will know."

"Marian," I whisper. "My name is Marian."

21

Wicked girl.

She's been—not exactly lying, but portraying herself as other than she is. A well-played trick that I would respect if I were not so angry. Because this isn't about some peasant woman playing a joke—this is a woman, trained to fight, disguising herself and working her way into my band.

And I didn't see it. That's what makes me so furious I can barely breathe.

I looked right at her. I had all the evidence before me, all the telltale signs, and I ignored them. I was too busy tricking her into thinking I was dead, and then I was too busy coming on her face. And then I began to suspect she was a young Fae male— or at least part Fae. It's pathetic, how frantically eager I was at the thought of another being like me here in Sherwood.

I am absurd, foolish, and pitiable.

"Marian." My voice doesn't sound like me. "You're a fucking liar."

"What I told you was the truth." Her voice shakes. It's lighter now, more musical. "I need to be part of your band, and I have no love for Prince John."

Interesting. She used nearly the exact words she spoke last time. Usually, when a human does that, it's because they are carefully using smaller truths to conceal a larger one they don't want revealed. She is lying without lying.

Enough of this.

I seize her curls in my fist and yank her head back. "*Why* do you need to be part of my band?"

She sucks a quick breath through her teeth. "I have no other options."

There's no warning twitch in my mind, which either means her words are true, or she believes they are true.

"Are you a spy for the Crown?"

She's naked before me, and defenseless, yet she meets my eyes anyway.

"Why would I spy for the Crown, when the Crown is a threat to me?" Tears shimmer in her gaze.

"Prince John is a callous, conniving, wretched, greedy asshole. And I'll happily tell him that to his face if I can ever do so without being killed on the spot. You're the only one who stands up to him, Robin. You help people. You give the wealth you take to the poor when you could keep it for yourself. You are *good*."

"Don't insult me." I shake her by her hair. "Does anyone else in the camp know you're a woman?"

"Yes."

"Who?"

Her lashes dip, hiding her eyes from me. "Will, David, and Tuck."

Fury roils in my chest. "All of them?"

"Yes." She licks her lips once.

And that tiny movement sparks a suspicion in my mind. "Where did you sleep last night?"

"With Will and David," she murmurs.

"Did they fuck you?"

"Don't be angry at them—"

"Fuck!" I use my hold on her curls to shove her backward. She stumbles a little, then shoves me right back, her eyes flaming.

"Don't touch me," she snaps.

My hand catches her under the jaw, gripping her throat, and I haul her to me. "Did you give me an order, little liar?"

In answer she twists and kicks me square in the stomach. I huff out a breath and let go, and she follows up with a sound smack to my cheek. Her breasts bounce enticingly as she moves.

"I said, don't touch me." She's facing me down, seething, her eyes glittering. She's spoiling for a fight just as much as I am.

"Sweet foolish Marian," I croon, pacing around her. "I'll touch whatever I please in Sherwood Forest." And with the flick of a finger, I guide a vine out of the woods to smack her bottom.

She yelps and spins around to look for her assailant. A raw laugh escapes me, and I wrap her waist in my arm, jerking her ass against the front of my trousers. I sway my hips, rubbing my erection against her through my pants.

"I've wanted to fuck you since the moment I saw you," I hiss in her ear. "That hasn't changed. I still want to fuck every one of your holes."

"Well, you're not trying very hard, are you?" she retorts.

Delighted surprise thrums in my chest. "Would you like me to try harder?" I keep my voice low and threatening. "Should I force you to take my cock?"

"Yes," she breathes.

Fighting and fucking are the two things Fae like best, and this woman has just offered me both. I'd be a fool to refuse.

22

DAVID

When the girl says "yes" to Robin, I grip Will's arm silently. We're standing with Tuck in the cover of the forest, behind some thick bushes.

I cannot believe our good fortune, that we get to witness this.

"You should strip first," says the girl. "Both of us naked. It's only fair."

She told Robin her name was Marian. I like the sound of it. I want to moan it aloud while my dick pumps into her mouth.

Robin lets her go and shucks off his trousers. He's bared to her now, his cock standing out proudly.

Quietly I reach down and unfasten my pants, releasing my own cock.

But Will tugs on my arm. The girl is hurrying toward us.

I don't dare move—I might step on a twig and give away our presence. Thankfully she seems to be searching the ground, not scanning for spies.

She picks up a sturdy branch, snaps the twigs off it, and whirls around just as Robin lunges for her. She strikes him across the forearm, and he snarls with pain.

"You're cheating," he growls.

"Come and get me," she retorts, breathless. I can see the pale globes of her ass, faintly marred by the bruises from Robin's staff yesterday. She's so lithe and lovely, with that trim little waist and those thick, creamy thighs…

Robin darts at her again, and she strikes his shoulder. He cries out, and heat throbs through my cock.

My god. I might come before he gets his dick inside her.

She's quick, but she's trembling with nerves—I can see her legs shaking. And she doesn't want to seriously hurt him, though I'll wager she could.

"Enough," says Robin, and two long, thick vines snake out of the forest, winding around Marian's wrists, pulling her arms apart until she's forced to drop the stick. Robin sends a third vine to collect the weapon and draw it back into the undergrowth.

"No fair using magic," gasps the girl.

"No fair using weapons," he counters.

"Fine. Just us then."

He nods, and the vines release her.

She bolts and runs, quick and catlike, along the bank of the pond, but Robin is a Fae of the greenwood, and twice as quick when the prize is precious enough. He catches her, picks her up, and carries her back to the beach while she kicks and claws at him.

"This is the best thing I have ever seen," breathes Will. I clamp my hand over his mouth immediately, but neither Robin nor Marian seem to have heard the whisper. She's squeaking and writhing while he tosses some clothes over the rock they sat on earlier. Then he pushes her onto it, belly-down, ass out.

He manages to get both her wrists in his hand, pinned to her back. She's still bucking, but halfheartedly.

"Lose your fight, did you, love?" Robin purrs. "Let's see if you're ready for me."

When he slides his fingers along her pussy, she whines.

I almost groan, stroking myself faster, picturing how I crushed her beautiful bottom with my hands. The way I bit her breasts, and how she asked me to do it again.

"Shit, you're dripping." Robin's voice is so soft with wonder I can barely hear him. "Were you this wet for Will and David?"

In answer she kicks at him and wriggles as if she's trying to escape. Robin laughs, squeezing her wrists harder against the small of her back. Then he shoves himself inside her.

My cock pulses in my hand, spewing cum across the dark leaves in front of me. Judging by Will's faint, rapid breathing, he's handling himself too. I rub my hand over my cock head, collecting some of my own release. Then I reach over, my hand still slick, and I find Will's shaft in the dark. I rub my cum along his length, and he lets me take over stroking him.

Robin is humped over Marian now, clamping his free hand across her mouth while he fucks her. It's a hard, punishing fuck, a half-angry, half-triumphant pounding of her body. She's entirely at his mercy.

"You're going to come for me." Robin's voice is taut with command, jerking with each thrust into her pussy. "You're going to come even if you don't want to, even without me touching your clit. You feel the pleasure circling inside you? That's my cock forcing you to orgasm, little one. You're going to come because you can't help it."

Her whimpers behind his hand are ramping up in frequency.

"Come," he orders. "Come now."

Marian shrills a muffled shriek, her thighs quivering with the force of her climax.

Will comes all over my hand.

Robin eases his pace for a moment, murmuring, "Yes, yes, you wretched little trickster. You're coming on Fae cock. Fuck—you—ah fuck—you feel incredible. What you do to me—gods—"

He groans, hips thrusting forward and stilling, his buttocks tightening as he comes inside her. He keeps coming until he's shaking all over. His cum overflows out of her, flooding around his cock, dripping down her legs.

He lets go of her mouth and wrists, helpless to his orgasm, and he braces himself on the rock, bent over her body, his cheek grazing hers. Marian reaches up and touches his face—and then a soft shrill cry breaks from her lips. I think she came again.

Will and I know all too well the intoxicating effect of sex with Robin. His Fae nature makes him especially skilled at extracting pleasure, particularly from humans. I love fucking Will and letting him fuck me, and we enjoy other partners occasionally, but both of us prefer Robin. Something about his cock and his mouth—both are magic. And his asshole—I'd live with my cock inside it if I could.

When Robin finally pulls out and lets Marian stand up, she nearly falls over.

He catches her.

And then he kisses her.

With a sweet moan, she props her arms on his shoulders, standing on tiptoe, eagerness in every line of her body. Robin rumbles low, clasping her ass with one hand and sinking the other into her hair, gripping the back of her head. They kiss with a breathless passion that blots every thought from my mind.

Robin Hood sometimes kisses the people he fucks—lazily, casually. But not like this. Not like he's trying to steal the living soul out of her body and inhale it into his own. Not like he needs the air in her lungs to survive.

Now it's Will's turn to reach over and squeeze my wrist. I pull free, only to wrap my arm around his shoulders. He's the one who struggles most with jealousy. He only fucks other people because Robin and I do. I think, if someone suggested the three of us remain faithful to each other, he'd be the first to eagerly adopt the idea.

Will worships Robin, and he adores me with a passion that stuns me sometimes. I love him just as deeply, but I struggle to show it. The most I can do is seek him out when I'm in dark places, and let him comfort me. He loves that.

In the darkness I comfort him in return. I shield him against his own personal demon, the insecurity that sometimes consumes his mind and turns his love to acid. He has always loved openly, fully, with his whole heart. When his family rejected him and tried to murder him, it wounded him deeply, permanently .

I will never abandon him. Though I may torment his body in the pursuit of bliss, I will never wound his heart.

Robin is kissing the girl more softly now, his hands traveling the curves of her breasts. He pauses when he encounters the two bite marks I left.

"David's work?" he asks, and she nods.

"Sadistic fucker," he says, but there's fondness in his tone.

He has loved me too, with a gut-wrenching, visceral power, ever since the night we broke each other on the floor of an abandoned cabin—baptized one another in blood and cum.

I understand him in a way the others do not. Like Will, I can empathize with his loneliness, his separation from his race, his people, his family. But I understand an aspect of his Fae nature that Will is too gentle to comprehend.

I understand that sometimes, Robin Hood needs to be cruel.

And sometimes, he needs someone he trusts to tear him apart.

23

TUCK

I watch Robin Hood fuck the girl, and I listen to Will Scarlet and David quietly huffing, stroking themselves in the dark.

I brace my forehead against a nearby tree, agonized by my own desire.

Why do I do this to myself? Why can I not simply walk away from these men, from this place, and never return?

The pain of grating my forehead against the bark centers me, but it doesn't relieve my aching balls or my straining cock.

After a moment I look at Robin and Marian again. They're face to face now, kissing as if the sweetest wine gilds each other's lips.

From my spot behind the tree, I can barely distinguish Marian's words when she says, "Will you let me stay?"

"No," Robin replies.

She stiffens, recoils a little from him. "Please."

"Women don't live in the greenwood with us. This place is for warriors, men who like to fuck each other freely, men who have cast off all human laws. Women come here sometimes, but only for a night. This is too rough and wicked a life for them."

She scoffs. "You have a poor view of women, Robin Hood. I'm a warrior, and an outlaw by choice. I may not be used to this outdoor life yet, but I could learn. And I… I like to fuck. I could be here for anyone who wants me."

Robin is pulling on his trousers again. "I cannot make an exception for you."

"You're a brute," she hisses. "A bastard. I told you I need this—I need to stay. You fucked me, and now you're sending me away?"

"Friar Tuck will take you to Nottingham tomorrow," Robin says, picking up her clothes and tossing them to her. "He'll be doling out some of the stolen gold to needy families there. You may take a share and go wherever you like. I cannot trust someone like you, and for my men's safety, I cannot

allow you to stay. Now get dressed, little trickster. I'm
done with you."

Robin strides away from her, heading straight for
our hiding place. He stalks past Will and David and
me, huffing in disgust when he notices us standing
there. "Enjoy the show?"

Will and David fall into step behind him, and
with a last glance at the stunned, naked girl, I follow.

Robin stomps through the undergrowth, finally
breaking out into the firelight of the camp. We're at
the far end, near the weapons hut. Most of the Merry
Men are at the other end of the settlement, drifting
away from the dinner tables into their own tents and
huts.

Will catches Robin's arm. "How could you say
that to her? How could you kiss her like that and then
reject her?"

Robin jerks away, then grabs Will's face in his
hand, a vindictive grip. "You kept this from me, Will.
You knew who she was and you didn't tell me."

"It was a joke, Robin," David interjects. "You've
played enough of them on us. Don't be a sore sport."

"You could let her stay, Robin," adds Will. "I like
her. She's strong, and kind, and she has suffered—"

"I don't trust her." Robin releases his face with a
rough shove. "Women don't belong here."

"That's your reason? Because you don't want a
hen in the cock-fest?" Will's voice rises. "She needs
us, Robin. And you're being cruel to her. I don't think

it's her gender at all. I think you care for her, and it frightens you."

"I'm not afraid of a woman," Robin seethes. "I already have one temperamental, meddling woman in my life, and I don't need another."

"You're talking about me now?" A harsh laugh breaks from Will. "I'm telling you what you need to hear. She may not have told us everything—I suspect she has secrets—but we can't send her back out there unprotected. You know what kind of world this is, Robin."

"Tuck can find her somewhere safe." Robin shoots a hard look at me. "He has found refuge for others—women and children who needed shelter."

I step forward, nodding. "There are some places. A few safe homes sustained by your generosity, Robin. I could find a bed for her. I agree with you— the Gloaming is no haven for a woman, especially not one of noble blood. You've defiled her already, doomed her immortal soul. I would hate to see you tempt her again and force her to heap sin upon sin. Best to let her go."

Robin stares at me, exasperated. "Don't help me, Tuck. Your arguments make me want to go fuck her into the next solstice."

"That wasn't my intent."

"I know, you big holy clod. What of *you*, and your constant ogling? You spy, but you never join in. I'll wager your balls are as blue as the summer sky." He closes the gap between us, his green eyes narrowing. "If I touched you between the legs now, you'd probably come at once."

"Leave him be, Robin," David says. "You're not yourself. Let's rest, and tomorrow we'll speak of this again."

"Marian is sleeping with me," Will says defiantly.

"She's all yours. One last night in the Gloaming. Take care that she doesn't stab you while you sleep." Robin stalks away to one of the tables and pours himself a drink.

Leaving Will and David to talk urgently in low voices, I return to my tent and pack up the rest of my healing supplies. Tomorrow I must leave the greenwood. There's a blacksmith in a nearby village who will melt down and restamp the stolen gold for me, so the villagers who receive it cannot be accused of theft. That will take a few days, and should give me time to find Marian a place in one of the safe houses I've set up with Robin's help.

The safe houses are packed with orphaned children, unwed mothers, the disabled, the sick, and the rejected. The shelters operate under my protection, and with Robin's secret funding I'm able to dissuade lawkeepers, churchmen, and others from interfering with their existence.

Perhaps, during our journey, I can speak with Marian about her soul. She has committed mortal sins while in the Gloaming, but maybe she will repent. Maybe I can persuade her to pursue forgiveness and absolution.

And perhaps, while I'm persuading her, I will also persuade myself.

24

DAVID

When Tuck goes to his tent, and Will goes to fetch Marian, I approach the table where Robin is guzzling ale. He's drinking more heavily than usual, gulping straight from a big jug. His near-death today and the incident with the girl have deeply unsettled him.

I pour some of Much the Miller's strongest brew for myself. The liquid heats my gut at once, and I slam down the mug, breathing hard.

Robin catches my eye over the rim of the jug he's draining.

He was cruel to the girl, savage to Will, and I can tell he's regretting it now. He's angry at all of us for deceiving him, for tricking him—and he's angry at the girl for not being Fae, furious because he revealed his longing for others like himself. He's frustrated because of how much he likes her. He's afraid she's dangerous. And he's torn between following his own rules and doing what he truly wants—keeping her with us.

Besides which, the assassin in the carriage brought him face to face with his own mortality. Small wonder he's a mess.

Now he will try to find distraction. The only question is what form it will take, other than the fiery liquor he's pouring into himself.

Alan of Dale is perched on the corner of a nearby table, strumming his lute—a slow, pleasant song.

"Alan," Robin says, without taking his eyes from mine. "Come here."

Alan is a lean redhead with ice-pale eyes and a hearty sprinkling of freckles. He's long-fingered, musical, and entirely in love with Robin, as many of the men are. But Robin has never loved him back.

"Sit there, Alan." Robin points to a stool, then stands up, pulling out his cock. "Keep playing, and open your mouth."

Alan obeys, blushing to the tops of his ears. He turns his head sideways so Robin can thrust into his mouth without bumping into the lute. The melody wobbles a little, and Alan's distended trousers show two wet dots of precum as Robin pumps harder.

Near the end of the song, Robin comes down the minstrel's throat with a fierce grunt. Alan swallows what he can, but he has to stop playing and spit out some of the copious release.

"Good boy," says Robin softly, cupping Alan through his trousers. The minstrel comes immediately with a broken gasp, wetting the fabric.

As Robin tucks himself away, I notice Will and Marian walking into camp together. She's in her boy's disguise again, and she looks less broken-hearted and discouraged. My Will, so talented at lifting the spirits of others.

Robin sees them too, and vents a jealous snarl under his breath. He strides away from Alan and me, toward his hut.

Once he has sealed himself in there, no one may disturb him for the night.

But I leap up and follow him. Just as he's about to enter the hut, I catch him roughly by the arm.

"You had her, and Alan," I say. "Are you done?"

He looks at me, and I see it in his eyes—the feral glint he tries to hide from the others. The wildness, and the loneliness, and the pain. There's an ache inside him, and he needs me to dig into his body and root it out.

"Are you done?" I speak harsh and low, with a shake of his arm.

"No," he whispers raggedly. "I'm not done."

He steps back, his head hanging low, and he lets me enter the hut first. He follows me in, and I hear the rustle of the hut sealing itself behind us, growing larger, thickening the walls with layer upon layer of branches so no one can hear what happens inside.

No one else is allowed to know what Robin and I do to each other in here. This is our personal den of madness, blood, and bliss.

I give him a moment to charge me, if he wants to be the aggressor. When he doesn't move, I understand he wants to be the victim this time.

We have a safe word between us. He will use it if I go too far.

Without warning I crash into him, a bruising attack. I force him to the ground on his belly.

Robin struggles, panicked gasps breaking from him as I tear down his trousers, exposing his rear. I slam my forearm against the back of his neck, pinning him while I rip open my own pants.

I almost get my dick in his ass right away this time, but he bucks me off and rolls free. He rises, feet braced apart, his trousers hanging so low I can see the base of his cock. His beautiful face is smeared with dirt.

Again I tackle him, slamming him down on his back this time. I wrestle his clothes off entirely, getting kicked in the jaw for my trouble. When I try to pin him, he bites my wrist so hard he draws blood. But I don't let him up.

While he's naked on his back, I seize both his legs in one arm and hold them together, straight up. There's his pink puckered hole, practically winking at me; I grab my cock head and wedge it into his opening.

He's dry. The groans shaking his chest as I begin to thrust are more like sobs, and I know it hurts, but he doesn't stop me.

When I come inside him, he has tears in his eyes, but he gasps with relief at the soothing flow of the liquid.

Soon it will be my turn, and he'll give me the same treatment. Worse, because he can use the branches and vines of the hut to pin me in place while he wrecks my holes. He lets me fight him sometimes. Other times, I'm helpless, except for the safe word.

When I'm done coming, I roll him onto his stomach and I beat his ass with my open palm until it's swollen and bruised. He comes twice while I do it.

Afterward I scoop a little of his cum off the ground and glaze his ass cheeks with it. He'll heal within minutes. I take a lick of the cum myself, too— it will help me get hard again more quickly so I can keep up with him.

He attacks me then, silent and furious, tears tracked through the dirt on his cheeks. He fights me like a mad wolf, both of us rolling over and over naked, snarling teeth, bare buttocks, and sinewy backs. It's a fight to see who can get a dick in a hole first. His cock slams into my mouth for a second, but

I jerk back and with a powerful effort I lift him whole, flip him onto the ground, and press my face into the seam of his ass. He yells out, a startled, throttled cry of desire.

And so it goes, the two of us slavering and grappling and grunting in the dirt, slick tongues warring with each other, erect cocks swinging and leaking precum. He has bruises and bites on both pectorals; my back is carved open and bleeding from his nails.

My neck aches. My head is ringing from a good punch he landed while I was trying to fuck his ass again. He gets me face down, grinding my cheek and jaw into the dirt with one hand while he ruts into me from behind. My insides are roaring with the burn of him, with the wild heat of him.

Robin is making the sounds I love—the young, helpless male moans that make me hard as a rock. My cock jerks as I come again, an involuntary compulsion, pleasure roaring through my belly and thighs.

He comes too, and there's too much cum for me to hold. When he withdraws, it pours out of me.

He spreads some of his release into the grooves he made down my back, and I can feel them healing at once. The fresher the cum, the faster the healing.

I climb to my feet, shaking, bruised, bloody, and filthy. He looks just as terrible and glorious.

We stare at each other, understanding locked between us.

This is only the beginning.
We have a long night ahead.

25

I'm very curious when David and Robin disappear into the hut together. The door seals over behind them, and the hut itself seems to grow much larger, with thicker walls.

"Sometimes he and David need to be alone," Will says in an undertone. "David gives him something I can't." He sounds a little wistful about it, but a moment later he shrugs off his mood and leads me into his own hut.

We don't engage in anything intimate beyond a few drowsy kisses as we fade into sleep. But when I wake up, he has one arm locked around my waist, as if he's never going to let me go. His blond braid is coming loose, tendrils wafting over his handsome face. I stroke his short blond beard with a fingertip before climbing out of bed.

It hurts that I may never see him again. But I try to ignore the pain, because it's foolish to feel so strongly for someone I just met.

As I push open the tent flap, I come face to face with Robin Hood.

He's naked to the waist, his black hair rumpled and his cheeks rosy. In the dawn light, his skin fairly glows. He looks as if he's had a very refreshing sleep. Whatever David did to him must have worked.

For a moment my heart bounds with hope, like a deer of the greenwood.

Maybe he will let me stay after all...

"I haven't changed my mind," he says quickly, gently. "I'm still sending you with Tuck. But I should not have said it the way I did, or left you there alone."

Biting my lip, I nod.

"It hurts me, you know," he says. "Sending you away. But we're a coarse, foul-mouthed, brawling, hard-fucking bunch, and despite your skills with a quarterstaff, I fear we'd break you."

I open my mouth to protest, but he shakes his head. "You can't change my mind, little trickster. Off you go, and see when Tuck is planning to leave. I'll wager it's soon—he likes to get an early start. I'll see you both off later. For now, I've got amends to make with my darling Will."

Breakfast is quick and cold, and then a couple of the Merry Men load a small cart with the stolen gold. It's hidden in bundles of firewood, tucked in packets of salted venison, and stowed beneath jugs of mead. A dull-eyed donkey pulls the load.

Robin has his bow in hand today, and several of the other men do as well. He steps away from the group and draws me aside, in the shade of a tree decked with fiery orange leaves.

"I haven't seen you with your bow since we met," I murmur. "It's a beautiful weapon."

"People seem to think I carry it all the time." He grins. "I prefer knives and magic, or my fists. Or a staff. But today we're hunting the king's deer, so—" He lifts the bow, scanning its length. "It is a fine piece, indeed."

"I wish I could see you use it."

"You saw me use my *other* fine piece." He winks. "That will have to do."

"Perhaps you're not as good as they say, anyway." I give him a small, teasing smile.

"I'm very good. Best in the kingdom—perhaps in the world. Once I hit the center of a target while my cock was buried in Will's ass."

"Holy Mother," I breathe. "I'd like to see that, too."

"It's a pity you won't. We won't see each other again, you and I." There's a raw, restive energy about him, as if he's a wild buck who might startle and spring away any moment. He bounces on the heels of his boots, biting his lower lip, and then he says, "Well, goodbye, Little John," and walks away as fast as he can.

Will and David approach me, glancing at Robin and then at each other.

"He may change his mind," Will says, low. "If he does, Tuck will know where you are. You won't be alone." His beautiful blue eyes are wet, and he clears his throat, looking at David.

"Take care of yourself, little one," David says.

And then they're walking away again.

Why do I feel as if pieces of my heart are attached to each of them—to Will, to David, to Robin? Why do I want to crumple into the dirt and sob, and beg them to keep me?

It's foolish and weak of me to entertain such a thought. I should be more worried about what the Sheriff of Nottingham will tell Prince John once he discovers I've been kicked out of Sherwood Forest. And I should be more concerned about the people I've known for four years, not the men I just met.

I failed my mission in just a few days. Besides Robin, Will, and David, I've memorized only a dozen names of Merry Men. And I have Robin's secret about his origins and his magic. Maybe I can get more information out of Friar Tuck today. Maybe it will be enough to buy the safety of my servants, and my own freedom.

Before we set off, Friar Tuck blindfolds me. He's apologetic while he does it, but the message is clear—

while Robin hasn't openly accused me of anything, he doesn't trust me.

"Hold onto my arm as we walk," Tuck says. "I won't let you fall."

I hate being led out of Robin's camp like this. I don't know what he told the Merry Men about my departure, but at least he let me keep my disguise. Maybe he did it to save face, and not because he wanted to spare me the dramatics of such a revelation. But the blindfold makes it clear he doesn't trust me not to betray the location of this camp.

The proof of his distrust feeds my despair, but at the same time I'm glad of his precautions. If I don't know the location of the Gloaming, I won't have to battle with myself about whether or not to reveal that information to the Crown.

With my hand tucked snugly in the crook of the friar's massive arm, I walk, step after careful step, heeding his directions every time he warns me about a root or a thorn bush.

He and I don't speak much, but after the noise of camp has faded, he begins singing prayers and psalms in a low voice. They're mostly pleas to be delivered from evil and temptation, which makes me feel rather guilty and uncomfortable. But the melodies are lovely, and his rich voice mingles pleasantly with the morning air, so I don't discourage him.

After a couple hours, the crisp autumn breeze pours over me more fully, and the light filtering through my blindfold changes. We must have left

Sherwood Forest behind, and we're walking through open country now. The road slants down, and my shoes scuff briefly on the stones of a bridge.

"The wind feels colder today," I say. "And the sun doesn't seem as bright as it has been. Are there any clouds? Signs of rain?"

In answer, Tuck speaks to the donkey, and I can feel him exerting force on the lead rope. With a rattling grind the cart stops.

Tuck's bulk shifts away from me, and for a moment I'm untethered and unseeing, breathing alone in the semi-darkness.

Then his thick, calloused fingers brush my cheekbones. He's easing the blindfold up, taking it off. I blink, a little dazed by the sudden light.

His massive chest is at the level of my eyes. I tip my head back, looking up into his handsome face. His rugged features are stern, but his hazel eyes shine with a concern that makes me want to rush into his arms and bury my whole self against his broad chest, against that big generous heart.

Maybe he reads the impulse in my face. He steps back, a muscle flexing along his jaw, and he curls one hand around the large wooden cross hanging from his string of rosary beads. As if the symbol of Christ is a weapon that can defend him against a whore like me.

"You despise me," I say quietly.

"No." He shakes his head, lets the crucifix fall. "I—I'd like to help you. If you'll let me."

"You're finding me a safe place to stay. I appreciate the kindness."

"Yes, but also—I feel I can offer you spiritual help."

I cock an eyebrow. "This from the man who watched Robin Hood fuck me over a rock last night? Yes, Will Scarlet told me you saw it, along with him and David."

"Yes, but they committed self-abuse while watching. I did not."

"And that makes you better than them? Because you didn't touch yourself?" I laugh harshly. "Such a pious man you are."

"I know, I know." He beats his forehead with the heel of his hand. "I shall have to do terrible penance to atone for what my eyes consumed during my stay in the Gloaming." His big shoulders shift uncomfortably, as if his back is twitching with some phantom pain.

"If it causes you such distress, why spend time with them?" I ask quietly.

"Because I believe in what Robin Hood does." He tugs at the donkey's lead rope, and we begin moving forward again. "The Crown is deeply corrupted, as are parts of the Church. They have forgotten what their purpose once was—to lead, guide, and help the people. They are to be shepherds, not wolves. But too many princes, lords, abbots, and priests are willing to sink their teeth into the helpless flesh of God's lambs. Robin is doing good work to rectify some of those ills, and when I work with him, I can be the hand of blessing to countless people who might otherwise suffer or starve."

He's so earnest. I can't help loving the passion he has for helping the weak.

"So yes," Tuck continues. "I go to Robin, again and again. I give him news so he can continue stealing from the rich. And I serve as his hands, doling out funds to the poor. In between my visits to the Gloaming, I travel the countryside, helping the sick and the needy. Yes, I mix his cum into the medicines and poultices I provide. It is a resource that God has allowed me to discover, so why shouldn't I use it on behalf of his injured or diseased children?"

Tuck casts me a burning glance, intensity laced with guilt. When I don't reply, he keeps speaking. "Robin could send someone to me so I wouldn't have to journey to the Gloaming. But I prefer to meet him in the forest. I tell myself it's safer that way. But the truth is—I succumb to the temptation of sight now and then. But I do not touch, or allow anyone to touch me."

"Doesn't the Scripture say that watching and wanting is just as terrible as committing the acts yourself?" I watch his profile as he marches along, noting the tension of his features.

"You are right," he says finally. "The words of Christ are impossible to refute."

"Your faith causes you so much agony. Why not let it go?"

"Is that what you have done?" He glances at me. "You've let your faith go?"

"Perhaps not entirely. But I've let my guilt go." I inhale deeply of the fresh fall wind, lifting my hands to it, palms-up. The sky is a keen, bright blue, with clumps of thick cloud dotting its arch and gathering in the west. We are in the center of a patchwork quilt of fields and thickets, streams and stiles, walls crisscrossing the verdant landscape, trees flaming copper and gold. "I feel so alive, Tuck. It's as if my whole body is singing, even though I'm sad Robin made me leave. I wish I could stay. But despite that sadness, my entire self feels more awake and refreshed than it has in years."

Friar Tuck nods grudgingly. "They say his cum does wonders for the body when he—applies it internally."

"Yes, but it's not only that. I felt wonderful after yielding to Will and David, too. As if a ball of dark, poisonous thread had been snarled and tangled up in my heart for a long, long time—and when I let myself enjoy pleasure, that horrible, sickening knot just dissolved. It's gone."

Strange how much I'm opening my heart to him. I'm telling him things I haven't yet admitted to myself—realizing, for the first time, how different I feel. How much freer and more relaxed, despite my worries about my castle and my servants.

"Sex with those men healed something inside me that I didn't know was bleeding," I murmur.

"Whatever happens in my future, I will always be grateful to them for it."

"And here I was hoping to convince you to repent and atone." Friar Tuck gives a rueful laugh. "It seems the harlot's path suits you, though."

I stop short on the path, stricken by his words.

He pulls the donkey to a halt. "I didn't mean—" He frowns, flushing deeper.

"You did, though. You meant what you said." I stare him down, my hands curled tight. "I've been called a 'harlot' and a 'whore' before, by the man I married. He called me those things because I had physical needs—because I, like a good wife, went to him for fulfillment—no one else. And he shamed me. He informed everyone in the village of my 'base animal desires.' Our priest told me a pious woman wouldn't have such urges, commanded me to satisfy my husband and deny myself. Truth be told, I was glad when my husband died."

I bite off the words, alarmed at how close I'm getting to the full truth of who I am. Robin, Will, and David know some of it. But I keep forgetting what parts I've revealed to whom, and when. If there's any sin I should be wary of committing again, it's lying. Lies are a fucking nightmare to keep straight.

"I didn't know that happened to you," Friar Tuck falters. "The Scripture says a married pair should not deny each other—"

"But what does that mean?" I exclaim. "Men have twisted those words and drawn the conclusion that they can rut into their wives anytime they please, even if the wife is begging and screaming to be spared—" My words choke off as memories crash through my fragile happiness, shattering it.

"I was glad when he left for war," I say, harsh and low. "I was glad when he died. Because he could not do that to me anymore. I won't let a man take me again without my consent, or without my delight in his mind."

"That is one thing I appreciate about Robin and his men," Tuck admits. "When they fornicate, they at least ensure that the women are well-cared for and thoroughly pleased. No one is taken by force, unless a few want to play at such things, like you and Robin did last night."

"Yes." I nod. "That was different. It was a game we both agreed to."

"I can't condone any of it." Tuck's voice is desperate, strained. "But I would never wish you harm, Marian. Only good things, and safety, and a place in heaven."

"A place in heaven—if I repent and grieve for my sin and do penance."

"Well… yes."

"And if I don't want to do any of that?" I look up at him while we continue along the road. "If I want to keep sinning, because it feels so deliciously wonderful?"

Tuck glances down at me. He doesn't speak, but his gaze lowers from my eyes to my lips.

Since our private moment in his tent, he has treated me with cautious distance, and with the kindness of a friend. But I can't forget what he said when I told him I liked his mouth.

He said he liked mine, too.

When Tuck doesn't reply to my question, I quicken my pace, walking in front of him, letting my ass sway a little more than usual.

"You can't keep walking like that," he says in a pained voice. "You have to keep up your ruse of being a boy. I can't be seen traveling alone in the company of a woman."

I give him a saucy look over my shoulder and stick out my tongue. He blushes so red from collar to forehead that I'm afraid he might have some kind of fit, so I slow down again and control the movement of my body as I walk. "Better?"

"Better." He clears his throat. "The blacksmith's shop is in a little hamlet up ahead, just beyond the hill. We'll give him the gold and stop at the tavern awhile. We didn't have much of a breakfast, and I'll wager you're hungry."

I am hungry, though I suspect he's thinking more of his stomach and less of mine. A man with such an enormous frame and muscles as huge as his must need to consume quite a bit of food to sustain it all.

"Didn't your Christ dine with harlots?" I say pertly as we walk.

"Yes, but I suppose they turned from their sins after meeting Him."

"Who knows?" I shrug. "Maybe they seduced a few of the disciples before going their own way."

He crosses himself frantically. "Don't talk like that. It's blasphemous."

Working him up is far too much fun, especially since it takes my mind off my own past struggles. I like this huge man who blushes so innocently and cares so deeply. I think I would like to render him helpless, to make him moan and come hard in spite of himself, just as Robin did to me last night.

But this journey with him might be the last chance I have to glean some more information about Robin's band. No time for fun.

I fall back to Tuck's side with a subdued air. "I'm sorry for distressing you. Perhaps I should confess my sins to you later. It would be a step toward my redemption, yes? Would that be a good thing?"

"I believe it would."

"Then before you deposit me at this safe home for wayward souls, you'll hear my confession." I squeeze his arm briefly. "Are there any among Robin's band who are still pious and confess their sins to you when you visit?"

"There's Adam from Owthorpe, and Clem the Tailor," muses Tuck, and I add the names to my mental list. "They don't participate in the nightly orgies, only the shooting contests and wrestling matches and such."

"Who's the best in the band at wrestling?"

"Robin's the best at everything, with David being a close second. Will is a fair hand at most types of fighting himself, especially knives. But as for wrestling—" He gives me a sheepish sidelong glance.

"You?" My eyebrows lift. "Of course! Why didn't I guess it? I suppose I thought a friar like yourself wouldn't be much of a fighter. You seem to prefer healing and service to others."

"I do. But I often carry alms to deliver to the poor, so I must be able to defend myself against bandits and thieves who do not follow Robin's creed. I need to be strong, so I can defend the weak and offer my aid to everyone. When I stop at a farm, a shop, or a town, I do whatever is needed, from herding cattle and fixing roofs to chopping wood or mending blankets."

He says all of it with the mild, matter-of-fact tone of someone who isn't looking for praise. I am entirely charmed by him. His allure is so different from Robin's wicked smiles, or David's gruff mystery, or Will's tender charm. Tuck isn't innocent in the truest sense of the word—he's seen too much sex for that—but he's so genuine, so pure of heart. I can't help wanting to hug him, kiss him, love him, and protect that good heart beating away inside his broad chest.

This is a man who gives everything selflessly. He deserves some comfort out of life, and not just the warmth to be found in a mug of ale. He needs someone to adore him and give him pleasure, to ease him into a new life of freedom from guilt.

If only he and I had more time together.

We crest the ridge he spoke of and descend into the tiny hamlet, no more than a handful of small shops. At the smithy's, Friar Tuck introduces me as an orphan lad temporarily under his care. We pull the cart into a shadowed stable behind the blacksmith's shop and transfer the stolen gold into a trough filled with hay.

"Give me two days, Tuck," the man says.

"Two days it is. And keep a few more coins than your usual share—Robin's orders."

"Bless him. God knows we could use the money! And my wife was asking if you happen to have any more of that tincture for chapped skin. You know her hands redden and peel something awful what with doing the laundry up at Lord Barrinworth's. She could use another pot of that cream."

"I've got some right here." Tuck rummages in one of his bags and produces a small pot.

"God bless you, Friar Tuck, and you as well, lad. And God bless Robin Hood. Safe travels to you."

Tuck and I leave the donkey and the cart at the blacksmith's. Once the gold is melted and restamped, he'll return for it and then continue on through the countryside, doling out provisions and coin to the poor.

"By then I hope to have you settled somewhere," Tuck says. "There's a safe haven near here that might have space for one more. We can visit this afternoon, once we've had lunch at the tavern. The blacksmith would have offered us food and drink, but he knows I can't linger long at his shop. It's best for both of us to keep our interactions brief so as to avoid suspicion."

I nod agreeably—but of course I have no plans to stay wherever Tuck puts me. Once he leaves me in someone's care, I'll head straight for Nottingham itself, which isn't far away. I have a general idea of where we are now, even though we're on a different road than the one I took to enter Sherwood Forest.

When I left court, bound by my deal with Prince John, I was escorted straight to Nottingham by the Sheriff's men, under cover of night. I was heavily cloaked, and no one was told my identity or why I was there. At the Sheriff's house, I dressed in my peasant boy garb and took up my quarterstaff. Near dawn, one of the Sheriff's men rode with me to the south and dropped me off on a dusty lane, which I followed into the forest.

The Sheriff of Nottingham doesn't approve of my arrangement with the prince, but he could not say much against it. He was at court that same day, with a contingent of heavily armed soldiers, to request the Crown's help in dealing with the Robin Hood situation. To which Prince John said, "If you have so many armored men with fine weapons, why can you not capture a handful of green-clad ruffians?"

Not the Sheriff's best day, but lucky for me, the prince was so frustrated with the Sheriff he decided to

accept my offer. I doubt he thought I would succeed.
I was simply a tool to shame the Sheriff.

Part of me wants to prove him wrong, to deliver
what I promised.

But another part of me, growing louder with
every step I take, simply wants to say "fuck the prince
and the Sheriff," leave behind everyone in my past
life, and let any lingering guilt float away, into the
bright fall air.

After a short walk, Tuck and I arrive at the *Blue
Boar* tavern, where he orders a gigantic leg of mutton,
bread, cheese, stewed apples, and copious amounts of
their best ale. I nibble at the food, my eyebrows raised
as I watch Tuck gulping enough ale to put any other
man under the table.

Our conversation must have agitated him even
more deeply than he let on, and he's trying to douse
his sense of guilt. It's interesting to me that he denies
himself sex, yet permits overindulgence in drink. He
needs to find a healthier balance.

Ironic that I'm judging him, when I keep
vacillating between the joys of my new life and the
sour guilt of my past.

Finally Tuck looks at me with bleary eyes and says in a loud, genial tone, "We'll be off soon, but I need a little nap first. Just a snooze. Just for a moment."

His head thunks onto the table, and he begins to snore.

Sighing, I pay the host with coin from a leather pouch at Tuck's waist, and then I settle in to wait. I left my staff in the cart at the blacksmith's shop, and I fret about that for a few minutes. It's a good staff, cut and smoothed for me by Master Blunt, the stablehand who trained me. I'd be sorry to lose it for good. Maybe I can go back and fetch it sometime. If not, he can make me another, I suppose.

Lord Flaymish told me he would look after my servants during my absence. I'm not sure I can trust his word, though. A toadie of Prince John, he's a man with some wealth but little influence, careless of anyone but himself and a few friends at court. He was personally horrified by my scheme, and insisted it be kept strictly secret. The idea of a woman dressing in a man's clothes is abhorrent to most these days. Had I not obtained the king's consent for the ruse, I could be in serious trouble with the law myself.

I run my fingers over the table, its surface worn smooth by the elbows and fingers of many tavern guests. Along the edge, letters have been carved: R-O-B-I-N. I press my fingertips over them, thinking of a certain sharp-eared, wickedly beautiful man in the greenwood.

Being fucked by him was like standing on the parapet of a castle during a lightning storm, being doused with fresh rain and seared by white-hot passion. I will never forget how my body leaped to obey him, soaring into climax when he commanded it. I will never forget the glittering, glorious sensation of his release flooding into me, bathing my insides, pouring down my thighs. It was a reckless, all-consuming bliss.

But it's over, and my mind must return to more prosaic things. Men have come inside me a few times in the past couple of days. I should ask Tuck if he has any tonics to prevent pregnancy. There must be no evidence of what I did with the Merry Men in the greenwood, or I will truly be cast out.

Still, I can't help stroking Robin's name, wondering if he carved it himself or if someone else etched these letters. Maybe someone who loved him.

I will likely never see him again. And if I do, it might be at his execution.

The moment I start to picture it, my heart begins racing, my breath quickens, and tears spring to my eyes.

I can't do this. I can't go to the Sheriff and give him names and secrets.

But I don't know what else to do. Return to court empty-handed? Marry Lord Guisbourne and suffer, along with my servants, for the rest of our days?

I can't return to Robin Hood. I suppose I could stay at Tuck's safe house and find some useful work—at least maybe then I could see Will and David and Robin once in a while. But then what of my people back home? How can I simply abandon them?

The door to the tavern bangs open.

"Welcome to the *Blue Boar*," calls the host. "Be right with you."

"Quickly, there's a good man," replies a gruff voice, and I look up from my perusal of Robin's name.

Three men have entered. Two of them wear the armor and colors of Nottingham, with arm bands identifying them as members of the Sheriff's personal retinue.

The third man is the Sheriff of Nottingham himself.

I hunch down, propping my elbow on the table and my hand against my face, praying that the Sheriff will not notice me.

He cannot see me with Friar Tuck. If he does, Tuck will be connected to Robin. Not only will he be in grave personal danger, but he won't be able to continue passing coin and remedies to the people of this area.

Once the Sheriff and his men are seated, the host bustles up to take their order. His wide back is a barricade between me and the three newcomers, so I jump up from the table and hurry out of the tavern by the back door, leaving Tuck to snooze at his table alone.

There's a skinny girl of perhaps ten outside, pinning wet sheets and towels to a clothesline. She stares at me, but doesn't question my sudden appearance or my anxious pacing.

I should speak with the Sheriff now. Then I won't have to walk to Nottingham alone tomorrow, or whenever Tuck leaves me.

But I have to be sure Tuck doesn't wake and see me chatting with Robin Hood's sworn enemy.

I still have a few coins left over from when I paid for our lunch. I kept them, because I have nothing else and money is power. I take one from my pocket, offer it to the girl, and whisper a message to her.

She nods and runs inside, while I continue pacing the back courtyard, watching the chickens amble about in their pen nearby. The tavern has a particularly fine rooster with vivid copper and emerald feathers. His pompous strutting reminds me of what I called Robin the first time we met—"a preening cock."

Damn me, I miss him. I miss them all.

The back door of the tavern opens, and the Sheriff of Nottingham steps out, crinkling his nose at the sight of the laundry, the chickens, and the refuse pile nearby. He looks nearly as pompous as the rooster, and has a similar wattle beneath his chin. His stomach swells far over his waistband—not something I would normally judge in a man, except I know his weight is a result of overindulgence at the expense of impoverished people.

Maybe he was once a warrior in his own right. But he has long since given up that effort. Why combat lawlessness himself when he can pay others to do it for him?

The Sheriff catches sight of me. "What is this?" He advances, deeper lines of cautious surprise carving into his craggy face. "Lady Marian?"

"Hush, please. Yes, it is I."

"You've completed your mission for the Crown so soon?" His eyes narrow with suspicion.

"I have gleaned some useful information," I reply. "But I wasn't able to get all the names of the Merry Men. Robin Hood discovered I was a woman and kicked me out of his camp."

Satisfaction lightens the Sheriff's expression. "I thought as much. It was a foolish and godless plan. And fruitless. Never send a woman to do a man's work, I say. Much less a simpering noblewoman like yourself."

His censure shouldn't pique me, but it does. "It wasn't entirely fruitless," I snap. "I made at least one significant discovery."

"And what is that, pray tell?"

I hesitate, agonized. What does it really matter if I tell the Sheriff that Robin is Fae? There are already plenty of rumors that he has magic, or that he's a demon. Even before I went into the greenwood I'd heard tales of him vanishing or making the trees move. Like most other people, I dismissed them as silly stories. Would it be so dreadful if I simply confirmed the rumors?

The Sheriff is watching me, his gaze full of contempt. "You have nothing. I knew it. Or perhaps you have the information, but you, being a weak woman, have succumbed to the rogue's wicked charms. Females have delicate minds and are easily swayed by evil. The Hood has turned you traitor, hasn't he? Perhaps you even let him between your legs. You know what happens to treacherous harlots, don't you, Lady Marian?"

"Robin Hood is Fae," I blurt out.

The Sheriff stares. "What?"

"He is Fae. He has power over the trees—they move at his command. That's why you can never find him—because he can change the paths through the greenwood. He can conceal his camp or his people within the forest."

"Is this a trick? The Fae do not walk these lands, if they ever did."

"It's not a trick. It's the truth. Believe it or not, as you like."

"And the names the prince requested?"

"I don't have them."

"You spent three days with Robin Hood's people and learned no names?"

"None that I'm sure of." I force myself to look him in the eye. "I need more time."

"But you said Robin Hood uncovered your disguise and made you leave. How do you plan to gather more information?"

"I have a source. I only need a little longer to extract the information."

The Sheriff begins to pace, just as I did earlier. "Do you know where the Hood's camp is?"

"I was blindfolded going into it and coming out of it."

"You need to get back there and devise a way to lead us in."

"That's simply not possible," I protest. "He's too careful for that, and so are the men with him. And with his magic, there's no way to ensure that any trail I left for you would remain intact."

"If we cannot get to him, then we must draw him out," says the Sheriff. "What does he like best? What does he take pride in? Is there some lure we could use?"

"Gold?"

The Sheriff pins me with a look. "He has certainly stolen plenty of that. I won't be putting any of my coin out as a lure, and I don't believe any nobles of this area want to risk theirs either. There must be something else he cares about. Any lovers? A wife?"

I certainly don't plan to give the Sheriff Will and David. But what else does Robin care about? He's cocky, of course. Proud. Defensive of his reputation, his accomplishments— "He's particularly proud of his skill with a longbow."

"Indeed," muses the Sheriff. "I believe I can use that. Yes, yes... we'll hold a tournament in Nottingham, within the very walls. A contest to determine who is the best archer in the land. The prize shall be a golden arrow."

"But you said no gold."

"Not solid gold—we'll gild the thing." The Sheriff brushes away my comment. "I'll do some investigation into this claim of yours, that he is Fae. There may be particular relics or charms that will help us trap him. You must worm your way back into his good graces somehow—get him to take you back into the camp, and then persuade him to participate in the contest."

"How am I supposed to go back?" My voice shrills with frustration. "I told you, he won't let me stay because I'm a woman."

"Yes, exactly. You're a woman. Buxom enough, when you're not strapped down. Pretty enough to gain Prince John's favor. Use your womanly wiles. Beg, cry, bare your breasts—"

"So first you accuse me of letting Robin Hood fornicate with me, and now you're advising I seduce him?" I scoff.

The Sheriff glances around, then seizes my shoulder in a painful grip and shoves me back against the stone wall of the tavern. His hot, foul breath bursts over my face. "You will do whatever needs to be done, do you hear me? I've been after this bastard for far too long. You're not the only one with something at stake. If I fail to capture the Hood within three months, I lose everything. My title, my position, my house—everything. Your virtue means nothing to me. Use your juicy tits, your leaking quim, that hole in your face—make Robin Hood take you back, and make him compete in the tournament. If you do, and I succeed in capturing him, I will personally advocate for you with Prince John. If you fail and I lose my position, I will find you, wherever you may go, and I will fuck you until you are raw and bleeding, after which I will peel the skin from your flesh. Then I will burn Elmwood Castle to the ground with your servants inside. Am I understood?"

My whole body is frozen in his grip. Terror paralyzes me, even as a voice in the back of my mind is screaming at me to push him away, to defy him, to protect myself. I want to be brave. But all I can do is nod meekly.

"Good." The Sheriff pushes himself back and straightens his doublet. "I'd better not see your face again until the day of the tournament, when you bring Robin Hood to me."

When the Sheriff goes back inside, I leave the courtyard by a low gate and stumble up a grassy hill, tears streaming down my face and breath hissing between my clenched teeth. I collapse in the tall grass beneath a scarlet tree.

I betrayed Robin. I told the Sheriff his secret.

Why? Why did I do it?

My heart is cracking with guilt, with fear.

And yet why should I feel guilty? This was my plan, my goal all along. To glean the information and give Robin to the Crown. To buy my freedom, and my servants' safety.

What if I tell Friar Tuck everything and throw myself on his mercy? Would he abandon me to the Sheriff's retribution? I can't imagine Robin Hood or any of his men would help me now, after this betrayal.

I should have gone to Robin first, when my marriage to Guisbourne was proposed. But I didn't know the Hood personally then—he was a legend to me. I couldn't be sure he would help. And I did not want to abandon the lands, the riches, and the castle that should be mine. Why should my servants and I be forced to leave it all and go live in the forest, just to be free?

Why can't greedy men simply leave me alone and let me exist?

A chill wind scours my wet face and pushes the gray clouds together into a looming mass. But in spite of the growing cloud bank, the sun still shines, illuminating the grass in golden splendor under the dark, smoky blue of the sky.

I have to make Friar Tuck take me back into the greenwood. Somehow, I must convince him that I need to see Robin Hood again. But I have no idea how to do that.

Perhaps, while we're journeying to the safe haven where he plans to leave me, I can talk to him about it. Or maybe I can tell him that the next time the Merry Men invite women for their nightly play, I would like to be one of those women.

I doubt the good friar would pass along *that* message, though, since he's so concerned for my immortal soul.

I stay under the tree, crying and seething by turns, until I see the Sheriff and his men mounting their horses and leaving the tavern. After wiping my eyes, I trudge back down the hill and re-enter the *Blue Boar*.

Friar Tuck is stirring, lifting his head from the table, wiping a bit of drool from his mouth. When I sit down across from him he groans, massaging his temples. "Forgive me. That drink was stronger than I thought."

"It's all right. I've settled up with the host, so we should go now. It looks as if it may storm later."

He drinks some water, rises, and walks toward the door. He's fairly steady on his feet, which is a good sign.

When we're a little way down the road, he veers off into the grass. "I need to piss. Wait a moment."

Perhaps he expects me to turn away. But he didn't tell me to, and I'm eager to have another look at the enormous cock I glimpsed in his tent back in the Gloaming.

He has his back to me as he lifts his robes, so I sidestep until I can see the huge dick in his hand, spewing a thin stream of liquid from its tip into the grass beside the road.

Tuck looks up at me suddenly. Our eyes lock, while he continues to piss.

When he's done, he shakes his cock lightly and lets his robes fall again.

"Filthy girl," he says, low. But it doesn't sting like when he called me a "harlot." There's a faint caress in his tone this time. Maybe his inhibitions are still soft from the drink.

"It's incredibly sad that magnificent cock of yours will never be shared," I murmur, as we continue walking.

"My body is reserved for God's service."

"Such a pity."

We journey for a while, while the dark blue clouds overhead continue to mount higher and climb farther across the sky.

We enter a thick belt of forest next. The trees are shedding their leaves in a riot of fluttering color, and my spirits begin to lift in spite of everything. When a gust of wind showers Tuck's bald head and brown robes with gold and scarlet leaves, some of them stick to the woolen fabric and catch in his cowl. I can't help laughing aloud.

"Here, I'll help you pick them off." I start plucking the leaves from his coarse garments, standing on tiptoe to extract one from the folds of his cowl. I sway a little, off-balance, bumping lightly into his chest.

And then I look at his face.

Our profiles hover near each other, breath mingling in the chilly autumn air. Everything is fresh, crisp color, and Tuck himself is so huge and handsome and close to me. His broad mouth is so tempting. His lips look warm and rough and delicious.

I nudge my face against his, gently, my mouth parted, drifting over his lips.

His hands close around my waist.

And then he moves me back, away from him.

"Enough, Marian," he says quietly.

Sighing, I relent, following him down the road.

Just as we break out of the tree belt, the cloud bank overhead begins to unleash its contents. Just a few fat drops at first, then more and more—a deluge of pent-up moisture breaking free.

I squeal, and Tuck shouts, and we run together as the road quickly turns slick with mud.

"This way!" He beckons me off the road. When I follow, he grasps my waist and lifts me right over a low wall into the pasture beyond. "See that?" He points to a building ahead—whether barn, shack, or abandoned cottage, I'm not sure.

The rain is streaming down in torrents now, soaking everything.

"Run!" shouts Tuck, and his voice seems strange until I glance at him through the rain and see that he's grinning broadly, almost laughing.

We pelt across the field, and he pounds on the door to the cottage. When no one answers, we charge inside.

26

Marian and I crash into the cottage together. It's just one room, empty except for a few pieces of rickety furniture and some clay pots. A hole in the ceiling admits a generous trickle of sparkling rain. Otherwise, the place is bare, and clean enough. No rats that I can see, and few spiders. Recently abandoned, perhaps.

I unsling my big, heavy satchel and unbuckle my money purse, laying both aside. Marian has been carrying my smaller satchel, and she unburdens herself as well.

I pull the door closed and immediately regret it, as the cottage interior becomes black except for a hint of gray light from the hole in the roof. Fumbling around in my bag, I manage to find a couple of candles and my tinderbox. The candles' golden glimmer relives the darkness of the room.

Next, I remove my boots. My woolen robe is heavy with rain, and it smells strongly of toil and travel, not to mention wet wool. Normally I would remove it, but with a lady present, I cannot.

Marian casts aside her sopping hat, cloak, and scarf. Then she removes her boots and reaches into her trousers to unfasten the codpiece underneath.

Before I can protest, she pulls off her tunic as well, revealing the bindings that give her a more masculine shape.

"Judging by those clouds, we'll be here awhile," she says. "And I'd like some relief from these wrappings. Do you have any extra clothes?"

"No. Friars travel with very little. But there's a thin blanket and a cloak in the satchel you were carrying."

"Thank the saints." She begins unwinding the cloth strips from her body, and I should look away— but I don't.

I've seen her naked before, when Robin was fucking her in the woods. It's entirely different to be alone with her in the candle-glow as her soft breasts are revealed. The curve of her graceful neck beneath the mop of curls, the swerve of her lithe bare body down to her slim waist, the soft skin of her belly right where the trousers sweep low on her hips—I crave it all. And I crave the round, luscious breasts with their tiny peaked tips. I want to suckle her. I want to squeeze her breasts together and run my cock up between them.

I want to touch someone else's warm flesh in a lascivious, wanton way.

My gaze lifts to her face again. Her plump mouth is twisted in a pretty little smirk, and her lovely eyes are dark with awareness and lust.

She wants me. She has hinted as much.

I've been wanted before. I've seen admiration in the eyes of weary mothers or faded widows when they looked at me, and I've endured Robin Hood's overt attempts to seduce me. I have always been able to say no—though with Robin, I have almost yielded more times than I can count. His wicked red mouth and the hard, perfect planes of his gorgeous body are too much for anyone to resist.

Marian finds the thin blanket in my satchel and pulls it around herself. But she lets the material slide off her shoulder, revealing her delicate collarbone and the upper swell of one breast. A cruel temptation, just for me.

Blood is pumping into my cock already, turning it hard with need. To conceal the protrusion under my robes, I sit down.

"You're not going to take that off?" Marian arches an eyebrow at my wet robe. "You could wrap yourself in the cloak. Here." She tosses the cloak to me.

Fuck. The sinful word echoes in my mind, a frustrated curse I've heard so often in the Gloaming that it has become part of my internal vocabulary. I shall have to beat myself in penance for thinking it.

Without answering Marian, I stand up, turn my back to her, and pull the robe off, over my head.

For a moment, my body is bared to her view.

She inhales sharply. "Tuck, your back. Those scars…"

"I punish myself for my sins. I hope that by suffering in this life, I may escape eternal suffering."

"Oh, Tuck." She sounds as if she's on the brink of crying.

Frowning, I wrap myself in the cloak. It was a gift, and it's a little small, so it doesn't quite close around my body. I have to arrange myself carefully so Marian won't be assaulted by the sight of my giant erect cock.

"I wish you wouldn't hurt yourself," she murmurs. "You're beautiful, you know. Gigantic and gorgeous."

"Physical appearance and comfort are not important," I tell her. "What's important is the heart. And sometimes the discomfort of the body is necessary to bring the heart to repentance."

"Hm." She sits crosslegged on the floor near me, her cloak slipping even farther down her shoulder.

"Repentance. Perhaps now is as good a time as any for you to hear my confession, Friar."

"Perhaps." I glance at the trickling rain and the shimmering golden candles. Then I look into the beautiful, sweet face of the woman in front of me. Her skin shines in the soft light, and her eyes are darkly luminous. She looks as innocent as an angel, though I know she isn't.

"These are strange circumstances," I tell her. "But God hears us everywhere. So yes, Marian, I will hear your confession."

"Bless me, Father, for I have sinned."

As Marian's plump mouth forms the words, my cock twitches.

This is going to be an exercise in endurance. Every nerve and muscle, every inch of skin on my body wants to be touching her.

But I remain where I am, holding the scanty cloak around my naked bulk. She is supposed to be the one baring her soul, but I feel more exposed than I ever have in my life.

Marian is rattling off minor sins. "I have taken the Lord's name in vain. I have told lies. I kept a few coins from your money-purse after I paid the tavern host—that may have been stealing. And worst of all, Father, I have been very, very naughty with men."

She pauses, blinking those doe eyes at me.

Hoarsely I say, "How have you been naughty, my child?"

A sparkle of mischief winks in her gaze. "I let three men spew their seed onto my face, Father."

"Very wrong. And what else?"

"I let one man tuck his hand into my clothes and pet my pussy." She scoots a little closer to me. "I let him play with me until I came on his fingers."

My whole body is blazing, and the heat is most acute in my straining cock. My balls feel painfully full and heavy, aching until I can hardly remain still. Through gritted teeth I say, "Was this the only sin of the flesh you're guilty of?"

"No, Father," she murmurs. "I crawled into bed with two beautiful naked men, and I let them touch me with their cocks and their hands. One of them rubbed my pussy from the outside, and then his cock slipped inside me. He was so thick, he stretched my little hole."

Marian's cheeks are flaming. She has let the blanket slip down to her waist, and both her plump breasts seem to beckon me.

My cock is swollen, burning—jerking uncontrollably every time another sensual phrase unspools from her lovely lips.

"Have you ever spoken like this to a man before?" I ask.

"No," she whispers.

"But it's all right, because you're confessing," I say hoarsely. "The details are important. You must face everything you've done in order to find true forgiveness." I've said those words a few dozen times to people who confessed immorality to me. I said them so I could hear all the titillating details I craved. I am a wretched, craven, greedy man despite all my efforts to be holy.

"David didn't finish inside me, so Will pushed his cock into my hole next," Marian says. "He has a lovely cock, and he came so beautifully, filling me up. But his cum began to leak out between my pussy lips, so David took the head of his own cock, and he pushed the cum back in."

"Oh God." My dick jerks uncontrollably, its sensitive tip grating against the rough cloak. I can't bear it any longer—I throw the cloak open, and my erection bobs in midair. The tiny hole at the head is leaking precum.

"After they both filled me up," Marian says softly, "I slept with their cum inside me all night. Just thinking about it makes my pussy flutter, Father. It's fluttering right now." Slowly she eases her trousers off, kicking them away, and she leans back on her elbows on the floor, opening her thighs wide, baring her sex to my view.

Her pink center is glistening, the lips trembling with arousal.

I devour the sight, while my belly tightens painfully and my cock jerks again—my balls are tightening—oh God—

A jet of cum spurts from my cock, and then another, and another. My nipples are tightly beaded, my belly ridged as every muscle contracts.

It feels good, but it's an incomplete pleasure. I slam a fist against the floor, groaning with frustration. I'm still hard, still aching.

Marian crawls to me. Straddles my lap, poised upright on her knees, with the tip of my cock a breath from her slick center. I should push her off, but I don't.

"Forgive me, Father," she whispers. "For I am about to sin."

She leans in slowly, giving me time to object. Her nipples brush the hot skin of my heaving chest. Her mouth closes with mine.

Lips, soft and warm. The delicate wet tease of her tongue.

I should stop this. I should stop.

I've fought so long to stay pure.

"Marian," My agonized whisper against her mouth.

"Do you want me to stop?" She pulls back slightly. Looks into my eyes with tenderness and understanding.

"I've taken holy orders. I am sworn to serve the needy—"

"Right now, *I'm* the needy," she breathes. "I'm a woman in great need. And you have it in your power to help me."

Relief dawns in my mind. "Yes," I whisper back. "Yes."

"I might go mad if I don't receive healing," Marian says. "Please, Friar Tuck—please heal me. Please satisfy my needs."

She's reaching down. Touching me—*touching me*—no one else has ever touched my cock, and I whimper, pained and helpless, as she pokes my tip inside her. She's sinking down, and I'm gloved in hot, wet suction. I bellow a groan of exquisite relief as finally, finally, my aching cock is swallowed up in a living, pulsing human body.

"God's bones, you're enormous," Marian gasps, but she keeps sinking lower, taking more of me inside herself. I fall back onto the floor, prone and helpless to the sensations racing through my body.

She's touching me more. Pressing both small hands over my pectorals. Rubbing her thumbs over my erect nipples—shit—a bolt of ecstasy zings through my cock.

This is what my soul has been crying for—to be touched by another human. I reach up and grasp her breasts in my hands. Tears fill my eyes because they feel just as I hoped they would, only better.

Marian notices my emotion, and her face softens again, a tender glow just for me. "Sweet Tuck." She relaxes fully, and slides down all the way so I'm seated to the hilt inside her. Leaning forward, she traces my lower lip with her thumb. "You big, beautiful man. You've been hurting for too long. Let me take the pain away."

27

MARIAN

I didn't think Tuck's cock would fit inside me.
I'm amazed that it did.

When I start to move on him, there's a rippling
burn with every surge of that enormous, thick shaft
through my channel. But my insides are well-
lubricated, coated with fresh slickness every time I
look down at his handsome face.

He's transfigured, practically glowing, his eyes
flooded with joyful tears and his mouth parted in
breathless wonder. I rise and sink on him, over and
over, while he gently cups my breasts. He's still
holding back, still unsure how much of me he can

touch, so I guide his hands to my ass. He catches on quickly and sits up, lifting and lowering me onto his cock with great surges of his gigantic arms.

The monstrous shaft inside me pulses, and Tuck groans, urging my body up and down faster on his cock.

"Yes," I gasp. "Come for me, come, come—"

A guttural, heart-wrenching moan bursts from him as he climaxes, throbbing inside me. His sinewy body tightens, then relinquishes every bit of its tension as he pants through the fading bliss.

He lies back on the floor, an expression of pure satisfaction bathing his face.

With his whole cock still inside me, I lean down to kiss his mouth, then his forehead. His eyes are closed, his great chest still undulating with heavy breaths.

When his eyes blink open, I meet his gaze cautiously, fearing the self-hatred I expect to find.

But he gives me a slow smile. "Thank you."

"Why?" I whisper, touching his cheek.

"I broke my vow in spirit a long time ago, and I've been tormenting myself, trying to keep that broken promise with my body. It was tearing me apart."

I smile back at him, trembling with relief. "I thought you might be angry with me, or hurt yourself."

"How could I be angry with you?" He pushes himself up to a sitting position again, still inside me, and he folds me against his chest. "You set me free. How can I suffer and sacrifice for an uncertain heaven when the joys here on earth are so incredible?"

A relieved breath rushes out of me, and I curl into his warmth, his strength, his kindness. I am safe here. Safe from everyone and everything.

But my heart is still unquiet with guilt.

After a few moments, Tuck lifts my body off his softened cock in one fluid motion. He lies back, pulling me forward along his torso, until my stomach thrills with the realization of where he plans to place me.

"Tuck," I gasp.

"If there's anything Robin and his men have taught me, it's to never leave a lady unsatisfied," he says. "Sit on my face, Marian."

"But I've never—and you've never—"

"I've seen it done. I've watched more sexual acts than you have, I'll wager. I'll do a fair job of it, or I'll drown trying."

"My god," I whisper, but he's already settling me into place, with my pussy right over his mouth. His nose nudges my swollen clit, which is already sensitized from the fucking. It won't take long for me to come.

I'm bracing myself, hovering slightly because I don't want to hurt him. Tuck's thick, rough lips nibble along my pussy, and then his tongue traces along one of my labia.

"I can taste myself here," he mutters against my folds, and I quiver at the exquisite vibration. "But I taste you, too, and you're so much sweeter, Marian. Come on my face, angel."

I whimper at the nickname. "I like 'angel' better than 'harlot.'"

"Angel," he growls against my sex, and his tongue lashes along my center. I squeal, my entire sex buzzing on the edge of climax. Again he licks me— again, again—and then, as if he has lost his mind to me, he seizes my hips, rams me down on his face, and begins mouthing and suckling with such wanton ferocity that I scream, while the orgasm splits me apart, lightning blazing through my sex, snaking up my spine. A crack of thunder from outside echoes the crashing pleasure in my body.

Tuck nibbles and soothes me, lets me rub myself against him through the last swells of bliss. Then he lifts me and drapes my shivering, whimpering body along his.

The storm continues for hours. We doze off, naked together, draped by the blanket, and then we rouse to eat some bread from Tuck's satchel and drink from a flask of ale. Afterward he spreads the blanket, lays me down, and takes his time thoroughly exploring my body. He licks my collarbone, sucks on my nipples, plants kisses along my belly, and nuzzles into my sex, breathing deep.

"I've never seen a whole naked woman this close before," he says.

I frown. "But what of the orgies with women in the greenwood?"

"I had to stay far away from those. The women they bring in are all from this region, and if they saw their priest at such a revel, they would be shocked and embarrassed. So for those, I stayed away entirely, or I spied from a distance, from the cover of bushes— which meant I usually ended up seeing only parts of the women as they were being fucked."

"But you said you've seen a woman sit on a man's face."

"Robin and a serving girl, at the *Suckling Pig* tavern," Tuck says, with a wry smile. "She was still wearing her dress, but she had it pulled up around her waist. She knelt astride him while he lay on the table. I was sitting at the head of the table, too drunk to leave without falling over, so I got the full view of how he did it. And what I couldn't see, he told everyone that night during dinner in the Gloaming. He loves to boast about his sexual exploits."

He gives my pussy an experimental lick. "The taste of you—I can't describe it. It's more addictive than ale."

I release a soft moan as he licks me again, over and over. Shifting my head, I notice the thick erection hanging between his thighs. I want it inside me again. I think from this angle it will feel even better.

I lower my hand to his head, where he's still lapping between my thighs. "Tuck," I murmur. "I need you."

28

WILL

Our hunt was successful today. The king's deer are roasting over our fires, and the men are in good spirits, playing games of dice, tending their weapons, drinking, and telling tales of the day to those who stayed in camp.

I enjoy hunting occasionally, if only to prove that I can lay aside my fine clothes and get my hands dirty. I'm better with a crossbow than a longbow, and best of all with knives. I pinned a fleeing squirrel to a tree with one of my knives today. My best throw ever, I think.

But I'm struggling to rejoice in the success, because I can't stop thinking about the girl. The absence of her itches at my mind, like a task that remains incomplete, or a precious thing I left behind somewhere, or an important name I forgot. I can't shake the unease.

When my heart is restless I seek out one of my beloveds. Robin is nowhere to be seen, but David is standing at the edge of camp under the eaves of the forest, holding a mug and glowering. He's shirtless, and the firelight glows on his brown skin, highlighting every glossy curve of hard-packed muscle.

I slink up behind David, wrap my arms around his waist, and tip my head against his back with a long sigh. Just touching him makes me feel better. I stand there for several moments, listening to the pattering of rain on leaves in the distant forest. The night is dark with clouds overhead, but no storm can touch the Gloaming itself. Some magic of Robin's, perhaps, or a remnant of the Fae charms that used to encircle this place long ago, when it was one of the favorite spots for his kind to gather.

"You seem more dismal than usual," I murmur to David.

"Same to you, Scarlet."

"Maybe we're out of sorts for the same reason."

"Hm." He sighs, turning around, pulling my face closer so he can kiss me. "The girl."

"She was so vulnerable, David, so wounded, yet so beautifully eager for sensual play. She was ready to be healed, body and soul. She needed us, and we sent her away."

He shakes his head slowly, his fingers twisting a lock of my hair. "I haven't felt this way about any of the other strays in camp, men or women. What is this hold she has gained over us, in so brief a time? I don't like it, Scarlet."

"We have both been deeply shamed and reviled in our past, you and I," I tell him. "We know what it is to have others sneer at our desires, to call us disgusting because of how we take our pleasure. We know how it feels to hide, to conceal our true selves. We understand the panicked despair of knowing that we have absolutely nothing of our own, and no one to call family or friend. We have been where she is. I think that's why we feel this way about her. That, and she took our cocks well."

"So well," he growls, kissing me again. "I loved mingling my cum with yours inside her sweet pussy. And she let me hurt her, Scarlet—she truly enjoyed it. I wanted more time with her. I wanted to unravel her, break her down until her trust in me was complete, until she had no more fear."

"You're so good at that, my love." I cup between his legs, humming with delight when I feel how hard he is. "I want her back, David. I want to fuck her while Robin fucks me, while you come in her mouth. I want her riding Robin's cock, watching us while you rut into me."

"Gods, yes," he says hoarsely. "I want her back, too."

"We need to find Robin and tell him," I say. "Together maybe we can persuade him."

"Or we could go find her ourselves, and bring her back, and tell Robin nothing until we return with her."

"A more dangerous option. I like it."

"Of course you do." David grins, catching my throat in his hand. "You like a little danger with your fun, Scarlet." He shoves me against a tree trunk. In preparation for the night's debauchery, I'm wearing only a scarlet robe, belted around the waist, with nothing beneath. He rakes my robe up with his free hand while I desperately unbutton the flap of his pants.

A moment later my legs are around his waist, and his cock is pushing into my asshole, a thick burn that I welcome with hoarse frantic moans into his mouth. He ruts into me against the tree, fierce grunts breaking from him with every thrust. The robe slips off my shoulder, and he pauses to crush a hand over my breast, working the flesh before twisting my nipple.

My cry of pain is muffled by his lips, and I feel him harden still more. My own cock is a burning rod pinned between our stomachs, and the sensitive underside grinds against his abs every time he rams into me.

"God, I love you." The breathless confession jerks out of me.

"You beautiful son of a bitch," he murmurs against my cheek. I smile, because I know that means he loves me too.

And then my smile is wiped away as my eyes glaze, as the ripples of bliss racing along my cock build into a wave, a hurricane, a thunderclap of nerve-shattering ecstasy. I come, sprinkling my chest and his with my release.

"David," I pant. "David…"

He kisses me again, bites my tongue until I taste blood, and then his body hardens as he shoves into me one final time, compulsively jetting cum into my hole.

"Scarlet…" His heavy breath gusts past my ear. "Scarlet, you're mine."

The crack of a twig near us startles me. I don't mind onlookers—we're fucking in full view at the edge of the camp, for gods' sake—but then a light, mocking voice sends my heartbeat into a frenzy.

"Starting the party without me, lads?"

Robin emerges from the shadows, his eyes glinting with lust and a hint of anger. Strange—he's usually not angry when we fuck without him. There's a restless energy vibrating in the air around him, which usually signals the start of a very long night of unnaturally intense climaxes. I'm getting hard again just thinking about how it feels when he comes inside me.

David locks eyes with Robin and pushes harder into my ass, a defiant surge of his powerful body.

Robin's savage grin widens, and his eyes sparkle. "That's how we're playing it tonight?"

"Play later," David says. "First, we need to talk. Scarlet and I want the girl back."

I close my eyes, wincing. That's certainly not how I would have broached the matter with Robin.

"No," Robin says, with undeniable finality.

"It's because she understands us. Or we understand her, because of her past—our past—Scarlet, how did you put it?" David looks at me.

"Let me down, darling. I can't think with your cock up my ass."

David actually flushes a little when he puts me down, and it's so adorable that I kiss him again, while Robin fumes nearby.

When I break the kiss, I whisper to David, "Suck on him while I talk. It'll put him in a better mood."

David smirks, and when we part he approaches Robin with his pants still undone and his cock hanging free. The expanse of his muscled chest is sprinkled with my cum. His glossy black hair curls around his handsome face, and his dark lashes are lowered, hooding his eyes. He looks like a depraved prince.

Robin is a lover of beauty, like all the Fae, and his eyes dilate as David approaches him. When David lifts Robin's tunic and reaches underneath, Robin swallows hard.

The Hood is slightly taller than David, as slender as I am, with an unearthly grace to his movements sometimes, when he forgets he's among humans. Sometimes I want to literally worship him. Kneel and lick his feet. I've done that more than once. He has lovely feet—fine bones, perfect arches, neatly-shaped toes.

Impulsively I kneel at the same time David does. He nods to me, and works Robin's cock free so it juts out between us. Together David and I lick along either side of our lover's cock. It's like a column of pure white marble, with that tiny gold orb near the tip.

I take the cock head in my mouth, suckling it. It's salty, delicious. Robin lets out a faint, weak sound.

When I release the head, David and I run our mouths along the shaft again. We repeat the movement a few times, until a string of gleaming precum is swinging from the tip of Robin's cock. I lick it up, and then I get to my feet while David takes Robin's whole length into his mouth and throat.

Robin cries out, his breathing ragged. And while David sucks him, I tell Robin about the girl, why we want her back.

"I'm half sure she's a spy for the nobility," says Robin breathlessly. "You're usually good at noting such things, Will—do you believe she'd betray us?"

"I don't know," I tell him honestly. "But I know she needs us."

"You're being too trusting," he replies. "That's *my* role. *I'm* the cocky one who lets the odd wanderers into camp, while you fume at my indiscretion... Shit, David—" Robin shudders as David quickens his pace.

"Tell me you don't feel it," I challenge him. "I saw the way you kissed her, Robin. You crave her like we do."

"I don't," he hisses. "I don't care where she goes, or what she does. I have you two—fuck, fuck!"

David pulls off Robin's cock immediately, leaving it glistening and naked in midair. Robin's dick bounces, one clever touch away from the moment of orgasm.

"Fuck you, David," Robin groans.

"Tell the truth, Robin." David's voice carries a note of command.

Only he can use that tone with Robin. If anyone else tried, they'd regret it instantly.

David flicks the underside of Robin's cock sharply, and Robin vents a quick bellow of agony. "You're a fucking bastard, David, you know that?"

"You're not being honest with us, or with yourself," David says calmly. "The girl, Marian—do you think sending her away was the right thing to do?"

"Imagine her living in one of Tuck's crowded safe havens," I murmur. "Working her little fingers to the bone doing everyone's laundry, helping with the cooking and the children. That beautiful body wrapped in coarse clothes, never to feel a man's touch again, because she won't have the opportunity for lovers there. She will have to conform to survive. She will never again enjoy the freedom of the greenwood, and no one will bring her pleasure like we could. A woman who takes cock so beautifully, who craves physical bliss, abandoned to a life of drudgery. Is that what you want for her?"

"It's the best I can offer." Robin cries out as David squeezes his balls lightly, and his cock bobs again.

We've done this with Robin before. His Fae nature makes him gleeful, dastardly, and charming on the surface, but that very demeanor serves as a shield over his true needs and emotions. David and I have found that sometimes our forest prince needs us to crack the shield, to break through and tease out what he's really feeling—otherwise he will never acknowledge it, and he will become increasingly morose, vengeful, and violent. A repressed Robin is a dangerous Robin, and he depends on us for this—the emotional purging as well as the physical release.

"You're so fucking stubborn," I whisper to him, cupping the back of his neck. "I fucking love you, my obstinate darling, you know that?" I pull his mouth to mine, and I pour all the tender passion I feel for him into the kiss.

As my tongue thrusts into his mouth, he comes—a heaving, quivering climax punctuated by groans. He clasps my arms, squeezing tight, and his head lolls back, breaking our kiss. When I look down, David has wrapped Robin's cock in one hand and is soothing him through the climax. He's covered in Robin's cum.

I hold my darling while he shudders through his prolonged climax, until he's limp and shaking in my arms. David cleans up Robin's cock with his tongue and tucks it away, rearranging Robin's tunic.

"You're right," Robin says, hoarse and jagged. "I think I need her."

"We all need her." David rises, clasps my shoulder and Robin's.

"She might destroy us," Robin whispers.

"Perhaps she will," I admit. "Or perhaps she will make us stronger."

29

Fucking Marian is the most wonderful experience I've ever had. Heaven help me, this entire night has been the best one of my life.

She and I keep dozing off, wrapped up together, and then waking only to fuck again. Marian has six orgasms, and then a seventh that's slower to come. By the time her pussy spasms against my lips with that seventh climax, my jaw is aching. A discomfort I don't mind in the least.

After that, she tells me her body is sated, but that I may fuck her while she sleeps, if I want to.

When I wake again, with faint dawn light leaking through the broken roof, she's curled on her side next to me, with her back to my chest and her knees tucked up.

It's the perfect position for me to slip inside her. I'm already hard again. It's as if my body is making up for years of self-denial.

Her pussy lips and the slit between them are still wet from our fucking. Some of my cum has dried on her thighs.

I shift on the floor, angling my body for access, and I swipe my cock head through her shining pussy, watching the squish of her plump flesh as I squeeze my cock deeper and deeper inside. She feels like a miracle. Like every blessing I've ever craved.

But this time, as I fuck her slowly, I can't help thinking of other holes I've wanted to fill. I've seen Robin's tight asshole a few dozen times—sometimes puckered into a rosebud, sometimes stretched wide around someone's cock. I've seen the gape of his hole, its slow close right after his partner pulls out— the creamy surge of cum pulsing from his entrance while he laughs and invites someone else to take a turn.

I want a turn. And I want to run my cock into Will Scarlet's pretty mouth. And I want David to throttle me and thrust into my ass.

I want to do all the things I've seen men do in the greenwood. And then I want Marian again, over and over.

Yielding to my lust didn't soothe it. If anything, it's stronger now.

I don't know how to reconcile my lustful surrender with the faith to which I still cling, half-heartedly. So I don't try. Not today.

I rock my hips, surging slow and steady into Marian's pussy while she breathes, pliant and peaceful and fast asleep.

And then a sound makes me freeze, horror pounding through my veins.

There are voices outside, and they're coming nearer.

Fuck.

The door of the cottage opens.

I'm paralyzed, my cock deep inside Marian, naked before the green eyes of the last man I expected to see—Robin Hood, swathed in a heavy, wet cloak.

He's on me in a flash, pulling me out of Marian, throwing me onto my back. The next instant he's astride me, my cock pinned to my belly beneath his crotch. His fist crashes into my face.

Marian is awake and screaming. "Stop, Robin, stop!"

Will Scarlet and David of Doncaster appear in the doorway, looking damp and weary. Their eyes widen at the sight of Robin hauling back for another blow.

"He was fucking you while you slept," Robin snaps at Marian.

"I told him he could," she cries. "Stop it! Stop hurting him!" She leans over, inspecting my eye and cheekbone. Both are ablaze with pain.

"You told him he could?" Robin repeats, dazed. "What the fuck?" And then, to my shock, he laughs. "Gods, men—didn't I tell you she'd be the one to break his resolve? Our sweet friar, thoroughly corrupted at last! What a glad day!"

"Why are you here?" Marian's voice is strained.

"We're here to bring you back," says Will from the doorway. His face is like sunshine when he looks at her, and her answering smile is just as brilliant.

Jealousy spurts in my heart.

What if they take her away from me? The three of them are the perfect triad—of course they want Marian, too. She's also perfect. They will be a merry foursome, and I will be left on the outside again. I, the clumsy, cloddish friar, the foolish idealist with my piety and my good works. I have never fit in with them or with the Church—but at least, until now, I had my vows, and my role in the community. Now, after what I have done, I have nothing. I belong nowhere.

"Tuck." Robin's voice, smooth and enticing, pulls me out of my dark reverie. He's still astride my naked body. I know he can feel my erection between his legs.

He's gazing down at me, with mischievous affection in his sparkling green eyes. "My apologies for the misunderstanding, Friar. Welcome to our merry band."

He leans forward, aligning his chest with mine. He's coming closer—saints, he's going to kiss me.

He's *kissing* me.

His mouth is warm, his breath sweet as fresh grass after rainfall. His tongue slithers between my lips as he deepens the kiss, and a groan of satisfaction rolls from me.

He laughs softly.

"Forgive the blow, Tuck." His lips are silky against mine. "I thought you were molesting our girl. But if she gave you permission, I can only say, well done. If you'll allow me, I'd like to mend the injury I've caused you."

30

ROBIN

Tuck could easily heal his bruised face with the tinctures and ointments in his pack. But he nods, accepting my offer of a fresher, more licentious type of healing.

I rise from my position astride his cock, and when I beckon, he moves to a kneeling position. I've seen his naked body briefly, during dips in the pool or when he was suddenly roused from sleep, but I've never gotten the chance to enjoy him like this. His sinewy arms, hulking shoulders, and muscled torso are an incredible sight. He's gigantic, godlike, a gorgeous Titan of a man. Just looking at him makes me hard.

Marian is naked too, her lithe, beautiful body defenseless and warm, utterly bared to us. And of course neither Will nor David can resist her in that state. They lift her to her feet and move in on either side of her, stroking her soft skin. She practically coos for them, arching into the petting they give her. The two sides of her fascinate me—the fierce fighter, strong and independent, and the submissive, sensual creature I'm seeing now.

"How did you find us?" she murmurs.

I reach into my pocket and pull out a small arrowhead, no larger than my fingernail. "I inserted this arrowhead's twin into one of Tuck's bags a long time ago. The two are carved from the femur bone of a Fae with tracking abilities. As long as I have one, and he has the other, I can find him anywhere."

"What?" Tuck looks shocked. "You can track me?"

"You wander this entire countryside weaponless, except for the occasional walking staff. If you were ever implicated in my doings and jailed, I wanted to be able to find you."

He stares up at me with heated affection in his eyes. Impulsively I lay my hand along his broad cheek.

Marian eyes the arrowhead curiously. "Does it work the other way? Could he track you?"

"Only if he had magic in his blood." I return it to my pocket.

"Oh." Her face shifts into a strange expression, half relief and half disappointment. An odd combination. I've been at war with myself enough times to recognize when someone else is fighting an inner battle. I've seen the look on Tuck's face a million times as he struggled with his desires. Clearly our little stray hasn't yielded all her secrets. But as Will reminded me, I don't have to trust her completely to know that I want her, that I need her, that she needs me.

We will take her home and make her truly one of us. Then we will see if she yields and discloses everything. If not, I can give her over to David. Will often gets results with his pleasurable methods of interrogation, but when it comes to digging secrets out of the most reticent people, David is the incomparable winner.

I pull my cock out, intending to stroke myself and bathe Tuck's injured face with my cum. But he leans forward a little and opens his mouth expectantly.

The thrill it sends through me, that this huge man is opening his lips obediently for my cock—it's exquisite.

I cup my fingers under his chin. "From now on, Friar, you pray only to me."

For a moment I wonder if it's a bridge too far, if he's not yet ready for such sacrilege. But he nods, breathing hard. He has stepped off the cliff on whose edge he wavered for so long, and he has crashed into the waiting sea of blissful depravity. He's more than ready.

I push my cock into his mouth, but I don't force it, or thrust. I let him taste me, suck me, while I keep one hand planted on the warm skin of his bare head.

Captive to the pleasure building in my gut, I still manage to look over at Marian. She's entwined with my lovers, her arms laced around Will's neck while he strokes her pussy lips with his fingers. David cups and massages her breasts from behind.

Her hooded gaze meets mine. "You changed your mind, Robin."

"I do that sometimes." I'm breathless from the stimulation to my cock, and she's panting too, from Will's ministrations.

"We convinced him." David kisses her neck, sucking the skin so hard she gasps. When he pulls away, there's a cherry-red mark on her white flesh, and he rumbles with pleasure at the sight. "Look at her, Robin. Our girl. One of us."

"Ah, but she isn't." I stifle a moan as Tuck takes my cock deeper down his throat. "She was christened 'Little John' under false pretenses. She will have to be reintroduced and re-christened. And we will have to find a way to ensure that all the men accept her. They might be displeased that we're introducing a woman into the band."

"What if I—oh—" Marian hitches a little sighing whimper as Will fondles her clit. He's watching her face, drinking in every shift of her expression, every darling sound. "What if I agree to make myself available to everyone? Not all the time, but—at least once?"

Will turns his head and meets my eyes, a startled glee on his face. "You would let all the Merry Men fuck you, darling? One after another? While we watch?" He sounds giddy at the thought.

Marian bites her lip and gives me a sidelong glance. "If I'm going to be a whore for the men of the greenwood, I may as well go all the way."

She and Tuck exchange a long, meaningful look, and he hums around my cock. "Gods!" I exclaim. "Do that again, Tuck—I'm almost there—"

"Faster, Will, please," Marian is gasping.

She and I lock eyes at the moment we both explode—I pull out and spray cum onto Tuck's bruised face, while Marian arches into Will's fingers.

I take a handkerchief from my pocket and wipe the cum on Tuck's eyelid, spreading it over the skin I bruised. He's heaving great breaths, his cock yearning upward, seeping clear precum from the tiny slit at its peak.

"Good boy," I tell him, low, and I kiss his mouth, tasting my release on his lips. I taste fucking amazing. One of the perks of being Fae—my cum not only heals and titillates—it's also delicious.

Tuck kisses me back experimentally. I can tell he's been practicing with Marian, but he's still a bit unsure. Time to leave him in the four hands I trust the most.

"Get dressed, Marian," I tell her. "Don't bother binding those pretty tits. You and I are going to walk down to the *Blue Boar*. The host there is a friend of mine, and he won't question your appearance. David, you and Will help Tuck with his needs." I nod to the friar's straining erection. "Will, make sure David is gentle."

"I don't need gentle," Tuck says, his eyes on David. "I can endure pain. He knows."

A twinge of jealousy flicks through my heart at the apparent intimacy between them. I don't know when they talked about such things. But the jealousy fades almost instantly, because it pleases me that the people I cherish most are deeply connected to one another, not just to me. The interlacing of our heartstrings can only make us all stronger as a whole.

Marian dresses rapidly, and I precede her out the door, holding it open with a sweeping bow. She looks surprised by my courtly manner, and her smile sends flutters of joy through my heart.

I suppose I have not treated her like a lady until now. I've battled her, crushed her against a tree, chased her, and fucked her roughly. But I am of royal blood, and she is nobility—and though I do not generally put stock in such things, I occasionally like to show my good breeding. I shall have to keep in mind that she appreciates the gesture.

"Will Tuck be all right?" she asks, with a wary backward glance as she follows me across the pasture. "What do you think they'll do to him?"

"Nothing he doesn't want," I assure her.

I leap onto the stone wall bordering the field and stare across the farmlands around me. The morning sun has turned the rain-wet grass into glittering diamonds, and the brisk air fills my lungs gloriously. Copses of dark evergreens, yellow elms, and bronze beech trees dot the landscape.

Marian hops up, too, and stands beside me, admiring the freshly-washed world. "You must have traveled through the rain to find us."

I shrug, feeling the weight of my wet cloak. "Perhaps you are worth the discomfort."

"Perhaps." I can feel her looking at me, but I continue drinking in the scenery.

The next second she shoves me with both hands, and I topple off the wall, crashing into the tall grass.

Giggling, Marian jumps off the wall on the opposite side and runs for the road.

"You little devil!" I can't help laughing as I leap up and vault the wall myself. I love the way she plays with me—the mingled violence and vulnerability of her. Her fighting spirit and her fragility.

I pelt down the road after her, catching up easily even though she seems to be running at top speed. I catch her up in my arms and seal her laughing lips with mine.

The minute I kiss her, she sobers—we both do, because the kisses between us have such compelling force, like a maelstrom sucking us both in, pulling us down into the dark liquid depths of passion. I'm physically sated for the moment, and that's how I know this is more than lust. Something inside this deceptive, intense, beautiful, sorrowful creature calls to me. Like summons like.

She breaks the kiss and looks into my eyes—an intense gaze, searching me out.

"I want to know you," she says softly. "You tease me and torment me, fight me and fuck me, but I want more. I want to know you like *they* do." She nods toward the abandoned cottage. "You've been a shadow to me, a myth and a mystery, and now an echo of some ancient magical race. But you're more than any of that, deeper and sweeter, and I want all of you."

She presses her lips together and looks down, as if she has said too much, as if she expects to be repulsed and denied.

"Marian." I set her down and lift her chin. "Such knowledge is a road going both ways. I know you're holding back, little trickster. I came for you in spite of it."

She averts her eyes. "I can't tell you what I've done. I'm ashamed. I'm horrified at myself. I can't—"

"Hush. It's all right." I take her hand and lead her along the road. "There will be time later for that, when you're ready. First, let's break our fast at the *Blue Boar*, and I will tell you of my youth among the Fae. Would you like that?"

Her eyes light up, and she nods. There's still a shadow in her gaze, and that irks me—but I push my unrest aside and speak cheerfully to her as we walk.

The *Blue Boar* serves a fine breakfast—mushrooms, eggs, bacon, sausage, tomatoes, and onions. I order two heaping plates for myself and Marian, with three more portions to come when my Merry Men arrive.

The host of the *Blue Boar* is a good friend of mine, and favorable to our cause. He and his family will warn me if the Sheriff or his men come anywhere near the place while I'm here. Still, I keep my hood up while I'm eating, and I speak low to Marian when I'm talking of Fae affairs.

We're halfway through the meal when a servant comes into the tavern and tacks a sheet of parchment to the notice board. There's a sketch of an arrow at the top, so I leave my chair and saunter over, careful to shade my face with my hood.

After reading the notice, I slide back into my seat. "Marian, such entertaining news! An archery tournament in Nottingham, with a gold arrow as the prize! It's to determine who's the best shot in the region."

"Oh?" She pokes at her food. "Sounds rather dull, don't you think?"

"A golden arrow! I must win it."

"But you already know you're the best."

"Yes, but this is my chance to show it to everyone in the region."

She jabs a sausage so hard grease squirts across the table. "What if it's some kind of trap? Your skills with the longbow are legendary. What if someone— maybe the Sheriff—has organized this on purpose to draw you out?"

I chuckle. "I'll go in disguise. And there's no trap he can set for me that I can't escape."

"What about the assassin in the carriage?" she counters.

"I'm here, aren't I? And flawless as ever." I pull open my collar to show my neck and breast, unmarred by scars. "As I said, I'll be in disguise the whole time. And I'll be alert in case there is a clumsy trap of some sort."

But Marian doesn't seem reassured, even though I regale her with more tales of my triumphant exploits since I became "the Hood."

She cheers up a little when David and Will arrive. Tuck is with them, looking deeply refreshed, if a little stunned.

"How's your ass?" I wink at him as he sets down his satchels and takes a chair. "Sore?"

He turns red and cuts a glance at David, who grins and says, "Nothing a nice healing cream won't cure."

"My ass, on the other hand," mutters Will, seating himself gingerly.

"Gods," I exclaim. "You took that massive co—"

"Hush, please," Tuck begs, glancing around. There's real distress in his eyes; he's not ready to let anyone know that his vows have been broken—not just broken—splintered into irretrievable fragments. I'd rather keep teasing him; but I care about him, and I can't cause him pain—not emotional pain, anyway. So I divert the conversation to the tournament.

Will, Tuck, and David all agree with Marian that my participation is a bad idea, which irks me. I like the notion of disguising myself, strolling right into Nottingham, and taking the prize right from under the nose of that pompous Sheriff.

But none of them seem to understand why I would risk exposure. They lecture me so long that finally I forbid them from badgering me about it any longer.

We spend a leisurely morning strolling the countryside before journeying back to Sherwood Forest in the afternoon. Will buys a fat chicken from some farmers, but it escapes from him almost immediately and runs off. Marian, David, and I laugh until our bellies ache while we watch him chase it.

Tuck tries to help, trips over a rock, and falls into a tiny stream that traces through the meadow.

It's a joyful day. A perfect day. One that will end with our lovely Marian being reintroduced to the Merry Men and yielding her pussy to be anointed by every outlaw who cares for a turn.

And that is something I would sell my soul to witness.

31

It has been the best day of my life.

I spent it roaming the countryside with four handsome men, all of whom made me feel deliciously desirable the whole time. There were sly, sultry looks from Robin, gentle squeezes of my ass from Will, a rough stolen kiss with David, and a bouquet of meadow flowers given to me by Tuck.

Now I'm back in the greenwood, standing with Will, Tuck, and David while Robin tells the story of my boyish disguise and his discovery of my gender. His green eyes gleam, and his sharp face is painfully beautiful in the dancing firelight.

I'm still clad in my coarse garments. I find trousers so convenient I doubt I'll give them up altogether—Robin promised me I can wear them in the greenwood anytime I like. But it will be nice to have softer, more comfortable clothing that fits me better.

"Until now, no women have been permitted to join our band and live among us here in the Gloaming," Robin says. "There are some men with wives and families who owe us allegiance but live elsewhere. This place has been a refuge for Merry Men—except when we invite some fine women to partake in an evening's carnal delight."

There's an appreciative roar from the men, and Robin's scarlet lips twist in a smile.

"I am making a single exception for our pretty maid Marian," Robin continues. "But it would be unfair not to make a similar offer to the rest of you. So from this night forward, if you know of a woman with a mind for pleasure and freedom, who would enjoy living here with us and will not balk at any of our debaucheries, you may bring her to me and I will determine whether she may stay here or not. Be warned—my approval will depend on several factors, including how well she takes my cock. We have no jealousy here, no rules or restrictions except free and willing consent."

The men cheer again, but Robin lifts a hand to silence them.

"Since we were all under a delusion when we admitted 'Little John' into our ranks, I have decided we shall have another christening," announces Robin. "And tonight—in the spirit of sharing without jealousy—once, and once only, anyone who likes may have a turn with Marian's pussy. She suggested this herself, and she is to be treated with respect and care at all times, both this evening and for all days and nights beyond. After this generous gift of hers, no one will touch her except David of Doncaster, Will Scarlet, Friar Tuck, and myself—unless she expressly says otherwise. Am I heard and understood?"

"Yes, Robin," chorus the men.

The moment Robin spoke of sex with me, a buzzing excitement seemed to race through the band of outlaws. Their desire for me is flattering in a way I hadn't anticipated. Blood rushes to my cheeks, and I smile at them, but I'm breathing too fast, feeling a little giddy.

Robin Hood leaps down from the table and moves through the crowd, talking with the men, admonishing some of them and joking with others, preparing everyone for the debauched entertainment.

Warm fingers weave together with mine, and I look up into Will's face. "Breathe, darling," he murmurs. "Deep and slow. You'll be fine. It's quite fun, taking as many cocks as you can in just one night."

"You've done it before?"

"Oh yes. David here, he's not interested in yielding himself publicly that way. And Tuck, I expect you need some time before you're ready to consider such debauchery."

"That he does." David smacks Tuck on the ass, then claps him on the shoulder. "Only one cock has opened that little bud of his—mine. Before he takes more, he will need time, and practice—and stretching." He grins wickedly.

"After tonight, I'll be going on my rounds through the villages to deliver the alms and gold," Tucks says stoutly. "After that I might come back for a while. For practice." He flushes, and both the other men laugh.

"You and Marian, by the gods! Your cheeks blush so beautifully," David says. "Sometime I'll have both of you bend over for me and I'll spank your other cheeks until they match your faces."

I squeal, covering my rear, and David laughs harder. Tuck looks cautiously interested in the idea.

"Come away, dearest," says Will to me. "I'll help you get ready while everyone else prepares."

It's time for the most sinful thing I've ever done—a fantasy I never dared to picture.

I'm going to be fucked by dozens of men, right in the middle of Robin Hood's camp.

They've draped a table in cushions and purple velvet. Will is sitting on it with his knees bent, and I'm between his legs with my sex positioned right at the table's edge. He's clothed in a soft robe, but I'm utterly naked.

Will's hands grip my knees, pinning my thighs apart as wide as possible. With my body curved and my legs spread, I have a partial view of my pussy.

David and Tuck linger together nearby. Their presence and Will's give me the warmest comfort, because I know they won't let anyone disrespect or hurt me.

Robin stands gloriously naked at my side. His godlike beauty is all I need to make me wet, and if that weren't enough, he keeps giving me little heated glances, sweet and savage and possessive all at once.

He scans the line of Merry Men waiting with their cocks out, and then he leans close to my ear, whispering, "You can have your fun now. But remember to whom you belong."

"I belong to you," I whisper. "To the four of you, and to myself."

"Good girl," murmurs Will, and Robin kisses my temple, quick and firm. Then he nods to the waiting men.

Alan of Dale is first. When he gives me a brief blushing glance, I smile encouragingly at him. He dabs his cock head against my slit and rubs the wetness along my pussy. My clit twinges with delight at the attention.

I can't help noticing that Alan keeps his eyes on Robin the whole time he's fucking me. After he comes, he rubs his thumb over my clit a few times, and my belly tightens, sweet little thrills racing through my insides.

Alan pulls out and moves on, with a final glance at Robin.

The next man lines himself up at my entrance. He's huffing hard, ready to come; he dips inside me, pulses three times, and then pulls out, wiping the excess cum from the head of his cock onto my thigh.

Another man approaches. His dick is stubby, protruding from a thick swatch of dark hair, but he has a merry smile and he jiggles my clit skillfully while he's thrusting into my hole. I come for him with a gasping shiver, and the men all cheer. When he pulls out, he pats the wet head of his cock on my leg, like a gesture of thanks.

My body is primed now, swollen and soaked and aching for more pleasure. I'm glad the next three men have nice thick cocks—one black, one pale, and one brown. Each surges deeply inside me, waking up all the little nerve endings and pleasure points inside my body.

After those three is a man with a monster of a cock, almost as long as David's, with a slight downward curve. He's stroking himself as he approaches, and when he sinks into my welcoming heat he groans, a rich, male sound that makes me flutter around his length. He plants both hands on my thighs and fucks me hard, never once looking at my face, only watching his wet shaft slide in and out of my hole.

I'm getting close again, so close—my body tenses and I'm whimpering, almost begging.

Will's soft mouth brushes my ear. "That's it, darling. Come on his cock, my love. Come for me."

Then David reaches over and pinches my nipple. I come with a squeal, writhing while Will holds me in place. With a fervent grunt the man inside me finishes, driving deep. When he pulls out, I can feel cum sliding down my pussy, glazing my asshole.

Eventually I lose track of how many men have fucked me. My breasts are flushed from being pawed and squeezed, and I'm full of so much cum. Whenever my pussy grows sore and red, Robin steps in and takes a turn, pumping into me while he holds my gaze with triumphant affection in his eyes. His cum bathes my insides and my pussy lips, soothing any irritation, helping my body reset for more pleasure.

Not everyone in camp desired a turn with me; some prefer men, and others have partners to whom they are loyal. But eventually, everyone who wanted to make a deposit of cum in my pussy has done so.

The rest of them wander off to clean up, to drink, or to sleep. It's just Will, Robin, David, Tuck, and me.

I'm a mess—damp and sweaty, my muscles limp from about a dozen orgasms and my eyelids drooping with weariness. When David approaches me with his cock in hand, I whimper. "No more. I can't come any more."

"Yes, you can." He drops to one knee and bites my inner thigh lightly. A thin bolt of pleasure traces from that spot straight to my sore clit.

"It hurts, David," I moan, exhausted tears slipping from my eyes. "It feels good, but it hurts."

"Sweet one, do you think that will stop me? You know I live for the blend of pain and pleasure." He looks up at Robin, who is stroking my hair. "I think she needs your cum one more time, Hood."

"And she shall have it." Robin cups my chin, turns my tearstained face up to his. "But I want to come on her with Tuck's cock inside me." He grins wickedly at the friar. "I've given you time, Handsome, but I'm done waiting. I've been craving your enormous dick for far too long."

David chuckles, and Tuck flushes nearly as scarlet as Will's robe.

Robin leans down and scoops some of the cum that's flowing out of my sex. He bends over, slathering his own asshole with it, sinking two fingers inside himself while his eyes drift shut with pleasure.

It's more than Tuck can handle. He jerks open his pants and steps forward, wedging his cock head between the ass cheeks that Robin obligingly holds apart for him.

Robin cries out as the massive girth of Tuck's erection stretches him wide. He gasps, tears filling his eyes.

"Fuck," growls David, stroking his own cock.

Will's arousal is prodding against my back.

Tuck gives Robin a moment to adjust, then squeezes in deeper. Robin barks a half-laugh, half-groan—agony and satisfaction mingled. Deeper… deeper… and then Tuck picks Robin up, his massive arms wrapped around Robin's slender body, and he begins to pump the Fae male up and down on his cock. The motion is hard, fast, compulsive—like Tuck can't help himself, like he's been wanting to do this, too, for a long time.

They're facing me, so close I could reach out and touch Robin's leg as he's being mercilessly used. He's staring toward me, but his green eyes are unfocused, glassy with tortured pleasure. His beautiful mouth is parted.

Another violent thrust, and his eyes pinch shut, his white teeth clenching. His cock is jerking up and down, stiff and swollen with need, drops of precum being flung off the tip.

"I'm coming," gasps Robin. "David, I'm coming."

David reaches in and grips Robin's cock, pointing it toward me. Streams of cum layer my already-drenched pussy, and I reach down to rub the fresh cum over my clit. Instantly it is soothed and healed.

Robin is groaning, almost sobbing, still coming. David lets go of him and turns his full attention to me, easing his cock into my gaping pussy. His shaft makes wet squelching sounds in my hole.

"Gods, Will," he moans. "You have to feel this. She's so full of all their cum."

"That's not the hole I want," murmurs Will.

David laughs, his glorious body rolling, hips slamming into me. "Give me a few seconds, and I'll help you lift her."

I'm so dazed I barely understand what they mean until David slips out, cups my thighs, and lifts my rear. Will reaches under me, collecting slick cum. He rubs some along his cock, then swirls more around my tight rear hole. He pokes a lubricated finger into the center of the puckered skin, and I tense.

"Easy, darling," he croons. "I'll be gentle."

And then the tip of his cock is nosing inside, pushing through that narrow channel.

I whine into David's broad shoulder as he lifts me, cradles me.

Will is all the way inside me now, deeply seated. And when David thrusts back into my pussy, I give a thin shriek at the strange feeling.

I am packed full of cock, impaled on two men who care deeply for me, and I think my brain and body might explode with the flood of sensation.

Together the men lift me, moving my body on their cocks. There's a beauty to the way they understand each other, the way they're synchronized in the rhythm. I can feel their mutual love, and their love for me. We're together, all of us, and David is kissing my mouth roughly, and Will is whispering tender, wicked things into my hair.

The beauty of it swirls deep in my belly, a building sensation, layer upon layer of glittering desire.

I'm going to come one last time. For them.

32

I'm still coming. Little jets of cum keep spurting from me, forced out by Tuck's massive cock in my ass. He came earlier, watching the men fuck Marian, so it may take him a while to come again.

I don't mind. Even when my bliss abates, I enjoy the burning rush of him fucking me, the fullness and friction of his body inside mine. Besides, I get to watch Will and David take Marian together, which is a magnificent sight.

She's clutching David around the neck, kissing him intermittently while they bounce her slim body between them. She's exhausted. It's a miracle she's still conscious.

In all my years, I've only seen a woman take so much cock once, during a Fae orgy. But Marian's pink shining pussy took every pearly deposit, man after man cumming inside her until she was full to overflowing.

I thought watching my entire band fuck our girl was the best time of my life; but this moment is surpassing it. My body is stretched and shaking, helpless to Tuck's massive strength, being taken raw while the men I love fuck the woman I love—it's bliss.

Tuck's burly arms tighten around me, and he roars, hot cum flooding my rear channel. He used me exactly as I wanted to be used. During all those months when he ogled me and I flirted with him, he was learning what I like, and I was falling for him.

I want him with me. I want him to be *mine*—one of us. The fifth in our group of lovers.

He's spasming inside me, huffing great breaths of bone-deep relief. "I've wanted to fuck you for so long, you depraved rogue," he gasps, finally hauling me off the length of his cock. I can feel cum dripping out of my gaping hole.

I turn to him, taking his face in my hand. He yields immediately, letting me drag his mouth to mine. I may have let him dominate me this time, but he knows who is truly in charge.

"Next time maybe I'll dangle you from some vines in midair," I muse. "Then I'll suck your cock until you almost come, and then I'll stop. I'll do that over and over. Such torture yields the greatest bliss—doesn't it, David? Never mind, you can agree with me later. Come here, Tuck, and look at their faces. Have you ever seen anything so beautiful?"

Marian is flushed, her dark curls damp and her lashes wet. Her legs and breasts tremble as she comes, while David hunches over her, his hips rammed hard against her pelvis. "I can feel you inside her, Will," he moans.

Will's golden head is tilted against Marian's hair, his handsome face taut with the moment of climax. As Tuck and I watch, his features relax, and he collapses a little, his forehead sinking against her bare shoulder.

I smile—truly, deeply satisfied in a way I haven't been for years. This lecherous ritual, this depraved ceremony—it has solidified Marian's place here and her bond with us. She's one with the greenwood now, linked to our merry band of rogues on a visceral level.

Among the Fae, sex has a unique function beyond pleasure. It heals us, fuels our magic, helps us control our wild emotions, and secures our loyalty to each other. Even among humans it has power—especially here, in the place that used to be the heart of my people.

David and Will slide out of Marian, and I step away from Tuck, toward her, drawn by the starry, liquid beauty of her eyes, the tremble of her lips. The men shift aside for me as I walk straight between her legs, as I tuck my cock inside her. It's half-softened, but this is not about pleasure. It's about comfort, and about being the last one in her pussy tonight.

Nestled inside her, I lift her right off the table and carry her toward the pool where we bathe. The others follow us quietly.

Marian wraps both arms around my neck and rests her cheek against mine.

She belongs to me.

Mine to trust, to protect, to fuck, and to love. And I am hers.

We are hers.

33

MARIAN

I sleep late the next day.

I spent the night in Robin's hut, in his enormous bed, with four handsome men lying all around me. My fantasy made real.

When I wake, only Will and Tuck remain—both fast asleep, with limbs tossed over my body—Tuck's arm, Will's leg.

Last night seems like a dream, from the parade of eager cocks to the late-night swim in the pond with my four lovers. Robin warmed the water for us using a spell, and we lingered a while, talking and laughing. They told stories of their lives in the greenwood, and

I drank their words eagerly, desperate to know everything about them.

Not for the Sheriff or Prince John. Just for me.

Gingerly I reach between my legs and palpate the delicate tissues there. Thanks to Robin's healing cum, I'm not sore at all. In fact, I'm wet again, as if my body craves more.

But there are other things I must do today. Robin mentioned that he would be doing target practice with his longbow, preparing for the upcoming archery tournament. I must persuade him not to go. And I have to figure out some other way to secure the safety of the people waiting for me back at my late husband's castle.

My ties to the Gloaming have grown so strong in such a very short time. They are compelling, all-consuming. Here in the greenwood I found a passion I'd always longed for, a love I didn't expect, friends and husbands I want to keep. But I cannot leave my friends of the past four years to fend for themselves or to suffer alone at the hands of Lord Guisbourne.

Yet part of me fears that abandoning them is the only way for me to be happy.

I can't tell Robin the truth now, not after all this. I can't confess that I told the Sheriff his secret. What if I lose all of them—these four beautiful men who, against all logic, seem to want me?

Carefully I shift the toned arm and the thick muscled leg off my body. There's a lovely red dress with green embroidery lying over a chair nearby, along with a small fur cape. It's safe to assume either Robin or David laid them out for me. I freshen up at the washstand and put on the dress and cape before going outside.

It's a little awkward seeing the faces of the men who enjoyed my pussy last night. But they don't behave strangely or lewdly to me at all—they simply greet me with a merry nod and a smile, or a few words of cheerful greeting.

Relieved, I approach the cook who's doling out the morning's servings of porridge. He's the man with the stubby dick, the one who gave me my first orgasm of the night yesterday.

"Where is Robin?" I ask.

"Target practice, I believe." He serves me a bowlful of porridge and sprinkles a generous handful of sugared berries over the top. "Have a blessed day, lass."

"Thank you." I give him a little smile, grab a wooden spoon, and head for the archery range, thankful for Will's guidance through the camp on my first day.

Robin is standing at the head of the range, legs braced apart and one arm stretched straight out, clutching the bow. His other hand pulls back the string, his fingers nearly touching his mouth.

None of that is surprising. What's surprising is that, once again, Robin Hood is stark naked despite the chill of the morning air.

More shocking still—there's a man kneeling on the turf, sucking Robin's cock.

I shouldn't be shocked, really. Robin boasted to me that he could hit a target while fucking.

"Faster," Robin says through gritted teeth. "Deeper. Try to break my concentration."

The man pushes forward and chokes on Robin's length. He has to pull away, gagging.

"Fuck, Tom," Robin sighs. "Go on, get out of here. I shouldn't have asked you—you've never been good at taking a whole cock."

"Let me try again. I can do it," insists the man.

But Robin's green eyes narrow, glinting dangerously. "Away. Go have a drink or something."

The man rises with a mumbled *fuck*, and stomps off.

I move closer to Robin, watching as he lets the arrow fly. It sails true and thunks into the dead center of the target.

"Perfect," I exclaim softly, and he whirls on me, his face brightening. The sharp tips of his ears are exposed today.

He has never looked more like a wild forest Fae, a spirit born to run gloriously naked through the greenwood.

"Marian," he says. "Perhaps you might help me."

"I don't want your cum on this dress," I warn him. "I love it too much. Thank you for the clothes, by the way."

Robin bows to me slightly, a graceful obeisance I find utterly charming. "I omitted the underthings, but you can borrow some hose from Will if you must."

"I noticed the omission of undergarments." I draw a little nearer to him. "I suppose, if you're very careful not to get cum on my lovely gown, I could help you out with your practice."

"So gracious of you." He whips another arrow from his quiver and sets it in place, the thin arrow shaft resting atop his finger. "Hike up your skirts then, little trickster, and bend over in front of me. Back up right onto my cock—that's it—good girl."

His length feels hot and silky as I ease myself backward onto it. I'm bent double in front of him, holding my skirts out of the way, with my rear exposed to the chilly air. But my skin is so hot and my pussy so warm and swollen already, I barely feel the cold.

Robin rocks forward, sliding deeper into me. He starts a slow, steady thrust.

I hear the whine of the arrow whistling overhead, and the telltale thunk into the target.

"Close to the mark," growls Robin. "Close isn't good enough."

He keeps thrusting slowly, rhythmically, while he nocks and shoots another arrow. Over and over he shoots, until he has struck the center multiple times.

"Now fuck yourself on me, Marian," he urges. "Really use me. Make yourself come while I'm shooting."

Gathering my skirts in one arm, I reach between my legs and massage my clit while I move on him. My bottom bumps hard against his lower stomach and thighs as I lose myself in the hot rush of his cock through my folds. I almost forget what he's doing, even though arrow after arrow whines above me.

"Keep your pretty head down, Marian," Robin warns. His voice is hoarse. "You're doing so well, precious. Harder."

With a desperate cry I rock harder against him, working my clit while my insides clench, and clench—almost, almost, almost— "Robin," I whine. "Robin, Robin—"

"Come for me, trickster," he grits out, and as another arrow sails down the range, a burst of pleasure explodes through my sex, widening outward, trickling along my nerves. It's not as strong as some climaxes I've had, but it's good.

"You need to move," Robin says in a strangled voice, "or I cannot promise your dress will remain clean."

I pull myself off him with a wet sucking sound, and I step aside, letting my skirts fall back into place.

"Touch me," Robin says hoarsely, and I circle his straining cock with my fingers, stroking it quickly, careful to stay out of his way and not touch him anywhere else.

He seizes five arrows, tucks them between his fingers, and fires one after another after another with inhuman speed—and as he shoots, he comes with a strangled roar. The first arrow strikes dead center, and each one after that shears a bit of wood or feather from the central arrow.

His cum paints long white lines on the turf. He lets himself sink into the climax, hunching over and huffing, thrusting into the comfort of my hand.

I envy him a little, as he cries out again, still caught in the throes of pleasure. What must it be like to have such lengthy orgasms?

At least his cum has a stimulating effect on my libido. Without it, I would never have been able to climax as many times as I did last night.

Once his orgasm abates, Robin turns to me, his eyes blazing with glad triumph. "I think I'm ready for the tournament," he says. "Let them bring on anyone they can find. I'll beat them all."

My inner echo of his joy disappears at once, drowned in my guilt. "Robin—"

"Don't." He makes a frustrated gesture for silence. "I've heard what you and the others have to say on the matter. This is something I want to do, Marian, even if it's dangerous. Why can't you understand that?"

Again I open my mouth, but he says petulantly, "Don't speak to me about it again. On any other topic you can say what you like, but on this, I am done listening."

He turns away, nocking another arrow—but I'm beyond concern, fueled by the same angry desperation that made me throw knives at Lord

Flaymish days ago, when I found out about my arranged marriage.

I snatch the arrow out of Robin's hand and cast it aside. "No!" I'm almost screaming at him. "You're not done listening. You will listen to *one more thing*, and if you kill me or cast me out, so be it. If I lose all I have, and if people suffer because of this choice of mine, so be it. Your life is more important to me than my own or anyone else's."

Robin whirls on me, white-faced with rage.

I spill out the words before terror can stop me. "I am in league with the Sheriff of Nottingham and Prince John. I came here to spy on you and your men, to learn your secrets and your names so I could betray all of you. I did it because I was threatened with marriage to a brutal man. I did it to keep my castle and to spare my servants from a life of misery. But my happiness and theirs isn't worth the lives of your people."

I gulp back a sob, and I hurry on before he can stop me. "The archery tournament is a trap. I told the Sheriff of your love for the longbow, and I told him you are Fae. He is planning a trap like no other you've experienced before. He will try to bind your magic and kill you. And I can't let you die. You must not die—none of you, because—"

Robin whips another arrow from his quiver. Drives me backward against a tree and sets the sharp tip of the arrow against my throat.

"Because what?" he hisses, his beautiful face bent to mine. "Because you *love* me? You love David, Tuck, and Will, after knowing them a few days? I've known them for years. They're my men. Mine to protect."

"I know," I whisper, tears streaming down my cheeks. "I'm sorry."

He scratches my neck with the arrow's point, right over the spot where my blood pulses hot under the skin.

"You're sorry," he purrs. "You're sorry for being driven to despair, treachery, and murder by a wicked prince and his lackey? You're sorry for caring about your servants, for wanting to preserve the only home you've known for years? You're sorry for trying to avoid another wretched, loveless marriage? Sorry for following the only path you could see out of the maze in which they trapped you?"

I can hardly breathe. I can only weep, my breasts hitching against his warm, bare chest with every sob.

"Don't be sorry, darling," he whispers. "I understand."

A low whining sob slips from my throat. Robin drops the arrow, throws aside his quiver. Collects me in his arms, pulls me so close I can hear his thundering heart.

"I suspected something like this," he murmurs.

"You knew?" I whimper against his chest.

"Not the details of it, but we knew you had secrets. One possibility we considered was that you were a spy for some noble or other."

"But you still came for me. You brought me back here to the Gloaming—you didn't blindfold me—"

I'm sobbing harder, because he's hugging me, because he said he *understands*. I think he's forgiving me, and that's almost worse than his anger, because I can't forgive myself.

"Will and David think they persuaded me to fetch you back," Robin says. "And perhaps they helped me take action on what my heart already knew—that you belong here with us, no matter what you've done or why you came to Sherwood Forest. I have been waiting, Marian, for you to tell me the truth. I thought I might have to wait much longer, but I'm pleased you decided to trust me now."

"But the Sheriff knows," I whisper brokenly. "He knows you're Fae."

"He should have been able to guess as much himself," Robin says. "Now that he knows it for certain, I'll have to be more careful when I go beyond the greenwood; but otherwise, nothing will change. He still can't touch me here in the forest."

"And you won't go to the archery tournament next week?"

"I really fucking want to," he admits with a laugh. "But no. I won't go."

Words stick in my throat, sodden and clumpy, but I force them out, because I must. "And will you send me away, now that you know what a despicable creature I am?"

He laughs, wild and gleeful. "Darling, we're all of us despicable creatures here in the greenwood. Untamable beasts. Most of us have done terrible things in our past. You're not the worst of us by far, and you're not alone. You will never be alone again, unless you wish it. And never fear—I will send some of my men to fetch your servants. Tell me where your late husband's land is, and it shall be done at once. If any of them would like to take refuge with us, or in one of Tuck's safe havens, they may."

His kindness breaks me, and I crumple at his feet, leaning my head against his thighs. He's still naked, but I don't care. I want to worship him. I cannot believe he's forgiving me this, my greatest sin.

"I should have told you at once," I murmur. "I should have come to you as a supplicant, not a challenger."

"If you had, I might have helped you," he says. "But we can't be sure. I'm fickle when it comes to aiding fallen nobility. I might have denied you my aid. And then you and I would not have had this chance to know each other." He takes my wrists, pulls me to my feet, and looks into my eyes. "And I'm glad to know you, Lady Marian. More than glad."

34

DAVID

Robin is fool enough to insist on going to this archery tournament, though it's clearly a trap for him.

So I am training, working my muscles to their limit, sweating through every pore despite the chill of the forest clearing where I sought solitude.

I need to be in the best shape of my life if I'm going to protect him.

I'm in the middle of a whirling series of sharp movements, combatting imaginary foes, when Robin appears between two trees, with Marian at his side.

I lose my momentum and crash to my butt in the crackling leaves. "Fuck, Hood. Why are you skulking around here? I thought you were shooting that confounded bow."

"I was. I'm done."

He draws Marian forward. Her dark eyes are more enormous than ever, and she's staring at me with a kind of terrified awe, edged with anticipation. I frown, confused.

"Marian has confessed her true purpose here," Robin says. "She is a spy for Prince John and for the Sheriff of Nottingham. She has told the Sheriff of my Fae nature. She says he will use that knowledge to make sure I don't escape the tournament."

"Fuck," I snap, getting to my feet and brushing leaves off the ragged short trousers I'm wearing. "You little bitch."

"I have forgiven her, David," Robin says sternly. "But I did tell her you would be less generous. And despite my forgiveness, I think her treachery still merits punishment, don't you?"

The pain-loving monster in my soul leaps up, eager for prey. "Yes. She must be punished."

"And you agree to this, don't you, love?" Robin looks down at the girl.

She glances up at him and nods. There's trust in her expression, despite her fear of what I might do to her.

This is the opportunity I've been waiting for, the chance to dismantle all her resistance and teach her the truth of herself. I learned my own truth through years of agony. I can bring her to clarity much quicker than that.

"Then I leave her in your care, David." Robin gives Marian a gentle push toward me. "I've thickened the walls of your hut. No one can hear what goes on inside, and no one will disturb you. Take as long as you like. Oh, and there's a cup of fresh cum by the bed, if you need to heal her."

"Fuck you, Hood," I snarl. "What if I'd thought it was milk and tried to drink it?"

Robin smirks. "Wouldn't be a bad thing. Might heal that gloomy spirit of yours." He blows me a kiss and saunters away into the forest. I stare after him, watching his ass cheeks shift under the taut leather of his breeches. Fucking gorgeous man.

Then I turn my attention to the girl.

She looks smaller than ever, burdened with the shame of what she has done.

But even in my anger, I find myself softening toward her. We knew she might be a spy, and we let her into our hearts anyway. And after all, she did confess to Robin. That's proof of her love, proof that she is altogether on our side now.

Still. Robin Hood has given me a task to do, and no sense of mercy will keep me from accomplishing it.

I lead Marian through the camp into my hut, and the vines close over the entrance, shutting us both in.

It's dark, but I know where the candles are. I light several of them, as well as two lanterns. I need plenty of light for what I'm about to do.

My hut contains several contraptions for torturous pleasure. I usually bring only one person at a time in here, although once I entertained both Robin and Will. I had them facing each other, strapped to wooden beams, the tips of their straining cocks barely touching in the middle, while I worked them both into a frenzy with alternating titillation and torture. It was a fantastic scene.

"Strip," I command the girl.

Slowly Marian divests herself of her cape and dress. She's bare beneath—no underthings.

"Walk to that frame and stand against it."

She obeys, with a cautious look at the X-shaped beams.

"Align your arms and legs with the X."

When she does, I begin buckling her wrists and ankles into the leather straps. Then I wrench the lever nearby, and the frame tips upward from the bottom. Her feet leave the ground—she's at an angle now, and I have full access to all the parts I need.

From a chest near the bed I take a handful of clamps, all different sizes.

"You betrayed Robin Hood," I tell her. "You are a filthy traitor."

She bites her lip, wincing.

"Say it."

"I am a filthy traitor," she whispers.

I place the first clamp on her nipple. She sucks in a pained breath.

When I attach the second nipple clamp, she whines, and my cock hardens.

I swallow, breathing deeply to keep my voice calm and steady. "Do you know why we betray and hurt others, little one?"

"I know I did it because I was afraid. I feared the loss of what little I have. And I feared harm might come to those I care about."

"Very good." My fingers trail down the soft flesh of her belly, and it trembles at my touch. I take one of her outer pussy lips, pinch it with a clamp, and pull it to the side, exposing the pink inner folds. I wrap a thin leather strap around her thigh and secure the clamp to it. Then I do the same to the other thick lip of her pussy.

She's pinned open now, those two flaps of flesh stretched apart, exposing what they're meant to conceal. With one fingertip I wiggle her inner labia, and she whimpers. Her hole is already wet, spasming slightly as I play with her. Her clit is more obvious like this, swollen and needy.

"You feared the outcome of circumstances beyond your control," I say. "So you tried to obtain control of the situation. Desire for control is the ultimate human evil, the root of all wars, abuses, and suffering. The craving for control turns the best of us into monsters."

I inspect the final clamp, a tiny one.

Marian begins to beg. "No, no, no, David, not there, please, not—aahh—"

She cries out as I place the tiny clamp on her clit.

"It's when we think we are in control that we're in the most danger," I say. "For example, I believe I'm in complete control now. I have control over you, yes?"

"Yes," she whimpers.

"But do I really have all the control?" I shuck off my trousers and stand naked before her, gesturing to my jutting cock. "It would seem I have no control over *this*."

Her pussy lips are pinned back, her seeping hole open to me. I could enter her now. And I want to—but not yet.

"What is the truth I'm teaching you, Marian?" I step over to the chest again and take out a short riding crop and a series of metal balls.

"You're teaching me that you like control?"

"Yes, but no."

I walk around behind her. Between the lower limbs of the X, her ass cheeks are partly exposed. I smack her there with the riding crop, lightly. Then I take one of the metal balls and push it deep between the buttocks, nudging it at the entrance of her ass. "This is going inside you," I say. "Don't let it come out. Say 'yes, my lord.'"

"Why do I have to—"

I flick the riding crop again, stinging her inner thigh.

"Yes, my lord," she gasps, and I push the ball through the sphincter muscle into her ass.

"Who's in control?" I ask calmly.

"You are."

"Wrong." I push the second ball inside. "Hold it in."

She whines, clenching her ass cheeks.

"Good girl." I pinch her inner thigh. "Who's in control?"

"I—I am? Because I'm holding them in?"

"Wrong." I push another ball inside her. Her soft moan makes my cock jerk.

"Who's in control?" I repeat.

"I can't hold them in," she says, panting. "Oh god, David—"

I circle back to her front, and I tweak both the clamps on her nipples. Then I slap her breasts around, several smacks to each one. Marian squeals, then murmurs, "Oh god" again.

"I'm your god now," I tell her.

She frowns, and I flick her clit. Her thighs jump and her belly sucks in, concave with frantic lust.

I twist the clit clamp just a little. "Say you want your god to fuck you."

"I want my god to fuck me," she repeats, breathless, half-sobbing.

I pick up a strip of black cloth and circle behind her again, tying it in place over her eyes. "You can't see anything now. Does that make you more or less afraid?"

"More," she whispers.

"You fear the lack of sensory input, because it feels like a loss of control. But can you really change anything I do to you, just by seeing it?"

"No."

Stepping in front of her, I take a moment to admire my handiwork—her naked body, sprawled helplessly against the tilted X, her pussy stretched open, her breasts flushed and heaving.

My cock is seeping precum, so I dab my finger in it and wipe the liquid over her parted mouth. She licks it off reflexively.

"What is that?" she asks.

"My precum."

A tiny moan escapes her. She's leaking arousal copiously now, so I swirl my finger through it. "Put out your tongue."

Her pink tongue ventures out, and I smear her juices onto it. "That's the taste of your own pussy, little traitor."

"Please, David—"

"Who am I?" I smack both her breasts with the riding crop, and she yells out, "God, I meant god. Please, god."

"Who is in control?" I repeat.

"God?"

"No."

She's sobbing as I trail the crop down her belly, over her mound, through her splayed-open sex. I smack her inner thigh.

"Are you holding the balls in your ass, little one?"

"Yes." A low whimper.

"Tell me the fears that drove you here. All of them."

In a shaking voice, Marian describes to me her one nightmarish week of marriage—the shaming and the rape she suffered from her husband. Then she tells me of the next four years, how she made friends with the servants and learned how to fight with a quarterstaff. She tells how news of her husband's death arrived, and how Lord Flaymish took charge afterward. How she was taken to court, shown off, and finally matched with Lord Guisbourne. How she protested the match, because Guisbourne is not known for valuing a woman's consent.

Finally she describes her audience with Prince John, and what she promised him in return for her lands, her servants, and her own liberty.

"So Prince John controls you?" I ask, tracing the hollow of her thigh with the riding crop.

She hesitates. "No."

"Good answer." As a reward, I jiggle the little clamp on her sensitive bud, and she starts to pant— quick, hitching gasps of desire. "He may seem to be in control, but you have choices. Can you control where those choices lead you?"

"No."

I bend, laving her open pussy with a long lick— another reward. She shrieks, her body tensing.

"Can Prince John control the choices you make?"

"I—not truly, no."

"Can you control him with your actions? Can you ensure that he honors the bargain he made with you?"

"No."

I reach between her legs, up to her ass, and poke a finger against the tight hole. "Good girl. You're still holding in the balls. Keep them there and tell me, who is in control?"

"No one," she whispers. "No one is in control of anything."

"And *there* it is." I drop the whip and lean over her, massaging one of her breasts with my hand, thumbing the clamp on her nipple. "Your fear is unfounded. Your illusions of control over your fate—they are false. Being governed by terror, anxiety, hate, and anger will destroy you. So what can you trust to make your choices?"

"I don't know," she whispers. "I thought this was the right choice."

"You thought betraying a whole group of men and their leader—men who curb the rich and help the poor—you thought sending them to the gallows by your treachery was the right choice?"

"It was foolish, I know. Foolish and wrong. I wish I'd never done it. But no—that's not true—I *can't* wish I'd never come here, because if I hadn't, I wouldn't have met Will, and Robin, and Tuck—and you."

Her voice on those last two words—delicate and sweet, despite what I'm doing to her. I have bound her, hurt her, torn her down to the root cause of her actions, and still she can speak to me with that exquisite gentleness in her tone.

I'm achingly hard, and not because of her pain this time.

"Beg me to make you come, little traitor," I say hoarsely.

"Please god, make me come, please, I beg you." She's half-crying, writhing, pulling at the straps that hold her tight.

I shift into her space, between her legs. With her ankles bound she is forced to remain wide open to me. When my cock noses at her entrance, she whines.

"This is what my relationship with Robin Hood and Will Scarlet entails," I tell her. "Sharing control. Being strong for the one in the group who is weak, and then yielding yourself to the others' strength and wisdom when *you* are weak. You and Tuck are coming into the group now—five of us, not three. You will no longer have to make decisions alone, unless you want to. From now on, if you don't know the right choice, or you need protection or advice, we'll be there for you. And the four of us men will trust you as well. Your protection, your wisdom, and your love will sustain us when we are weak or uncertain. Are you willing to be part of that?"

"Yes," she whispers. "That's what I want. It's what I've always wanted, though I didn't know it."

Her small hole is gaping, pink and wet. I push my cock inside, and she inhales, a long slow breath of relief.

"You will not come until I tell you," I command. "That will be a sign to me that you've truly learned your lesson, that you know when to surrender control."

"Yes, my lord."

I run my cock deeper into her silky warmth, groaning in spite of myself. "You're stealing *my* control now, little one," I moan. "You feel so good."

Slowly I thrust, torturing both of us with the slick gliding sensation, until I can't bear it any longer. I ramp up the intensity, fucking her, letting myself grunt, loud and primal, with every slam of my cock into her body. She answers me with her own shrill cries, matched to my rhythm.

"Now?" she gasps. "Can I come now?"

I tweak the clamp on her clit. "No. Don't ask me. Wait."

She whimpers, agonized, her whole body straining with the effort of holding back the orgasm.

I want her to succeed in this obedience, so I only make her wait a moment longer. "Come for me. Come all over your god's cock."

"I'm coming on my god's cock," she pants, and then she screams, high and shrill and free, a primal ecstasy that I echo with a bellow of my own as cum shoots from my balls through my cock into her womb. She's pulsing around me, gasping through the aftershocks, shaking against her bonds.

I do a few more slow pumps into her pussy, and then I pull out. Creamy white drips from her slit, and I rub my thumb through it, then unclamp her clit so I can stroke the thick liquid over it. She jerks, so utterly sensitive.

"I think you can come again," I tell her. "But first, I want you to push out the balls from your pretty little asshole. Can you do that for me?"

"Yes," she breathes.

"How did it feel, coming with them inside you?"

"So good. So fucking good."

I grin at her intensity and lean forward to kiss her mouth. Then I go around behind and watch each smooth, shiny ball squeeze out of her rosebud hole and drop into my palm.

"I'll release you soon," I promise, squeezing her creamy bottom. "But first, I'm going to make you come so hard you see stars."

When I circle back to her front, she gives me a lascivious smile that makes my body thrill all over.

"Take your time, my lord," she says. "I'll stay here as long as you like."

35

When David finally sets me free, my muscles are so loose and my limbs so relaxed I can barely walk upright. The lovely dress, soft as it is, almost feels too harsh against my sensitized skin.

Will is perched on a table near David's hut, both his long, scarlet-clad legs swinging. He holds out a cup and a dish, and I hurry over, suddenly conscious that I'm both famished and thirsty.

I slide onto the bench by the table, wincing a little. David swatted my bottom with his riding crop several times, and he refused to use Robin's cum on me there.

"I want you to remember what we did for the rest of the week," he said. But he did dab some healing cum onto my nipples and my clit, as well as on my wrists and my ankles, where the straps chafed a bit.

Will watches me gobble the stew and gulp the water, a lazy smirk on his face. "I always have a big appetite after a session with David." He leans in and says, low, "Are you all right? Was he too harsh?"

"Not too harsh." I smile up into his handsome face, touched by his concern. "I'm fine. I feel refreshed. And I feel like he—he *knows* me. Maybe better than I know myself."

"He does give a person that feeling." Will nods, stroking his golden beard. It's shorter now, barely a smooth golden scruff. He must have trimmed it today. The sharp angles of his jawline are even more noticeable.

"Did Robin tell you what I did?" I ask, nervously watching for his reaction.

"Yes. It wasn't anything I hadn't suspected. I was disappointed, darling, but I understand why you did it. All of us do. Well, I'm not sure if Tuck does—he was gone when I woke up. Off to collect the newly stamped gold and do his rounds among the poor. He won't be back for a week, I'll wager. Hopefully he'll still want cock by then."

"I have a feeling he will. Lots of cock, and pussy, too."

Will laughs and chucks me gently under the chin. "Look at you, love, spewing naughty words. Finish your stew, drink your water, and then come with me. I want to test these excellent quarterstaff skills I've heard so much about. And then maybe I'll teach you how to throw knives."

The next few days pass in a blur of weapons training, walking the greenwood, dancing and singing by the bonfires at night, bathing in the pool, and fucking my three insatiable men. I'm glad they have each other's holes as well as mine, or I might not be able to keep up with them, even with the stimulating effect of Robin's cum.

My monthly bleeding is due to begin, and when it doesn't, I'm concerned that I might be pregnant—no wonder, after taking so much cum. But when I express the fear to Will, he assures me that in the Gloaming, fertility is negated through the placement of a spell. Anyone who spends time in the Gloaming is rendered temporarily infertile. Once they leave, the spell takes a while to wear off. So I've been protected the whole time, even when I was with Tuck in the cottage during the rainstorm.

The messengers Robin sent to my late husband's castle have not yet returned. It's a long journey—a couple days each way—and there have been storms lately, which may have delayed them. Besides, if any of my servants do decide to join us and live under Robin's protection, they will need time to pack up some of their belongings—and the trip back to

Sherwood Forest will take longer, since they'll need to travel more slowly with their luggage. I doubt they'll want to remain in the debauched environment of the Gloaming, but Robin has established a sort of secondary camp not far away. When he took me to see it, he claimed it wasn't solely for my people.

"Tuck has told me that our current havens are packed to bursting," he said. "We needed a new safe place anyway."

And then he sauntered off to weave more huts out of branches and vines, while I smiled, because I know he did it for me.

Despite the delights of Will, Robin, and David, and despite my eagerness for more training in the art of combat, I miss Tuck. The gentle, gigantic friar hasn't returned. I find myself scanning the forest or peering down the path that leads out of the Gloaming, looking for a broad-shouldered figure and a donkey cart.

It's nearly time for the Sheriff's archery tournament, which Robin Hood still claims he isn't attending. I feel safe here in the greenwood, but I can't help worrying about what the Sheriff might do when Robin doesn't show up and I don't appear either. I can only imagine his rage. He'll take it out on the poor people of the surrounding villages, no doubt.

Two nights before the archery tournament, I'm lying on a table in the Gloaming, being slowly and lazily fucked by Robin Hood. My head is turned aside so I can savor Will's cock with my tongue and lips. My fingers are curled around the base of his length.

The Merry Men of Sherwood are watching us, palming their own erections, humping urgently against each other, or fucking outright. There are a couple of other women involved in the orgies now—I don't know them well yet, but they seem thrilled to finally get the chance to purge the lust they've been repressing.

But no matter how many women join us, my three men have assured me that I will remain their queen. Robin has fucked all three of the newcomers, but he informed me that I transcend them all. "She took my cock well, but there's something of magic between us, love," he whispered to me after a tryst with one of the newcomers.

Even now, as he's thrusting steadily into me, he's watching my face with a tenderness that warms me to the core. I angle my gaze to his, still sucking Will's cock, and Robin pushes deep into me, leans over my body, and squeezes one of my breasts lightly, fondly. "Devilish darlings," he murmurs. He bends, kissing the corner of my mouth and Will's cock at the same time. "I love you both."

His confession sends a thrill through my belly, clinching the climax that's been building inside me. Ecstasy spears through my body, and my sex pulsates around his cock, while he hums, "Yes, yes, little trickster. Yes. Such a good girl."

I moan around Will's dick, and he echoes the sound. He pulls out and comes on my face, painting my cheek and lips, urging the last bit of pleasure out of his cock with firm strokes while he groans deeply.

Then Robin drags Will's mouth to his and comes hard inside me, with his tongue down Will's throat.

The sparkling flush of Robin's cum through my body sends me into a euphoric daze, an afterglow stronger and more delicious than I get from anyone else. I'm still lying on the table, limp and dazed, when a shout sounds from the edge of camp.

"Robin!" It's Alan of Dale's voice, breathless and frantic. "Robin, dreadful news!"

Robin slides out of my pussy, and his abundant cum pours out of my sex, drizzling onto the blanket on which I'm lying.

"Come here, Alan," Robin says. "Breathe, man. Tell us your tale."

Alan staggers over. He's sweating, gasping as if he has been running a long time. "It's Friar Tuck," he pants. "The Sheriff of Nottingham has him."

36

Quickly I tuck my cock away, and I hand Marian a cloth to wipe her face and pussy. She sits up, turning pale beneath the rosy sensual glow on her cheeks.

"The Sheriff has Tuck?" Her voice is thin, strained.

"Tell me everything, Alan," Robin says.

"I was at the *Blue Boar*, playing for everyone and listening for news, as I do at taverns throughout the region," Alan says. "A couple of the Sheriff's guards came in, out of uniform, and they started drinking. And then they started arguing with a few of Lord

Barrinworth's men, talking about *you*, Robin, and what's being done to catch you. So one of the Sheriff's men bragged that they caught an ally of Robin Hood's, a wandering friar with pockets full of gold. No mention of how they knew he was a friend of yours, but someone must have seen him in the wrong place at the wrong time."

"Maybe when he and I were at the *Blue Boar* together, the Sheriff figured it out." Marian leaps off the table and pulls on her robe. "Robin, we have to save him."

Robin lays a hand on her shoulder, both a comfort and a quieting gesture. "Where is he being held?"

"At the jailhouse in Nottingham," Alan replies.

"Fuck." The word escapes me before I can stop it. The Nottingham jailhouse is notoriously secure and well-defended. The Sheriff has trouble catching renegades and villains, so he likes to make sure they stay put once he's got them.

"Fuck, indeed." Robin runs a hand through his black hair.

"They're torturing him," Alan ventures. "So said the Sheriff's guards."

"Oh my god." Marian's voice quivers with a sob. "Poor Tuck."

I know how she feels. I can't bear it when the people I love are hurting or in danger—it cleaves my heart open, and I bleed until I know they are safe again.

And that this should happen to Tuck, who is arguably the best of us—it's horrible. His very bones are forged of kindness and benevolent strength. When he eased into my asshole that first time, back at the cottage, he kept asking me if I was all right, if he should stop. His sweet concern helped me withstand the searing fullness of his massive shaft in my rear.

I keep myself always ready for cock. I watch my diet carefully, and I cleanse my rear channel repeatedly each day. Robin has some magical way of preparing himself—I've never asked him about the details, but he has never had any unfortunate incidents in that regard. David is a little less careful with his diet and hygiene, but I've always found his hole to be clean and welcoming. He doesn't mind if someone else's hole isn't pristine, which is why he took Tuck's ass himself that first time. The way Tuck roared and groaned echoes in my mind—but more powerful still is the memory of what he said after he came in me, and David came inside him.

He looked at both of us, and with gruff emotion, he said, "I could not dream of two better men to guide me into Hell."

There was a triumphant pathos in that statement—his full surrender to pleasure and physical connection here on Earth, despite his lingering fear of eternal retribution.

He is a man with more layers than one notices upon the first meeting. He is humble and self-deprecating—self-debasing, even—and he's utterly focused on the good of others. He denied himself and chastised himself strictly for years, and yet he can be as wantonly indulgent of his fleshly passions as any of us.

My sweet contradiction, my beloved dichotomy. My holy man of darkness. I know he must be in the worst kind of pain right now, and I cannot bear to think of his great body being broken. The Sheriff is notorious for his brutal treatment of prisoners. Thumbscrews, racks, amputations, tongue-slitting, ear removal, blinding—I've heard of it all happening there, in the jailhouse at Nottingham.

"We must get him out, Robin," I say hoarsely.

"I know, I know." His face is taut and paler than usual. "Go find David. I think he is spanking Watt the Tinker's ass in the trees over there. Bring him to me, and we'll discuss plans for breaking into the jailhouse."

"But Robin," Alan interjects, "it's impossible. It's never been done. No one has escaped or been extracted from that place, not in any of the awful stories I've heard of it."

Robin steps sharply toward him, a fierce threat, and Alan retreats, wincing.

"It's Tuck," snarls Robin. "I will get in or die trying."

"There's one more thing you should know," says Alan faintly. "The Sheriff has announced an additional prize for the archery tournament. Whoever wins gets to pull the lever on the gallows and make Friar Tuck hang."

Robin huffs out a frustrated breath. "The Sheriff is making sure I'll be at the tournament. Fucking bastard. Apparently he didn't trust you to convince me to compete, Marian."

She looks down, twisting her hands together. "He suspected I had feelings for you. That I—that I love you, and wouldn't turn you in. I'm so sorry, Robin. This is all my fault."

"It's not." Robin catches her by the chin, tips her face up for a swift kiss. He inhales while he kisses her, as if he wants to suck her essence into himself, as if she is the air he needs to survive. "It's not your fault, precious. It's the fault of the nobles who hate me, and the prince who condemns the land to poverty while he lounges on a golden throne. It's the fault of the foul Sheriff and his men. You are not culpable."

She nods, and Robin lets her go, with a sharp glance at me. "What are you standing there for, Will? Go and fetch me David. Alan, call Clem the Tailor— he's a fair hand at drawing and I believe he delivered goods to the jailhouse once. He can sketch what he recalls of the layout."

I jog away from them toward the treeline. As I duck beneath the branches, I can hear sharp slaps and incoherent cries of pain mingled with ecstasy, coming from somewhere among the trees.

In a clearing lit by a pair of lanterns hanging from branches, David of Doncaster stands with his cock out, facing a naked Watt the Tinker, who is bent double. Watt's hands are tied together and tethered to a tree limb. As I watch, David strikes the tinker's ass again with a pliant switch cut from a birch tree. Then he reaches in and slaps the tinker's balls.

"David." I step into the lantern light.

He looks at me, and in the orange glow I'm struck by his beauty once again—a body worthy of a god, despite the old scars seamed across his torso.

"Friar Tuck has been captured by the Sheriff as an accomplice of Robin Hood," I say. "He's being held in the Nottingham jailhouse until the day of the archery tournament, when he will be hanged by the winner. They're torturing him, David. Torturing our Tuck."

"Fucking shit," growls David. "Watt, I'll send someone to finish you. I have to go."

"What?" The tinker whimpers. "You're leaving me out here? It's cold!"

"Fine." David jams his dick into the man's ass without warning and begins thrusting at a frenzied pace. I help by reaching under the tinker's belly and fisting his cock. Between David's rough thrusts and my quick jerking of his dick, Watt comes in a few seconds.

David pulls out, still hard, and puts himself away. His lack of care for his own pleasure is a mark of how much he cares for Tuck's wellbeing.

"Wait!" calls the tinker. "Untie me!"

"Ah, I forgot." I bend swiftly, yanking a small knife out of my boot, and as I rise I throw the blade. It skims past Watt's head and plunges into the loop of rope that circles the tree limb, severing it neatly. "Pull yourself loose. Return the blade to me later."

I hurry to catch up with David, who is striding through the trees with the malevolent purpose of a man bent on someone's doom.

"Nice throw," he mutters.

"Thank you, darling."

"We'll need your skills for this adventure. I wish I could make you stay behind where it's safe, but—"

"But it's Tuck, and I'm going," I finish.

He nods. We break out into the main area of camp, where Robin is leaning over the shoulder of Clem the Tailor. Clem is sketching the layout of the guardhouse on a broad piece of parchment.

"Where's Marian?" I glance around, not seeing her in any of the clusters of people nearby.

"Off to bed, I think." Robin peers more closely at the map. "What's in this tower, Clem?"

We pass the next several hours poring over the sketch, pondering modes of attack and entry, and talking with several of the Merry Men who know Nottingham best. Every plan we devise feels flimsy, likely to get too many of our people killed. Robin is growing more frustrated by the minute.

"We could leave him be until the tournament and rescue him then," suggests David. "Tuck will be out in the open that day. We wouldn't have to conduct a full-scale assault on a defended jailhouse."

"Leave him in there another two nights and a day?" I exclaim.

"I don't like it any more than you do," Robin says. "But David may have a point. I think it's the only way to do this without losing so many of our men."

"But that's what the Sheriff wants. He will have set traps for you, Robin—traps that restrain your magic."

"I know of no relics or magic he could use against me," Robin counters. "None that he could have learned or obtained in such a short time, anyway."

"Don't underestimate him," I reply. "He's a vicious man with much to lose and many resources at his disposal. Such a man may be capable of more than you think."

At last we lay aside our planning to take a few hours' sleep in our separate huts. Marian isn't in my bed, which surprises me since she seems to prefer it to all others in camp. But perhaps she decided to sleep in her own hut, or David's, or Robin's.

When she doesn't appear at breakfast the next day, an acidic uncertainty begins to curdle in my stomach. I peer into all the huts and tents, including the one Tuck uses when he's here. Nothing. And she isn't in any of the training areas, or on the shooting range.

She couldn't have left the Gloaming on her own... could she?

When Tuck left to deliver his alms, Robin changed the placement of the path that leads from our camp to the edge of Sherwood Forest. He told Tuck where he could find the mouth of the new path when he came back, and which turns to take to reach the Gloaming.

Was Marian nearby when they discussed it? Or— My god.

She was standing nearby when Robin gave the same instructions to Alan of Dale, before he left for his musical circuit through the local taverns.

She knew how to get out of Sherwood Forest. And she knows the surrounding area well enough, from living here when she was a child. She knows how to get to Nottingham.

My stomach drops.

She has gone to do something wildly foolish, I know it.

Robin is bent over the new sketches Clem has made—drawings of the entire town of Nottingham this time, including its walls and gates. I approach him on leaden feet, trembling with my fear for Marian and my apprehension of how my Fae lover will react when I tell him my suspicions.

"Robin," I venture. "Have you seen Marian today?"

"No." He doesn't glance my way.

"I cannot find her. I think she has—gone."

He looks up at me sharply, realization and dread in his eyes.

"Fuck," he hisses.

And with the force of that single explosive word, the entire forest around us shivers.

37

My breath seeps raggedly between my blood-crusted lips. My shoulder joints are screaming from holding up almost my entire weight for hours, and my wrists are raw and bloody from the shackles. My toes can barely touch the floor. If I stiffen my feet, I can take a little weight off my arms for a few seconds at a time.

I'm fairly sure one of my toes is broken, though.

I can't see out of one eye. It has swollen shut, and my other eye has crusted blood along the lashes from a wound on my skull.

One of my ears has been shorn off, and I'm missing both my littlest fingers. My tongue throbs from being scorched with a hot poker.

I want to die. The hanging that awaits me on the day after tomorrow will be a mercy.

I don't know how the Sheriff discovered my connection to Robin Hood. Someone must have seen us together when we left the *Blue Boar* the morning after the rainstorm. We didn't exactly hide as we strolled along the roads together, a merry group of five. Most folk of this region are sympathetic to Robin and wouldn't betray him, but I suppose it only takes one to report the local friar keeping unsavory company.

That heavenly day I spent with Robin and the others seems like a lifetime ago.

This evening, before he left to go home, the Sheriff promised to relieve me of my dick and balls tomorrow. "You aren't using them anyway," he said, smacking my limp cock.

So I have the worst torture of all to look forward to when dawn comes.

Maybe I'll be lucky enough to die from the blood loss. Though knowing the Sheriff, he will cauterize the wounds so I'll live to be hanged.

The cell I'm in smells of shit and mildew. It's four walls, a high ceiling, and a wooden door with a barred window. Nothing else. No chance of escape even if I had the strength. If I did manage to wrap my legs around a guard's neck and snap it, I'd have no way to free myself. Nowhere to go, because we're underground here, and there are several guards between me and the stairway leading up to the main jailhouse.

I'm being punished for my carnal sins. I broke my vows, and this is the price I must pay. This, and an eternity of agony in the life beyond death.

Tears burn cracks in the dried blood on my cheeks.

Despite my misery, my fear of Hell has abated since I met Robin Hood. I've never seen God, but I have seen one of the Fae, proof that magic and the old gods existed. Perhaps I need not fear Hell at all, or long for Heaven. Perhaps there is a milder sort of Afterlife, like Robin told me once—a place of meadows, pleasant wandering, and meetings with old friends.

If God, Heaven, and Hell do not exist, there is no reason I should have taken any vows, or kept them.

I am glad I took some pleasure while I still could.

Outside my cell, booted feet echo along the corridor—multiple sets of feet. Surely it cannot be dawn yet.

A key clanks into the lock, and my door grinds open.

I blink and squint with my one good eye.

I must be dreaming. That's the only explanation for the figure I see in the doorway—silky curls clustering around a sweet face with enormous dark eyes. A slim neck, creamy skin, slender fingers clutching scarlet skirts.

Marian. She's here.

But she can't be here, because she's safe with Robin in the greenwood. They're all safe, and that's the only certainty that has buoyed me throughout the hours of misery.

"Oh, Tuck," she says brokenly.

"Angel," I wheeze.

The Sheriff is behind her, pushing her into my cell, gesturing for the two guards in the corridor to unchain me.

"I've no more need of you, Friar," he says. "I have a more tempting lure for the little Robin I plan to catch. I should hang you, after all, but you are a man of the cloth. So I think I'll let you go. You'll toddle off to the Hood and tell him the change of plans, yes? Tell him to come to our little tournament if he wishes to see Marian one last time. If he even wants to after I've had her."

He tucks Marian against his body, one hand sliding down into the neck of her dress to squeeze her breasts. She winces, but submits without protest.

"No," I whisper over my scorched tongue. "Angel, no. You can't do this. Keep me here, you bastard, and let her go."

"I'm saving you, Tuck," she says firmly. "Now hush, and go with the guards. I'm sorry we didn't realize you were here before now—sorry you endured this so long—I'm so sorry—"

Her voice fades as I'm half-hustled, half-dragged out of the cell. I try to break free of the guards' grip, but I'm too weak. One backward glance shows the Sheriff bending Marian over, pulling up her skirts. I vent a low, pained roar and wrench at my captors. One of them strikes the base of my skull with the hilt of a dagger, and my vision slides out of focus, my legs turning watery.

Halfway up the steps to the surface, I vomit. I'm dealt another blow, this time to my temple.

My vision blackens entirely.

When I come to my senses, I'm being dumped off a wooden cart at the border of Sherwood Forest. The grass is golden in the light of late morning, and the trees rear overhead like judgmental watchmen.

The cart rattles away, accompanied by the Sheriff's men.

I roll over and vomit a little watery bile. I've had nothing to eat for days.

I have failed my girl, my angel, my Marian.

She sacrificed herself for me, body and soul. She's to be raped, tortured, and murdered in my place.

I can't bear it.

Greater love has no one than this—laying down one's life for one's friends.

The scrap of Scripture tears at my brain. I despise the words, and myself.

I may not be able to return to Nottingham to save Marian, but I must make it to Robin Hood alive.

I must warn him, tell him—he must save her, whatever the cost.

38

MARIAN

Taking the Sheriff's dick wasn't as bad as I feared. I was able to relax my body and think of other things—like my poor Tuck's mangled face and torso, and how my sacrifice has spared him any more pain.

Yielding myself to the Sheriff's lust was only part of the bargain I struck. I convinced the Sheriff that Robin Hood loves me, that he's jealous over me, and that he'd be far more likely to come and save *me* from the gallows than some placid friar.

The Sheriff accepted the deal, because he is desperate to lure Robin within the walls of Nottingham. He seems oddly eager for the tournament, almost jubilant. He must have found something to counter Robin's Fae magic.

When the Sheriff is done with me, he shoves me to the floor and leaves the cell, slamming the door and locking it.

"You'd better hope Robin Hood comes to town tomorrow," he says through the barred window. "If I catch him, you'll be free to go. If not, you'll be hanged."

"And how will you explain my death to Prince John and Lord Flaymish?" I ask.

"You confessed to sympathizing and fornicating with Robin Hood. The guards who were in the room when you told me are witnesses."

"And they are also witness to you defiling yourself with me."

"Ah, but no, you see—they are not. They left with the friar before we began." He leers through the bars. "If the plan succeeds, I will let you go, and we will never speak of this again. If it fails, you die. Do you think your noble blood gives you any value at all, in the eyes of the Crown or anyone else? You are a woman. You are holes and a womb, meant to serve a man's pleasure and bear his children. There are many more like you. No one will miss you, or weep for you. You'll be forgotten a moment after the tale is told at court, of the woman who promised to bring down Robin Hood and became his whore instead. Respectable folk will revile your name, if they remember it at all."

He steps back, chuckling. "Count yourself lucky I don't put you through the same torture I dealt to the Friar. Keep that cunt warm for me; I'll be back to use it again later."

His footsteps recede down the corridor.

The dreadful anticipation of servicing him again curdles my stomach. But he doesn't return for many long hours. Perhaps preparations for the tournament have distracted him. He has a wife, as well—maybe he was forced to remain in her bed to avoid suspicion.

Whatever the case, I'm spared another session with him. Instead I'm left with the long hours of another day and night. I'm brought a little water and a hunk of bread, but nothing more.

When I'm finally hauled from the dank cell and out into the jailhouse courtyard, bright sunlight assaults my eyes. It's the day of the tournament—the day when Robin Hood will come to save me.

Or perhaps it's the day that I die.

One man binds my hands in front of me, and then a dozen armored guards flank me, hustling me along a narrow wooden passage, like a chute to guide sheep to slaughter. It's a ramshackle corridor, and through gaps in the boards I glimpse a crowd gathered in the town square of Nottingham. They're here to see both the archery tournament and a hanging. Strange how human beings crave the spectacle of a death even more than they delight in a contest of skill.

Perhaps watching someone else lose their life is a reassurance for the onlookers—a visceral reminder that *they* are still alive.

The scent of roasting mutton, warm sugar, and sizzling fried fish fills my nostrils. There's a faint stench of unwashed bodies, but it's bathed in crisp fall air, so it's not too overwhelming. Small mercies.

At the end of the chute through which I'm being led, I can see wooden steps.

"Up you go, lass," grunts one of the guards. "The tournament is under way, and they wish to have you on display."

"Do you even know why I'm being hanged?" I ask him. "Do you care?"

Another guard cuffs me across the mouth so sharply I taste blood. "Quiet, bitch," he snaps.

The first guard looks away, ignoring both my question and the blow.

In my head I debate whether the person who ignores an evil is worse than the one who perpetrates it. I can't decide, but the question distracts me a little from what's happening—from the imminence of my own death.

I'm shoved up the steps, still corralled by armored guards holding shields. The Sheriff is clearly afraid that Robin Hood will try something before the tournament's end. It comforts me a little that he still fears the Hood's wrath, if not his magic.

"Stand here." One of the guards shoves me so that I'm forced to step onto the trap door in the floor of the gallows. When the lever is thrown, the trap door will drop, and I'll plunge through the gap. If I'm lucky, my neck will snap immediately and I'll die at once. If I'm unlucky, I'll have to struggle through long moments of strangulation.

The Sheriff's voice booms over the cacophony of the crowd. He's standing on a dais nearby, also surrounded by armored guards, wearing a gleaming suit of armor himself.

"See there?" he calls, speaking to the crowd but pointing to me. "I promised you a hanging. Perhaps you expected to see a certain local friar, but here I have something even better for you—the whore of Robin Hood. She's a wicked traitor to the Crown and a devilish temptress—a witch who must be destroyed lest she corrupt the hearts of the good sons and fathers in this fair town of Nottingham."

Murmurs and shouts of assent ripple through the crowd. I scan the gathering, noting the revolted, angry faces of two shrewish middle-aged women.

One of the guards settles the noose around my neck and draws it tight. It's a snug fit, though I can still breathe, for now. The coarse rope burns against my skin.

If Robin doesn't come, I will be hanged. And I suspect that even if he does come, and the Sheriff succeeds in trapping him, I'll be killed anyway, whether by hanging or by some 'accident.' The Sheriff can't let me go, not after this public condemnation.

"We are entering the third round of the tournament," the Sheriff continues. "Remember, gallant archers—the winner among you receives this fabulous golden arrow." He points to the arrow in question, which is being cradled on a velvet pillow by a servant. "And they will also win the privilege of sending the devil's wife back where she belongs."

Another cheer from the crowd. I lift my eyes from the strangers' faces, and my gaze latches onto a row of contestants with longbows. I don't recognize any of them, but a few are wearing hats or thick scarves. One especially tall, gangly fellow has an eye-patch. If he's good enough to make it to the third round with only one eye, he might be the one to watch.

Blue sky arches overhead. It's a beautiful autumn day, a blessing after the chain of stormy, rainy days we've had lately. As the Sheriff signals for the target shooting to begin again, a trio of musicians stationed right beside the gallows starts up a merry, lilting tune, one that reminds me of dances in the greenwood.

At least, if I must die, it's on a bright day like this.

39

I'm so full of rage I can hardly see the target. Tears are clouding my vision.

I'm Fae. We don't cry.

Correction—we rarely cry. And when we do, we don't usually weep for human girls.

But *this* girl—this beautiful, brave woman standing so calmly in the hangman's noose—this woman who gave her own body to spare Tuck—I could cry oceans for her.

I can't afford the luxury of tears right now. So I blink my eyes swiftly, clearing my sight. I block out the mental image of Marian standing on the gallows platform behind me, with the sea of the crowd between me and her.

I focus on the target in the distance.

I close the eye that's hidden beneath the patch, and I mentally adjust for the change in my vision. This is a new challenge for me—shooting one-eyed. And what is life, if a man cannot show off a little? Especially on a day which might be his last.

The moment I walked into Nottingham, I could feel the oppressive influence of the sigils the Sheriff has placed on the walls of the town. I didn't think he would be able to get access to the lore and the symbols he would need to bind my magic, but somehow he did. He probably tortured some hapless fen wizard or hedge witch to obtain the information. Humans with magic are few and far between nowadays, thanks to persecution by the Church, but they still exist.

The roots of Sherwood Forest extend far. Whenever I leave its boundary, I tease a root or two to follow me, snaking along deep underground, waiting to surface and spring into living action if I need it. But when I passed through the gate of Nottingham, my sense of the forest and my access to it was instantly cut off. I could feel a weakness in my bones and muscles—a strange, unsettling fragility instead of my usual strength. That sense of fragility has been increasing with each passing hour.

No matter. Without my powers, I am still a match for this paltry Sheriff. Even if I cannot heal myself or anyone else while I'm inside the town's walls—even if I cannot draw on the power of Sherwood Forest—even if I am not as fast or strong as usual, I can best him.

I must.

Because if I don't, Marian will die.

So I anchor my bowstring near my mouth, and I breathe. I pretend the center of the target is the Sheriff's heart.

And I let the arrow fly.

It strikes dead center. No other man can match that shot, and none of the six remaining contestants seem hopeful about their chances. One throws down his bow immediately and says, with awe in his tone, "I yield to the man who made that shot."

The other five men shoot at the target, and though two strike near my arrow, no one touches it.

"The three archers nearest the mark will now compete in the final round!" calls the town crier.

A couple of boys hurry out to switch the current target for a fresh one.

Meanwhile I glance over my shoulder at the Sheriff of Nottingham.

I could have shot him immediately, during the first round of the tournament. But he was more cautious then—not only armored and helmeted, but surrounded by guards with shields. He seemed to expect an attack of some kind.

But since no attack has been forthcoming, he has relaxed his own guard a little, and so have his soldiers.

Their shields have dropped a bit lower, weary arms yielding to the long exertion. If I move fast and time this perfectly, I can strike the Sheriff right in the eye. The arrow will sink into his brain, and in the ensuing chaos my men and I can claim Marian and escape.

If I can move quickly enough. My bow skills remain the same as ever, but my speed and strength are diminished. There's a strange weakness in me, growing worse the longer I remain within these walls.

After several minutes the new target has been set up, this time at a greater distance. One of the three remaining competitors steps forward and takes his shot. A good effort, with the arrowhead striking near the center.

I shake out my fingers, frowning at the numbness that seems to be gathering in them. Blinking hard, I set the arrow and pull back the bow.

I pretend to aim at the target, but in my mind I am picturing the Sheriff's position, behind me, off to the left of where I'm facing now.

Another second, and I will whirl around and let the arrow fly.

If my aim is true, he will die. If not—

I spin on my heel, and I shoot.

40

DAVID

Robin isn't himself.

I know his body as intimately as I know my own.
I know the span of his skin, the hollow of his thigh,
the curve of his bicep. I know his body language,
from the tilted hips when he's flirting to the braced
legs when he's determined. One look tells me if he's
angry or sorrowful, lecherous or longing.

Since the tournament began, I've watched him
from my perch on a rooftop, in the shade of a
chimney. I know he's not feeling like himself.
Inwardly I've been cursing him because he didn't take
the threat to his Fae nature seriously, and now he's

suffering the consequences. Though truthfully, it's not his fault. We didn't know if the Sheriff would have the means to weaken him or not. And Robin had no idea how to counter such repressive magic if the Sheriff did use it.

We had to come, risk or no risk. After Tuck was found wandering in the forest and was carried back to the Gloaming, half-dead, all three of us knew we had to go after Marian. The entire band rallied on her behalf, clear-eyed and steadfast, determined to save her. As well they should be, when she was so generous with her body and her kindness.

Many of our men are positioned on rooftops all around the square. We had to dislodge a few of the Sheriff's men, who had thought to cover the square with their bows as well. But we managed to dispose of them quietly and take their places.

More of the Merry Men are among the crowd in the town square, ready to move against the Sheriff and his men if need be.

We must try to accomplish this without bloodshed. Much as I like pain with my pleasure, I don't like killing. I did enough of that in the war, fighting for causes that weren't my own. I will defend the people I love without hesitation, but I hope Robin can make this shot and lives can be spared.

Cut off the snake's head, and the body will flail uselessly. If we take out the Sheriff, our chances of extracting Marian quickly will be far greater. But if Robin fails and the Sheriff moves out of our reach, he can continue to command his men, and we'll be in for a bloody battle.

I risk a quick glance at Will, tucked into the shadow of a gable on a nearby roof. He's dressed in a dark, rusty red that nearly matches the color of the roof tiles. His golden head is swathed in cloth of the same color. I admire the lean grace of his body, the way he's crouched with catlike poise, with his crossbow ready. Knives are tucked into the bracers along his forearms, and more knives are concealed in his boots.

He looks over, catches me staring at him, and jerks his head sharply toward the square, a wordless command for me to pay attention.

It's Robin's turn to make the final shot at the target. The winning shot, in more ways than one. Except his true target isn't the one at the end of the range.

He draws back the bow. Hesitates.

Then he whirls around and shoots right at the Sheriff of Nottingham.

The arrow sails true. Almost.

The Sheriff turns his head slightly at the last instant, and the arrowhead pings off the metal cheekplate of his helmet.

"Fuck," I hiss.

The dais where the Sheriff sits explodes into action as men raise their shields to protect him. Guards are leaping to restrain Robin—I shoot the first one who touches him, and Will gets the second.

They're armored, but parts of them are still vulnerable—the eyes, the joints, the seams and gaps of the armor.

I vent a piercing whistle, the signal for everyone else to fight.

Among the crowd, Merry Men draw knives and cudgels. They throw off capes, revealing the signature green of our band. Some attack the Sheriff's men, while others fight their way to Robin and attempt to form a protective ring around him.

He's fighting on his own behalf, but his movements are slower than usual. Do the sigils on the town walls have a cumulative effect, weakening him more the longer he's under their influence? If so, we must finish this quickly.

I won't risk losing him.

My gaze skips over to the gallows, where our sweet Marian stands with the noose around her neck and her hands bound in front of her. She's ringed by guards, who have crowded onto the platform with her. One of them is holding a knife to her throat.

Fuck.

If we get too close trying to rescue her, that guard will spill her blood.

41

MARIAN

Everything went wrong so quickly.

I'm not sure what I was expecting from a rescue attempt, but I certainly hoped it would go more smoothly than this. But I suppose Robin Hood and his band operate best within the bounds of their forest, where Robin has full access to his magic. They're less used to fighting in a town.

Robin is sluggish, fighting like a drunken man, swaying on his feet. And that concerns me more than the knife to my throat. Whatever the Sheriff put in place to curb his magic is clearly affecting him, more so with every passing minute.

People in the square are screaming, mothers pulling their children back to safety, young women shrilling and clutching each other, old men yelling curses in cracked voices. Robin's men and the guards are engaged in bloody, bruising hand-to-hand combat, and since the guards have armor, Robin's men seem gravely outmatched. They can only win with more numbers.

Where can we get more numbers?

I scan the square again, noting sturdy women and strong men standing back from the fray. People from Nottingham, yes, but also from the hamlets and villages all across the region, come to see the tournament. People who might be sympathetic to Robin Hood.

I suck in a breath, preparing to shout, to try and stir them up to help him—but the guard beside me jams the knife harder against my throat, and I feel the grinding sting of its edge beginning to split my skin.

"Hush, bitch," he snarls.

I'm considering defiance when I see a tall, broad, brown-clad figure coming down a side street, moving into the crown. A man with a handsome face and a bald head that glows in the noonday sun.

Tuck is wearing a huge crucifix, and both his big hands are raised, all fingers intact.

He looks so much better. His shorn ear has regrown, too. Robin's work, no doubt.

"People of Nottingham!" he bellows. "I am Friar Tuck. I'm the man you came to see hanged today, before the Sheriff put this sweet girl in my place. But I am no traitor—not to the true king of the land!"

Tuck is making his way toward Robin, and every time a guard moves to attack him, an arrow whistles through the air and strikes that guard in the elbow, the knee, or the side. Robin's men, carefully placed on nearby rooftops, are defending Tuck.

"Stop him!" squalls the Sheriff.

But Tuck keeps moving, a bold, unstoppable force, like a galleon sailing onward through churning, stormy seas. He pays no attention to the fighting, or to his own safety. He has almost reached Robin Hood now, and he's still speaking in a booming, commanding tone.

"You all know me. I've given you tonics, ointments, healing poultices," Tuck says. "I've done work for you—mended your roofs and carts, shorn your sheep, shoed your horses. I've raked hay, dug weeds, and scrubbed your pots. I've given you coin when you had nothing left. But what some of you don't know, though you may have suspected—all those good things came straight from this man. From Robin Hood."

Tuck grips Robin's wrist, raising his arm high. "Will you now allow the dastardly Sheriff, who steals from you and enforces cruel laws, to destroy this man who fights on your behalf? Stand up, good people, and fight for the one who defends you! He needs you now! Do not fail him!"

A woman cries out her agreement, brandishing a frying pan, and a couple of men's voices join her cry. The people in the crowd surge forward, stirred to revolt by Tuck's voice and by gratitude.

My heart swells with love and admiration for Tuck. A brave man, to return so quickly to this town where he suffered for days. A wise man, who knew exactly the right words to stir up the people.

God, I love him.

He's got a thick cudgel in his hands now, and he's laying into anyone who dares approach Robin.

I desperately want to join the fight and help protect my men, but with this fucking dagger pressed to my vein, I dare not move. I can only watch.

Movement to the left catches my eye. One of the musicians beside the gallows has slung his lute onto his back and is shimmying up a post to the gallows platform.

None of the guards pay him any mind—they must think he's trying to escape the churning panic of the crowd, finding a coward's refuge up here with us.

But my eyes lock with the lute-player's, and I almost gasp.

It's Alan of Dale.

There's something else slung on his back, too—something with a gnarled, polished end I recognize. My quarterstaff—the one Master Blunt made for me.

Alan whips the quarterstaff from its strap and strikes a well-aimed blow to the skull of the guard whose knife is poised at my throat.

The knife drops, and the guard topples off the platform.

The other guards cry out in surprise, forced to defend against the incoming arrows as well as Alan's flailing quarterstaff, which seems to be everywhere at once, thunking heads, knees, and groins by turns.

Alan backs up to me, wielding the quarterstaff one-handed while his other hand fumbles with the rope around my neck. After a moment it loosens, and he tosses it off my neck, over my head.

But my hands are still tied, and he's struggling to keep the guards off us. One of them is unslinging a crossbow, seating a bolt, aiming it at Alan—

But before he can shoot, a tall, lithe figure swings down from a rooftop and crashes onto the gallows platform.

Our savior is David, his dark eyes blazing. He draws a sword and begins hacking at the remaining guards.

"Get her hands free, Alan," he orders.

Alan whips out a knife and saws through my bonds, while David deflects incoming blows and slices straight through whistling arrows, protecting us with the skill of a man who has seen many battles. If we survive this, I must get him to tell me his life story.

My hands are finally free, and I shake them out to restore the blood flow.

Alan tosses me my staff. "Tuck said you would want this back."

"Fuck yes." I smile at the familiar heft of the weapon, and I charge into the fray, battling the few remaining guards on the gallows platform while David keeps fending off arrows and crossbow bolts from the Sheriff's men. Alan takes his lute from his back and uses it as a club, helping me knock the rest of the guards off our perch.

"We're too exposed here!" David shouts. "We need to get down!"

He's right. And the gallows platform is built too high for us to leap off—we could end up with sprained ankles or even broken bones. There are steps leading into the chute from which I came, but that way goes back to the jailhouse, and I don't want to be separated from Robin and the others in the square—I want to help them.

Energized by a sudden idea, I step over to the hangman's rope and adjust the length, allowing more slack before knotting it again. Then I grip the dangling loop of rope with one hand.

"Pull the lever, Alan!" I shout.

He obeys, and the trap door falls. I tense my arm as I drop, so the sudden jerk of my weight on my shoulder isn't too drastic. Thanks to the extra length of the rope, I'm nearer the ground now. When I let go I land on my feet without damaging my legs or ankles. The other two follow me.

With manic glee I plunge into the fight, screaming all my pent-up fury as I slam the quarterstaff into helmeted skulls and slam it against the backs of knees or exposed elbows. There's a satisfying crunch of bone after more than one blow.

After everything I've endured from wicked men in power, a full-on brawl like this is deeply satisfying. Through violence and blood I purge my hatred for the Crown, my sense of helplessness and despair, and my rage at having taken the Sheriff's cock.

With David of Doncaster and Alan of Dale at my back, I work my way toward the Sheriff's dais.

I want nothing more than to kill him.

I've never felt a bloodlust like this in my life. It's a scarlet haze across my mind, a scorching fire in my chest.

Somewhere in that haze, I become conscious that the guards are fewer and farther between now, that most of them are crumpled on the ground where citizens kick at their bodies and faces.

I'm nearly to the dais. And even there, the guards have been thinned—struck down by arrows. As I watch, a knife flies straight into the gut of one of the last three guards.

A glance over my shoulder shows Will Scarlet, swathed in clothing the color of old blood, with the devil's fire in his eyes. He's holding two more knives.

Robin and Tuck are approaching too. The last of the Sheriff's soldiers are dragged off the dais by townspeople.

Only the Sheriff himself stands there, sword in hand. His wife cringes in a chair behind him.

Tuck charges with a roar of anguished rage—a cry of vengeance for his own pain and mine. The Sheriff tries to block the blow, but Tuck's full strength is in it, and the Sheriff's sword snaps in half.

Screaming a swear, he throws it down.

Tuck is about to follow up with another blow when Robin says, "Wait, my love. This vengeance shall be mine."

Robin Hood is pale and sweaty, looking more human and vulnerable than I've ever seen him. But the hand holding a blood-slicked arrow doesn't shake.

Robin lifts his longbow. Sets the arrow and draws the string, aiming directly at the Sheriff's face. A shot no man could miss.

It's over. We've won.

But the Sheriff steps forward, his left arm held out straight. Something in his hand glows suddenly, a burst of red light that travels through the air, strikes Robin in the center of his chest, and returns to the stone in the Sheriff's palm.

Robin jerks backward, like a puppet tugged sharply by a string. His limbs go loose, and he's falling—he's crashing to the ground.

He lies startlingly still, his green eyes staring fixed and vacant at the blue sky.

Will Scarlet screams. Yanks a dagger from his boot and flings it, straight and true.

The knife skims right beneath the Sheriff's left arm, which is still outstretched—right into his armpit.

Right in that vulnerable spot where there is no armor, where the blade has direct access to his heart.

42

WILL

The Sheriff falls. His wife screams.

I couldn't care less about him, or her, or anyone but my Fae prince, my darling, my beautiful Robin.

I crash to my knees beside his body and gather him in my arms, hungry for the beat of his heart, for breath from his lips.

There is nothing.

Wildly, desperately, I look up. "Someone help him! Tuck! Tuck, fix him!"

But Tuck's eyes are wide and wet, his lips trembling.

David kneels beside me and places two fingers against Robin's throat, where his pulse should be. "Fuck," he says brokenly. "Fuck, fuck, fuck. No, fuck—no, he can't. No, you don't." His voice rises—he's yelling at Robin. "Wake up, you bastard! Wake up!"

The crowd has gone silent around us. It thickens slowly as people press in, craning their necks, eager for a glimpse of death.

I hate them all. Don't they realize who he is? He gave his life for them, but he belongs to me.

Through the awed murmurs of the crowd, through the strident cursing of David and the hoarse sobs from Tuck, I hear something else.

A woman's voice, calm and cool.

It's Marian. She's got the Sheriff's wife by the throat, and she's carving a thin slice into the woman's cheek. "Tell me what that weapon is, and where he got it. I know he told you. He would have bragged about it. You tell me, or you die with him."

"There's a hedge witch in the jailhouse," whimpers the Sheriff's wife. "She's been there ever since I can remember. She told him about the sigils, and the stone."

Marian rises, dragging the sobbing woman upright with her.

In this moment, standing on the dais in her battle-torn scarlet dress, our Marian looks like a queen. There's a regal glint in her eye and steel in her voice when she commands, "Some of you get into the jailhouse and bring out the hedge witch. Quickly! There's a bag of gold for whoever brings her to me!"

The wait seems interminable, but it must be only a handful of minutes before the hedge witch is hustled through the crowd to stand before Marian.

"The stone the Sheriff used on this man." Marian points to Robin. "What is it, and how do we reverse its effect?"

The hedge witch blinks rheumy, pink-rimmed eyes. "I don't take orders from you, bitch. What's in it for me if I tell you?"

Marian smiles a little—amused, not offended. "Your freedom, and a cottage of your own, with as much gold as you need to live out your life comfortably. We'll hire you a servant, too. You won't lack for anything, if you tell us how to save him." Her voice has the barest quiver on the last two words, the only sign that she feels Robin's loss like I do—like a devastated wasteland in her heart.

The hedge witch puckers her mouth, smacks her wrinkled lips, and nods. "The stone is a soul-capture. It sucks the life out of a Fae. You must put the stone in his mouth and leave it there until his body reabsorbs the soul again."

"How long?" Marian asks.

"A week. Maybe two."

"You'll come with us until he recovers," Marian says. "And then, if you spoke true, you'll get your reward."

David is already moving, prying the stone out of the Sheriff's cold, lifeless hand. He pushes Robin's jaw down, opening his mouth, and he wedges the stone inside. It's palm-sized, and it barely fits.

"Close his lips," says the hedge witch, and David obeys.

Some of the townspeople make a stretcher so we can lay Robin on it, and several small children approach quietly, tucking flowers around his body.

The old hedge witch refuses to walk, so Tuck carries her while David and Alan bear Robin on the stretcher. The other Merry Men fall in behind us, and the crowd follows.

It's a somber procession as we wend our way through the streets of Nottingham to the gate. I ready my knives, but there are only two guards there, and when they see the size of the crowd in our wake, they let us pass without question.

Marian comes abreast of me. In one hand she carries her quarterstaff, and in the other she holds the gilded arrow that should have been the prize of the archery competition.

When she sees me looking at it sidelong, she says tightly, "Robin will want it."

"Yes, he will." I slip my arm around her waist as we walk, and she sighs, agony and relief mingled.

"He'll be all right," she says. "Robin will survive this. He has to."

43

Halfway through the journey, David yields his spot at the stretcher to another one of the Merry Men, and he takes over the job of carrying the hedge witch.

"You need to rest. You're still not fully yourself, Tuck," he says, and I can't deny it. When I was found in the forest and brought back to the Gloaming, Robin applied fresh cum to my wounds and came inside me twice, all with the goal of healing me fully before he and the others had to prepare for the tournament. Yet even with Robin's help, I don't feel quite myself. I barely got any sleep, food, or water during my days in the jailhouse.

So I accept the relief of traveling burdenless, and I move to walk beside Marian.

The words I need to say stick in my throat, but I push them out, one by one. "He raped you. The Sheriff."

"I allowed it. It was part of the bargain I made to free you."

"You saved my life." I swallow hard. "But you should not have—I would never have asked that of you, Marian. I—"

She slips her thin fingers between mine. "Tuck, you're worth all I had to give."

"I wish I could have stopped them. Saved you."

"You saved all of us back there, in Nottingham. You were glorious." She squeezes my hand.

"I spoke from the heart. That's all." For a moment I struggle, trying to find the right words. "Do you need healing? From the—did the Sheriff hurt you badly?"

"I'd rather not talk about it," she says. "I'm trying to forget it. Maybe you can help me with the forgetting, later."

There's not a hint of teasing or seduction in her voice, and I understand. Sex isn't only sly looks and naughty words and the hitching gasps of orgasm. It is also quiet and soothing, vital and healing. It is connection, absolution, benediction.

When we reach the edge of Sherwood Forest, the townspeople and the other villagers stand at a respectful distance while we pass beneath the eaves of the wood. Without Robin to shift the trees and make a straight path, it's a long trek back to the Gloaming, but we manage to find our way.

The Merry Men who stayed behind stare in sober horror as we carry Robin through camp. Will begins to tell the tale of the battle, and whenever he chokes up, Alan of Dale steps in to fill the gaps.

We settle Robin Hood in his hut, on his bed, surrounded by fall flowers and branches decorated with scarlet autumn leaves. It's the most we can do while we wait to see if the hedge witch's remedy will work.

Marian and I give the witch a hut of her own, and we appoint a couple of the Merry Men to wait on the elderly woman. The witch seems pleased with the arrangement.

"A real live Fae," she cackles. "Well—a sort-of dead Fae, but still—it's a wonderful thing. Never thought I'd see another in my lifetime. Incredible. I do hope the stone yields his soul again—I'd like to see him up and walking around. Pretty fellow, isn't he? What's the chance of an old woman getting a warm bath?"

While the two Merry Men set about the task of heating water for the witch's bath, I take Marian by the hand and lead her to my tent. We strip to our bare skin and couple quietly, lying face to face, a sorrowful desperation threaded through our pleasure. She comes on my cock, panting against my neck, her tears wetting my skin. My climax is a piercing, beautiful thing, and my cum pumps into her slowly.

We drowse together like that, with my cock still inside her.

When David and Will find us, they remove their clothes quietly and lie down with us. There is a soothing comfort in the warmth of skin, in the rush of bare limbs and the soft breath of deep, heartfelt passion. The air of the tent grows heavy with lust, with the smell of sex.

We sleep in a tangle of bodies all night. To me it doesn't feel like sin—not anymore. It feels like redemption, like a baptism. Like salvation.

Other Merry Men watched over Robin through the night, and we continue the watch throughout the day, all of us taking turns.

Around noon, Marian's servants arrive in camp. Will and I accompany her to greet them. We escort them to the other safe haven—a separate clearing in the greenwood where families can reside in safety without being involved in the debauched revels of the Gloaming.

Two of Marian's maidservants hold hands while we show them around the place. It's subtle evidence of the sapphic love Marian told me about. Here they will be able to express and enjoy that love to its fullest, without fear of judgment and cruelty.

One of the servants is an older man with a twisted leg, strong hands, and bright eyes. He's Master Blunt, the one who trained Marian with the quarterstaff. When I suggest he might train some of the newer Merry Men, he agrees wholeheartedly.

Martha, a woman with twin boys, seems uncertain at first, but when we show her the large, furnished hut we've prepared, she smiles and instructs the boys to help her unpack their meager belongings. She asks about the possibility of continuing with her weaving and knitting—a passion of hers—and Will assures her he will personally see to it that she receives all the supplies she needs.

Another of Marian's servants, George, was the gardener at Elmwood Castle. I speak with him about starting an herb and vegetable garden for the communal needs and the health of those in the safe haven, and he seems eager to manage that project. His son Otto, who cannot walk, is thrilled with the gift of a sturdy rolling chair, crafted at Marian's suggestion by a carpenter among the Merry Men.

Will, Marian, and I stand by, watching the boy roll himself across the smooth turf between the huts, while the tow-headed twins run around him, shouting encouragement and admiration.

And for the first time since the rescue, I feel hopeful that everything will be all right.

44

DAVID

We pass two quiet weeks getting the newcomers settled, making improvements to the new haven, and continuing the evening tradition of wrestling matches and fucking. Without Robin, there's a zest lacking from the events at first, but when Will takes over, his charisma and golden beauty soon have everyone participating with the usual enthusiasm.

One night I'm balls-deep in Alan of Dale, who has become rather more popular with our group since he freed Marian during the rescue. He's a needy fellow, but he has a good heart, a musical soul, and a delightfully plump, round ass. He seems to have switched his puppy-like affections from Robin to me, though I'm not sure why. He can't handle much pain, but it's fun to push him farther each time I fuck him.

Marian is sprawled on the table in front of us, stroking Will's cock with her fingers, arching and mewing while Tuck eats her pussy. She's a delight to watch, and I'm close to coming. Just a little more pain is all I need. Robin always knew exactly what to do for me…

A set of teeth bite savagely into my shoulder, while at the same time ten strong fingers clutch my ass cheeks, nails digging deep.

My cock jerks, spurting wildly into Alan, the orgasm blasting through my lower belly, ripping a startled groan from my lips.

The man behind me smells like rain-washed leaves, like fresh grass, like wild magic. His lean, naked body presses against my back, and I cry out again, aching relief mingled with my pleasure this time.

"Robin," I croak, shaking through the orgasm, shattered by joy.

Robin Hood nuzzles my neck. "I've fucking missed you, David."

"Robin?" Marian squeals her delight, but she's helpless to pleasure, her legs hitched up and her breath coming in ragged gasps as Tuck's tongue works its magic.

Robin laughs, walking over and gripping Tuck's big shoulders. Tuck pulls away from Marian and looks up, his broad mouth wet. Deep dimples pop into his cheeks as he grins. "Robin, thank god!"

"Told you he'd live," the hedge-witch cackles from her nest of pillows on a table nearby, where Master Blunt is heavily thrusting his cock between her wrinkled legs. It's their second time participating in the evening's pleasure, and they seem to enjoy it, although they both take a long time to achieve a climax. Some of the men complained about them participating—said they weren't young and attractive enough—but I ordered silence on the matter. Sexual need can be just as strong with the aged as with the young, and why should our elders not enjoy themselves openly as well?

"My thanks to you, milady." Robin walks over to the witch, stark naked, healthy and beautiful as ever, and he kisses her mouth.

The hedge witch presses a fluttering hand to her sagging breast. "You'll send an old woman to her grave with those Fae graces, lad. Tend to your lovers there. They can handle your goodliness much better than I."

He laughs, merry and musical, and trails his fingers along Tuck's back. "Let me finish her, will you, my heart?"

"Gladly." Tuck rises, leaving Marian's shining pink pussy open and helpless. She's quivering on the edge, and I look forward to watching Robin take her over the brink.

I tug my cock out of Alan's ass and smack him hard as a reward. He moans, and I reach below his belly to grip his cock, jerking my hand along it swiftly. "Come for me, Alan, there's a good lad. And then you can play us some music."

With a shudder, he comes, huffing through his pleasure. Absently I wipe his cum from my hand onto his ass, fully engrossed in the spectacle of Robin Hood sliding inside Marian's pussy. Robin leans forward across her body, and Will leans in to meet him. They kiss with a sweet, pained passion that echoes my own emotion. Robin's recovery has flooded my heart with golden joy, but I still feel the keen sorrow at its edges, the aftertaste of nearly losing him.

"Marian, you can stop stroking Will," says Robin. "I'll be sucking his cock in a moment. And then Tuck will take my ass—god, I need a thick cock in my hole. It's been an age."

He turns the full force of his green gaze on Marian then, while she gazes up at him with a kind of fierce, joyful worship. He slams both hands on the table on either side of her and begins to fuck her, wild and fast, like he did that night by the pool. She grips his shoulders, her nails digging in, her blazing gaze joined with his. There is always a special magic in watching the two of them together, the way they need each other so recklessly, so violently.

Marian shrieks, high and pure, her legs curled tight at Robin's hips, her eyes rolling back with the force of the orgasm. Robin roars aloud, a bellow of sheer fucking relief, as he comes inside her. He keeps coming, convulsing, his gorgeous muscles hardened, his pale skin glowing in the firelight.

He's alive. Alive, and ours.

I will never want anything more than that.

45

MARIAN

The night Robin Hood reawakens, the five of us fuck for hours, over and over, in every configuration we can think of. The next day, we do nothing but sleep, eat, and orgasm.

And then, a few days later, Robin disappears, and for three weeks I don't see him at all. At first I'm nearly frantic, afraid perhaps his healing regressed somehow and his soul slipped away—afraid some agent of the Crown has found and assassinated him. But Will, David, and Tuck don't seem concerned.

"Have a drink, little one, and stop fretting," says David. "His magic is stronger than ever, strong enough to protect us from Prince John for years to come. He's just away on business."

"Business? What business? *Thieving* is his business, and he usually takes at least one of you with him!" I retort.

"We can't tell you any more than that, darling," Will says, sidling up to me and fondling my breasts through my tunic. "It's a surprise. Now don't worry about Robin. Come to bed with us."

Despite my anxiety, heat is pooling at my core, thanks to Will's delicate tantalizing of my nipples.

"I'll do that thing you like, the one with my tongue," Tuck promises. He weaves his great hand into my hair and pulls my head back, bending down to kiss me.

I can't resist them, and they know it. Grumbling, I let them lead me to Will's bed, where they slowly take me apart and melt all my resistance into a river of bliss.

The next day I'm pinning a few of my underthings to a clothesline when Robin Hood strides out of the greenwood, looking thinner than ever, with a frenetic gleam in his eyes. He returns the merry greetings of his men, but he doesn't pause to talk with them—he makes straight for me. Walks right up to me, cups my face in both his hands, and kisses me, inhaling deeply like he has missed my scent.

My eyes drift shut, and I lose myself to his delicious mouth for a moment.

Then I remember I'm angry with him, and I pull away.

"You've been gone for three weeks," I chastise him. "I've been so worried. Will, David, and Tuck all seemed to know where you were, but they wouldn't tell me. I don't like being kept in the dark, Robin. You know I've sworn off lying, and I don't like being lied to, either. You really shouldn't run off. I don't care what wild Fae things you thought you had to do—it's too dangerous. You could be killed. Again. And this time it might stick, and then what would the boys and I do? We'd be missing part of ourselves without you. You need to take your own health and safety more seriously—"

"Will you hush?" He's half-laughing, half-exasperated. "Come on, trickster. Come with me, and all the questions in your pretty head will be answered."

"Very well," I grumble, and then I gasp as he picks me up and begins to run, out of the Gloaming and along a path, with a strength and speed so much more than human.

"What is so exciting that you must race me to see it?" I say, breathless, clinging to his neck for dear life. His hair is soft as feathers against my fingers.

"This." He sets me down as suddenly as he picked me up, and draws me through a belt of trees into a huge clearing, in the center of which sits—

My castle. Elmwood Castle. The castle I should have inherited from my late husband.

My vision swirls, and I nearly topple over. Robin catches my arm.

"Will wasn't sure you'd want it, because of the things that happened to you here," he says. "But David told me you would. He said judging by what you went through to keep it, you must deem it worth having. And whatever you want, I procure. A fair exchange after you saved that lovely golden arrow for me."

Sobs are clustering in my throat, threatening to choke me. "Robin, how—how—" My voice cracks. "You—you *moved* it."

His eyes are bright as stars, and his smile is just as brilliant. He's practically squirming with excitement; he can't stay still. "I extended a strip of Sherwood Forest out to the place where your castle was. Then I grew some roots underneath the castle—deep, deep down, you see. And then the forest and I just—lifted it up, earth and all. I cleared a path, and we brought it here. So when Lord Guisbourne or some other pompous noble goes to take possession of it—why, it will be clean gone." He laughs, a glorious ripple of sound. "My best trick ever, I think."

"You brought me Elmwood Castle," I choke out, dazed.

"I thought we could throw out anything that reminds you too much of your bastard husband. And we can steal some new things to furnish the rooms—I hear a new Sheriff is moving to Nottingham—he's bound to have good furniture. We can intercept some of his carts on the road. Some of us can live in the castle with you, if you want. Although I will occasionally sleep outdoors—I can't bear having a roof of stones and tiles over my head for too long. Forest Fae, you know." He gives me an apologetic smirk.

Footsteps crunch behind us, and David's voice says, "Fuck me. You really did it, you insane Fae bastard."

"It looks ugly on the outside," Will says. "Perhaps it's better inside, though. How do you feel about it, darling? Are you pleased?"

Tuck walks around me and bends, looking deep into my eyes. "Yes," he says softly. "She's pleased."

A sob breaks from my throat, and I throw myself into his strong arms, soaking in the heat of his broad chest.

"That's all very charming," says Robin dryly. "Don't mind me, I'm only the one who towed the damn thing here in the first place—"

I reach out, clutch the front of his tunic, and pull him right into Tuck's embrace with me. Will moves in too, kissing my tear-slicked cheeks and then kissing Robin's mouth. David's fingers squeeze my ass fondly, then settle with reassuring comfort on my waist.

I have never felt more alive, more accepted, more secure.

"I love you all so much," I breathe into the warmth of our circle.

My words are echoed by each of them except Robin. I twist in the tangle of male chests and arms, cocking an eyebrow at him.

He grins. "I said 'I love you' with a *castle*. I win."

"Preening cock," I throw at him, with a teasing smile.

"Naughty little sparrow," he retorts. "Men, I've just realized we've an entire empty castle here, with many rooms ripe for christening. Shall we see how many of them we can fuck in before we fall asleep from sheer bliss?"

Tuck and David roar their agreement.

"First one there gets to top," Will says, and starts running—but Tuck quickly matches his pace, picks him up whole, and throws him over his shoulder, with a sound smack to Will's bottom.

Then David passes them both, shoving Tuck's shoulder as he runs by. They collide on the castle steps in a tangle of passion and muscle, already beginning to tear each other's clothes off.

"Animals," says Robin, clucking his tongue. "What are we going to do with them?"

"Fuck them into submission?" I suggest.

"Wicked girl. I like the way you think. I'll have that plump little pussy of yours first, though."

"You'll have to catch me, then." I leap into a run, racing at my top speed toward the castle, a helpless giggle escaping my throat as he growls with predatorial glee.

I know he'll catch up in a moment. And then we'll have all our lives to cuddle, and kiss, and fuck, and play. We'll have this whole wonderful castle as our home, protected by Sherwood Forest and Robin's magic.

Everything that has happened to me was only the beginning—the first notes of a song that will only grow more beautiful as years pass. And though I know there will one day be an end to it all, I'm not afraid of endings—not anymore.

Not when my story is going to have such a beautiful middle.

MORE
RAUNCHY RETELLINGS
YOU NEVER KNEW YOU
WANTED

by Jessamine Rue

Phantom's Thrall
Pirates' Witch
Robin's Maid

Ingram Content Group UK Ltd.
Milton Keynes UK
UKHW022227070423
419836UK00013B/2431